I0667361

A Genuine Disguise

The Billionaires' Reunion, Volume 4

Rose Fresquez

Published by Rose Fresquez, 2024.

Join my Insider Group and get an exclusive Novella, THE THERAPIST'S NEIGHBOR [1]

---

1. https://dl.bookfunnel.com/pucr7p3use

CHAPTER 1

Morning light seeped through the mobile home's bent blinds, splashing golden hues across the timeworn countertops. It played off the deep ebony of Whitney Reed's skin, accentuating its rich undertones. With the aroma of brewing coffee a comforting companion, she searched the cabinet for her preferred mug, the one with a verse that reminded her that each day held the promise to do better.

Then she cringed at the unwelcome memory—she'd shattered it yesterday. She'd placed it too close to the table's edge, and it tumbled to the floor. Hopefully, that didn't mean she'd shattered its promise as well.

Reaching for a souvenir cup she rarely used, she flipped it, but a clear bag beneath it froze her in place. Her fingers closed around the small zip-top bag that must've been purposely hidden, and her pulse quickened, thudding with the weight of betrayal. She gripped the Formica countertop, lightheaded, either due to her health or anxiety about the impending confrontation with Mama.

The almost-forgotten waffle iron signaled its readiness with a sharp beep. Whitney tucked the bag into her floral apron's pocket, grabbed the tongs, transferred the golden-brown waffle onto a plate, then poured in more batter for the next one. Doing so, she caught her reflection in the chipped mirror lining the space above the cabinets. With strain tightening her mouth and the corners of her brown eyes, she seemed too weary for a twenty-eight-year-old. And her coiled black hair pulled up in a hasty bun made her look like Mrs. Powers, the older librarian at Jada's school.

The craving for ice gnawed at her, a habitual yearning for the cold crunch that dulled the edges of stress. Her tongue flicked against the roof of her mouth, seeking that familiar, icy relief. But the rhythm of approaching footsteps broke through her focus. Mama had woken up from her spot on the living room sofa after another late night.

"Morning, baby girl." Weariness tinged Mama's raspy voice. She stretched, every motion saturated with a fatigue that tugged at Whitney's heart. The chair's legs grated against the linoleum as Mama prepared to sit.

Grinding her teeth, Whitney pulled the bag from her pocket and tossed it onto the table. It splatted before Mama, and the sight magnified the betrayal she felt. "Again, Mama?" The bag's significance tore a further rift in their already fragile relationship. "When will this end?"

Mama's lips pressed together, her eyes misting over with the burden of countless regrets. "You think I don't notice the disappointment in your eyes every day?"

"It's not just about my disappointment, Mama. It's about the damage you're doing to yourself. To us." Emotion clogged Whitney's throat as fragments of an old hymn echoed in her memories, along with the times Mama's face lit up, so joyful during the hymns they'd once shared in church. "We need you, Mama. Jada and I. Dad's loss isn't yours alone."

Mama's face hardened from a fleeting understanding to defensiveness. "You think you have the right to judge me?" She slapped the table, sending the bag bouncing. "I don't need no judgment from my kids."

Fatigue weakened Whitney, despite having slept for six hours. Retreating a step, she leaned against the counter's support. "I'm not judging. I just want my mother back." Her legs quivered, nearly giving way beneath the desperate frustration, and heat radiated through her from the emotional turmoil. The struggle seemed endless, this uphill battle to open Mama's eyes to Whitney's relentless effort to prevent their family from unraveling. An effort constantly sabotaged by Mama's own needs. "Please," Whitney whispered, clenching her fists into the folds of her apron.

"Perhaps you should quit mothering me." Mama's eyes flashed, yet beneath that fiery anger burned coals of a profound sadness.

The soft patter of footsteps announced Jada's arrival. Her brows furrowed as she took in the scene. Whitney's younger sister's eyes, usually brimming with vibrancy, were now clouded, capturing and reflecting the stormy air between them.

Whitney's chest tightened.

"Why's it gotta be like a twisted family movie in here every morning?" Jada sighed, shoving her messy braids behind her shoulder, clearly upset but trying to bring a semblance of normalcy back to their fractured family.

Whitney drew in a deep breath, her cheeks warming. She'd always wanted to set a positive example for Jada, yet here they were again, another disagreement with Mama playing out. Heart heavy, Whitney forced a smile. "I made your favorite breakfast. Could you grab the fruit from the fridge for us?"

Jada bit her lip, hesitating. Then, with a deep breath, she slung her backpack from her back and retrieved a paper. She held it toward Whitney. "Need a signature."

"Ask Mama." Whitney nodded toward their mom, as always attempting to let her take her role in the family.

Mama's gaze drifted to the fridge where their last family photo with Dad was magnetized. Lips pressed tight, she stiffened. "Whitney's got that pretty handwriting."

"I was only doing you a favor." Jada huffed, rolling her eyes. "Perhaps Whit should be my mama."

Whitney exchanged a look with Jada and took the permission slip from her sister's hand. At the thirteen-year-old's challenge, Whitney raised her brow in silent communication for Jada to respect Mama—*always*.

"Sorry," Jada muttered, her shoulders slumping. She then sidestepped to the fridge and pulled out a bowl of diced cantaloupe.

Whitney's frown deepened at Jada's top. It clung a tad too closely, even if it wasn't revealing. She bit back the comment since Jada already had the fruit bowl out and now focused on setting the waffle plates, seeming to have shaken off her earlier mood. Some battles could wait.

Distracting herself, Whitney picked up a pen from the counter's cup holder, skimmed the form for a museum trip, signed it, and handed it back.

At the table, Mama's silence persisted. Still, Whitney led grace, and soon, the waffles were under attack.

"Working late?" Jada probed, her focus on her plate. No doubt she had an oncoming request.

"I'll shoot you a text," Whitney replied, her hours at the resort unpredictable. Bills loomed on the horizon. She drizzled syrup over her breakfast and passed the container to Jada. "Might take on an extra shift if it's available."

"Going to Lily's after school." Jada's fork cut through the waffle.

Whitney's eyebrow arched, a grin tugging at her lips. "For homework, or to see Lily's brother?"

Jada, feigning innocence, smirked. "Thought boys were off-limits for me."

She was thirteen, too young to entertain deeper ideas for her crushes.

"Making sure you remember." Whitney smirked back, bubbling up a slight chuckle. "Always have that pepper spray handy."

Jada's eyes sparkled. "Our self-defense moves? Better than any pepper spray."

"That's right." Whitney smiled, a genuine one this time. "Those defense classes weren't a waste after all."

Her throat tightened at the innocence aglow in Jada's eyes. Whitney's desperate plea was that God protect her little sister. Reaching out, she tucked a stray braid behind Jada's ear. It wasn't the first time Mama gave a cold shoulder after Whitney called her out. When Jada glanced at Whitney with a content smile, the trailer's stormy emotions vanished, and the warm promise of a happy family took over. It might take a lot longer for Mama to get back on track, but there was still hope, as long as she was home under Whitney's care.

Almost an hour later, in the resort's dimly lit meeting room, Whitney's hand rested on the table, one finger flicking at its chipped edge. Housekeeping staff filled the mismatched chairs, their collective gazes riveted on Charlotte, the resort manager dressed in a black blazer, at the head of the table.

Papers rustled, creating the only sound as Charlotte sifted through reviews, each more negative than the last. "This won't cut it." Her voice cut through the heavy air, and her sharp gaze drilled into everyone. "If things don't change soon, we're toast. Should new management step in, our jobs are on the line."

River Oasis Resort had once been a symbol of opulence. Now, its splendor was fading. Staff departures were frequent, and of those who remained, commitment levels varied. The late owner's death left a void filled with rumors and questions about the resort's future.

Tina across the table appeared contemplative, while Jake was busy with a fidget spinner. Whitney's shoulders stiffened beneath the weight of it. She couldn't afford to lose this job.

"So, what's our plan?" she asked, her words were no doubt filled with urgency. The resort had become a second home to her. Starting somewhere else wasn't an option she relished. "How do we turn this around?"

Charlotte's sweeping hand gesture underscored her point. "The complaints? Most of them point to housekeeping." Her tone made it clear—everyone needed to pull their weight. "I can't micromanage every corner. Do your jobs."

With Charlotte juggling multiple roles since the housekeeping manager's departure, the stress deepened the wrinkle marks on her forehead. Whitney had eyed the housekeeping manager position in the past, but she'd never had enough to pay for training costs. Since the housekeeping manager departed, now would be a good chance to attempt for the position, but with the resort's stretched finances, they didn't intend to hire another manager.

"Whitney, can you double-check all the rooms to make sure they meet the standard from now on?"

"Of course." Given varied interpretations of "cleanliness," it was no shock when Charlotte singled her out, but Whitney's affirmation wasn't thought through. The extra workload meant job security and perhaps bonus pay now and then—a necessity with her circumstances.

Old-timer Tina piped up, "I remember the glory days." Her brow furrowed. "And Alice? Where's she slacking off now?"

"Right?" Jake lifted his fidget spinner. "I missed the other day and couldn't hear the end of it."

"We're a team of five," Whitney interjected, forestalling the brewing negativity. "Pointing fingers won't help. We roll up our sleeves and dive in."

Charlotte, rifling through newspapers, turned to Whitney. "One more thing. Can you cover the restaurant tonight?"

Despite her growing responsibilities, Whitney agreed. She had pressing medical issues to consider and could only hope she'd have enough time to get the money, provided the leaky valve symptoms didn't intensify.

Tina, ever eager, started to offer her services, but Charlotte held up a hand. "Whitney's done solo nights at the restaurant. And our budget? It doesn't allow two on overtime." Flicking the papers, Charlotte added, "Also, Whitney, training on Wednesday."

Whitney gave a nod. Another task on her ever-growing list. She'd managed before, and she would manage again. Being a longtime employee and having proven she could handle any task got her extra shifts where they needed help most.

At times, she assumed she could handle any task, but today was grueling. With one twenty rooms of their five hundred needing attention, the day became a whirlwind of linens, vacuum noises, and cleaning solutions. When Tina balked at cleaning up puke in two rooms, Whitney stepped in. Taking on the responsibility of ensuring perfection in each room, she felt like she was everywhere and nowhere all at once. By the time she swapped her housekeeping outfit for the restaurant uniform, every bone in her body screamed for rest.

By ten twenty, Whitney's fingers throbbed as Charlotte approached. "Mind covering the bar? Just one customer left." Charlotte discreetly pointed to the lone figure beneath the dim lighting. "Give him ten more minutes. If he's still here, remind him of our closing time."

Charlotte's walkie-talkie interrupted Whitney's intention to refuse.

"On it!" Charlotte responded and left, signaling Whitney to handle the bar since the restaurant shift was over. Seeing Charlotte hustle just as hard always reignited Whitney's drive. If Charlotte could give her all, why couldn't Whitney?

***

Things got complicated twenty minutes later when the burly man mumbled in annoyance to himself. The ice jingled in the glass as he clenched his jaw, and frustration etched the deep lines of his face. He slammed the empty vessel against the counter, sending a discordant note into the soft background music.

"More whiskey!"

She resisted the urge to inquire about his day. That would further the conversation and fuel his consumption.

"I'm sorry, sir." She explained she didn't work at the bar. "I'm only here to lock up."

"Too bad." The man's words slurred, and he teetered on the barstool as if his limbs had betrayed him. His thick brows knit together, creating shadows of his eyes. His gaze trailed over her, and a lecherous grin curved his wide mouth.

A chill pricked her skin, and she found herself taking an involuntary step back. She grabbed a napkin needing a distraction.

"I'm not ready to leave."

Too bad the resort got rid of the security team two months ago. Otherwise, she'd be calling them to handle this customer.

Her heart pounding, she surveyed the darkened restaurant where she'd worked earlier, straining to find someone, anyone, to provide a sense of security. All she found were empty tables and chairs in place for opening tomorrow morning. A place once bustling with workers twenty-four seven now closed by ten thirty p.m.

"I'll have another." The man's voice drew her back.

Summoning the warmth an employee in the service industry should muster, she leaned against the counter and kept her voice gentle but firm. "Sir, if you're not a guest, let me call a cab for you."

"Don't need your help." His lips twitched into a smirk as he staggered to his feet, unsteady and unpredictable. He stumbled toward the door leading to the east parking lot.

After he vanished, she exhaled a shaky breath, her thoughts tangled in prayers for his safety. With trembling fingers, she slid the metal drape into place, sealing off the bar area, and then snagged her handbag. She headed to the restaurant kitchen to clock out on the computer.

She made her way toward the parking lot along a scarcely illuminated path shrouded in the shadows of dense shrubs. At this late hour, she should cross paths with one or two employees, but tonight, an unsettling quiet overtook the space, leaving no one in sight.

A prickling sensation crawled up her spine, hinting her night was yet to unveil more disconcerting moments.

Then an unexpected grip encircled her waist, pulling her sideways into the shrubs and knocking her off balance.

She ignored the brush of leaves against her arm as she held her breath, not wanting to inhale the reek of alcohol. Without a second thought, her body responded, pivoting on the spot, and her foot shot out and connected with her attacker's groin.

He doubled over, letting out a strangled cry of pain, and the weak lamppost light flooded his face—the same intoxicated customer from earlier.

Her thoughts raced to Jada and Mama. Jada needed her, and while Mama could be just as incapacitated at the moment, she also relied on Whitney. She couldn't afford to be a victim. She bolted, gripping her purse and needing to get as far away as possible.

Breathless, she fought the urge to retrieve her water bottle from her handbag to tend to her parched throat. Instead, she fumbled for her pepper spray from its side pocket. Just in case the man followed her.

Her heart racing, she sped along another paved sidewalk, and her shoes clapped a swift tempo against the path.

Shrubs closed in on both sides. Their looming forms cast eerie and elongated shadows that seemed to converge ahead of her.

In the moment the shadows started playing tricks on her mind, a man's silhouette emerged from around the corner, jolting her into action. Her hand shot to the pepper spray, unleashing it at the unfamiliar face. Then the realization of her mistake crashed down when an agonized groan cut through the night. The voice wasn't the one she dreaded, the air wasn't heavy with the drunk's reek, and something else was off.

"Oh no!" She gasped, the regret instant and heavy as the man spoke through evident discomfort.

"You've got to be kidding me." Hands pressed to his eyes, he staggered off the path, sought momentary refuge by a grassy area, and lowered himself into a squat, overtaken by the pain.

"I didn't mean... I thought you were..." Panic tangled her words. Watching him hunch over, she cringed, then rummaged through her bag for her half-empty water bottle.

"Let's see if this helps." She crouched, uncapping it. "Here, tilt your head back some." She couldn't speak fast enough. Holding his chin, she began to pour, and her gaze fixed on his, looking for any sign of relief. "Just keep blinking. Let the water do its thing."

He complied, but he seemed preoccupied with the sting.

Guilt overwhelming her, she needed to explain. "I mistook you for someone else, someone who..."

Oops. Was she revealing too much about the resort's security issues? If he caught on, he didn't show it, more focused on soothing his eyes.

With the bottle emptied, she let herself inspect him through the dim lamp post light. His attire and demeanor—jeans paired with a casual button-down as well as an upscale watch gleaming on his wrist—pointed to him being one of their guests.

Finally, he blinked a few times. "You always greet people this way?" His voice, although strained, carried a hint of humor.

A flush warmed her neck, and she took in a deep breath, then retorted playfully, "Only when they sneak up on me in the dark."

He looked her over as he strained his eyes before chuckling. "Well, that's an unforgettable introduction."

What a relief to hear his voice so rich and laced with a teasing undertone despite the circumstances. A silent prayer passed her lips in gratitude for his well-being. "I thought you were someone else."

A playful tilt touched the corner of his mouth. "That much was clear."

"Let me escort you back to the main grounds. It's the least I can do." Offering her hand, she added, "Whitney—that's my name."

"Theo." His tentative smile, a subtle shift beneath the well-groomed beard, brought out the defined lines of his strong jaw. "It appears you need an escort more than I do."

He didn't give her the impression he was a creep, but, if he were, the spray might have put an end to his mission. Under the resort's dim lights, this unexpected encounter sent her body rushing with energy. But while she thought she had energy, she could use him as a bodyguard right now.

"I wouldn't mind an escort."

CHAPTER 2

Theo Stone rubbed his eyes with the back of his hand, trying to soothe the remnants of the burning sensation. Ugh. He should've known better than to get reeled into his brothers'—especially Wade's—infectious enthusiasm for going undercover at the resort. Wade had a talent for finding potential blockbusters everywhere, and now, Theo was caught in a real-life drama.

Forget the room he meant to critique tonight. With housekeeping complaints and now a dash of questionable security, more seemed wrong at this resort than met the eye.

Strolling next to Whitney, their footsteps resounding along the paved path, he relished the freedom of not being cooped up in the room. Every so often, he caught her uneasy side glances at the dense shrubbery lining the path, her shoulders taut.

"I feel terrible." She apologized for what seemed like the hundredth time.

"With so many apologies, no wonder my eyes are still burning." He tried to lighten the mood.

Overgrown shrubs encroached, their shadows swaying to the whims of the breeze, and he mentally cataloged the necessary upkeep. The greenery required tending to, starting with the unruly shrubs. To the left, the glow of an almost-vacant parking lot flickered, accompanied by the distant hum of the highway—a muted undertone in the night's tranquil symphony.

Curiosity had tugged him toward the parking lot's quieter parts, an innocent exploration that left him a pepper-spray victim. Who had she confused him for? He thrust his hands into his pockets, the phone grazing his fingertips, then gave her a quizzical sideways glance. "So, it seems I was an unintended target. Who were you bracing yourself for?"

Her grip tightened on the handbag strap resting against her shoulder. With a slim name tag affixed to a crisp white blouse tucked into her black trousers, she belonged to the league of waitresses. Yet the expected aroma of lingering foods was absent, replaced instead by a delicate floral scent that floated from her presence into the night.

"A customer..." A shaky breath punctuated her words. "He'd consumed far too many drinks."

Theo's fists clenched in his pockets as she relayed her ordeal about a man lunging from the bushes, the liquor in his system more than the resort bartender would ever serve.

"I was just filling in, waiting for him to leave."

His jaw tightened as well, a rising tide of anger heating him. "Are there no surveillance cameras?" he snapped, unable to conceal his frustration. "It seems this man allowed alcohol to embolden his already deviant intentions."

"The resort operates on a tight budget," she explained. "Luxuries like security often get sidelined."

"Your safety is *not* a luxury."

"Ensuring safety for our customers..." She halted her steps as though selecting her words, wary of tarnishing the resort's reputation. "The resort is safe. Please, don't let tonight taint your perception. It's just this one incident."

She then launched into one good thing after another about the resort, probably to take back any negative. "I'm sure you've heard of the place's charms. Why else would you stay here?"

He scratched his neck, evading her gaze, unready to share the reasons for his presence, especially not to an employee. Now wasn't the time to delve into the details of his supposed job title at the resort. "It's just for a night. I've recently moved to Houston. Heading to a different hotel tomorrow."

Her face brightened. "Well, welcome to Houston."

"Thanks." Eager to shift the focus from himself, he asked, "You like working here?"

"It's always been a good place to work. Things aren't the same now."

He didn't need to ask how things were different. Not if they'd cut security and whatnot.

Approaching the bustling street and amber streetlights, he found his gaze lingering on her as she spoke of the resort's good old days. Soft-featured and slender with flawless brown skin, she seemed almost ethereal in this light, and the glow caught it all—the subtle curve of her lips, the arch of her forehead and cheekbones, the spark in her eyes, the bounce of her hair. All of which he had no business paying attention to. He blinked to steer himself from gawking. He had a purpose here and couldn't afford personal entanglements.

As they neared the bus stop, a solitary bench waited in silent vigil. The notion of offering her a ride flitted across his mind, but he squashed it, sensing the delicacy of the evening's events.

The bus roared into view too soon, halting their companionship. "Thanks for walking with me." Gratitude softened her voice. "And for keeping me company."

"I hope we bump into each other—" He caught himself, almost having mentioned he'd be working at River Oasis soon. He raised his hand in a half wave, the distance between them already growing.

"Nice to meet you." Her voice trailed her as she entered the bus doors.

Entranced, he found himself watching the bus pull away, the warmth of their exchange lingering. Yet his purpose here pressed on him, as did the tasks ahead.

When he returned to his room, unexpected cobwebs slapped his face as he entered. Flicking the sticky threads off his face, he reaffirmed his decision to stay just one night to gauge the resort's neglect.

His phone buzzed a subtle vibration against his trousers pocket. He pulled it out and frowned at Gomez's name flashing on the screen. His pulse picked up, an instinctive reaction. Every call from his second-in-command involved pivotal business decisions. TSF Media was in the final stages of negotiating a crucial deal with a major South American telecommunications company.

Clearing his throat, he answered the call. "Updates?"

"We've made headway, but they're being stubborn about revenue-sharing percentages." Urgency heightened Gomez's Portuguese accent as he detailed their negotiation progress with Valce's Distribution Rights. "I think we can push them further, but I wanted your input."

Valce's Distribution Rights were a potential game changer, but nothing was easy in business. The vital exclusivity terms would give Theo's company the sole rights to distribute their original content in the new region.

He marched to the window, scanning the horizon, and the familiar weight of responsibility, the burden of leadership, bowed his shoulders. He rubbed his taut neck. "Gomez?"

"I'm still here."

The slight pause allowed Theo to collect his thoughts. "Push for better terms, but be mindful not to burn bridges. We need them as much as they need us. If they won't budge on revenue sharing, see if we can negotiate better exclusivity terms for our original content."

As the conversation reached a temporary lull, Gomez cleared his throat. "There's something else, Stone. About Miranda."

Their hardworking accountant with an infectious laugh. "What's wrong?"

Gomez exhaled, the weary sigh traveling the airwaves. "Her daughter. A cardiovascular diagnosis."

The news hit like a sucker punch. Illness, death, hospitals. Why was it so hard to escape it all? It was best to ignore the conversation of illness and loss, but it was inevitable.

"Miranda, our Miranda?" Theo's chest tightened, even though he'd only seen her family photos on her workstation during corporate visits.

"Yes, the very same," Gomez confirmed. "The treatments will be—"

"Can you handle it?" Theo shivered. This woman could lose her daughter. Hospitals. If he could, he'd steer far and pray for the family to recover. Ignoring the tragic realities of life was how he grasped for happiness in any form. Not the right way to deal with things while God was in control, but Theo still struggled to understand God's operation. He squeezed the bridge of his nose. "She gets a bonus. And ensure she understands she can take as much time as she needs. Our employees need to know we care for them."

Gomez's chuckle was soft, filled with respect. "This right here? It's why I work for you."

Theo snorted. "You only work for me because you get the big pay."

"You're not wrong about that."

The lighter exchange offered a needed reprieve, a moment to breathe. They bantered, having addressed the urgent issues. Gomez was the closest friend Theo had outside his family. Limiting his social life, Theo preferred to spend more time with his family. His siblings, particularly his brothers, were his best friends, and there was never a dull moment.

"How's your secret mission going?" Gomez's question pulled Theo back to the present.

"It's not a secret mission."

"Isn't undercover a secret in itself?"

That was the question Theo was figuring out too.

"I'm hoping to wrap things up here within a month," he said as the conversation stayed on his whereabouts. A knot clenched his gut. The fact that he'd come undercover was becoming more problematic, especially after meeting Whitney. Her genuineness and enthusiasm about the resort made his forthcoming deception harder to swallow.

After the call, he collapsed onto the bed, grappling with his current double life. A little over a month ago, an attorney contacted him about an uncle who'd died and left Theo the sole owner of River Oasis Resort. He'd almost thought they had the wrong person until the attorney confirmed details of Theo's foster home and deceased Mom.

The resort was now his, an unexpected inheritance from a family tie he hadn't known existed. No doubt he'd sell it, regardless of his siblings' urge to get closure to some unknown uncle. As CEO of TSF Media Holdings, he already had a massive empire to oversee.

Yet here he was, undercover in a strange place and about to lie to Whitney—an employee who believed in the place with all her heart. Just how was he to navigate this mission and keep his integrity intact?

CHAPTER 3

The recessed lights bathed the staff gathered in a relaxed circle, in a warm, golden hue. They convened in the main storage room – an unusual choice for a morning meeting about cleaning rosters and toiletries. Yet, the room's expansive grandeur provided ample space to accommodate everyone comfortably.

Whitney twisted the irritating tag on her shirt, its rough edge scraping against her neck. Meanwhile, Charlotte, armed with her clipboard, stepped forward to capture their attention.

"We have a new employee today." Charlotte scanned them, perhaps skeptical the supposed employee would show.

Whitney had become accustomed to seeing new housekeeping hires get cold feet and didn't show up. Which could be because Oasis wasn't offering them convincing pay to get them into the door.

"He must be running late." Charlotte frowned. Her wristwatch became the momentary focus of her icy gaze. "HR thought we could benefit from a floater—someone versatile to fill different roles as needed."

That sounded good. Hoping their new hire would show soon, Whitney shifted her gaze to the doorway. Then her stomach fluttered at the sight of a familiar face before his broad frame emerged fully.

"Sorry, I'm late." Theo's deep voice flowed through the room, causing a few heads to turn and Whitney's heart to skip a beat. There he was, stepping into the circle as though he had walked out of her head and made her imagination real. "I had a few things to sort out."

"That's not the best first impression, is it?" Charlotte's brows snapped together like two magnets. "Let's hope tardiness doesn't become a habit."

Theo's hand brushed his stubble as though trying to swipe away the disapproval landing on him. "It won't happen again."

Whitney's gaze locked with his briefly. Beneath the soft embrace of recessed lights, a heartbeat of connection pulsed between them. The room's formal predictability seemed to step aside, making room for something unfamiliarly spontaneous.

Charlotte's voice droned on, a monologue about resort rules and expectations. Each syllable uttered became mere background noise, blending into a dull drone, while every detail about Theo sharpened in Whitney's mind.

Their gazes met again with heightened awareness, and her stomach somersaulted. Despite the climate-controlled room, warmth rushed over her as if they were standing in the Houston humidity on an isolated part of the Oasis's sprawling golf course.

When Theo refocused on Charlotte, the invisible bubble popped, leaving Whitney relieved and bereft.

"You can grab a uniform from the drawer," Charlotte instructed, her chin gesturing toward the wall chest.

Theo—the man Whitney sprayed in the eyes two nights ago, the man she'd taken for a guest, the man who'd escorted and intrigued her—was now part of her everyday landscape. Her embarrassment that night had short-circuited any curiosity about why he'd just moved to Houston. Odd he hadn't mentioned he'd be working here.

As Charlotte continued her briefing, Whitney did her best to maintain her composure, though she stole glances at Theo. He looked anything but a stereotypical cleaner, standing there with an air of casual self-assurance, not the least bit beaten down by the anticipation of scrubbing tubs or making beds.

His groomed buzz cut almost faded from the picture, letting thick brows and trimmed beard take focus. That beard graced a chiseled jawline, and those brows highlighted gleaming amber-brown eyes, all set in clear skin rich with olive undertones. As he smiled, a hint of a dimple emerged in his left cheek.

His tall frame towered over most of the staff, exuding a quiet confidence mirrored in his disciplined, gym-honed build—after all, those forearms could probably deadlift her. Dark jeans clung to muscular legs, and a broad chest stretched the untucked cotton shirt that made him look more like a figure from a home improvement magazine than a typical resort house cleaner.

Her gaze drifted down to his shoes, the white sneakers seemed out of place among the mops and brooms. Unless he was working at the Oasis as a corporate stepping stone.

Get it together! She touched her too-warm cheeks. How long had it been since she'd noticed an attractive man? Probably never?

But here she was acting like a teenager with a crush. Not professional at all.

"This is Theo, by the way." Charlotte, unaware of Whitney's coiled emotional currents, pulled Whitney back to the present. "Let's help him adjust." She frowned at him as if also taken aback by his not-so-housekeeping demeanor. Then she clapped, signaling the meeting was coming to an end. "All right, everyone. Let's make today a good one. Whitney, you're showing Theo the ropes today. I trust you'll make him feel at home."

"Will do." Whitney offered a smile she hoped masked her turmoil. She might need to apologize again for making his eyes a watery mess that night.

"And, Theo." Charlotte's voice shifted focus. "Whitney is one of our most experienced team members. She'll be able to answer any questions you have."

"I have no doubt." His eyes twinkled, and his smile seemed to hint this would be interesting. "Looking forward to it."

The words hung in the air, heavy with potential. Whitney managed a nod, her heart fluttering as if trying to keep pace with this rapid change. How much training would she need to give him? Had he done housekeeping before? Worked at a hotel? A cleaner who could afford to stay at River Oasis even for one night was something else.

Theo extended his hand, making introductions to the staff. Everyone seemed to take to him, a magnet drawing them in.

"You'll do fine. Trust me," Tina reassured him, holding his hand a moment longer after their introduction. "As long as you don't fuss about cleaning each nook and cranny as Whitney does, it's easy work."

Theo eyed Whitney. "I'll keep that in mind." His playful undertone tingled down her spine. "I can use all the advice I can get."

Heat rose through her once again. As the meeting dispersed, the day's hum sprang to life. With Theo in tow, it was hard to know how this day would unfold.

Several minutes later outside one of the hotel rooms, she clipped her walkie-talkie to her belt, a subtle exhaustion lurking in the back of her mind. She prayed today wasn't one of those days where her energy tanked within an hour.

"We always need this." She handed him his walkie-talkie. "It's good for reaching the maintenance team or other departments." She stopped short of mentioning security since that department didn't exist anymore.

Theo clipped the radio on, then held up his hands, showcasing his radio perched in his black uniform's front pocket. "Is it good like this?"

"Perfect." She rapped on a door before she slid the key into the lock. "Housekeeping?" She announced it, more out of routine than a necessity. The front-desk list marked the guest had checked out. "We always double-check if a room is vacated. Best to be sure rather than barge in."

She pushed the door open and, after confirming it was vacant, maneuvered the cleaning cart and wedged it against the partially ajar front door. She then gestured toward the rumpled beds. "You can strip the linens off, and I'll gather the trash."

While he scanned the beds as if they were an unsolvable puzzle, she moved toward the window and drew back the curtains. Sunlight splashed into the room, warming the cool colors—each room reflecting the resort's river-oasis theme with a water-toned color palette and river or riverside watercolor paintings.

Theo still stood there contemplating the beds.

Seriously? "Do I need to show you how it's done?"

His mouth quirked, and he raised both hands. "I'd hate to mess this up on day one."

She shook her head. Just how much did he know in this industry? She went over to one of the beds and began pulling off the linens. "Be careful when doing this. You never know what you might find. Could be vomit or worse."

"Shouldn't we be wearing gloves?"

"Grab some from the cart." She moved toward the other bed. "I put them on when I'm cleaning the bathroom."

"Okay." He crouched beside the opposite bed. "I'll grab the gloves when it's bathroom time, then."

"We yank the bedding off." A warmth she didn't intend lingered in her words as she stripped the duvet and sheets off at once. "Now you'll want to bundle them so they can be taken to the laundry. Like this." She demonstrated.

"Like this?" His movements awkward, he peeled the linens off. With that concentrated frown and clenched jaw, he could've been defusing a bomb rather than removing sheets and a duvet cover.

"Not bad," she said when he tossed his sloppy bundle next to her tidy pile.

His face broke into a genuine smile. "Thanks to a good teacher. How long have you been doing this?"

"Since I was eighteen." She ducked her head, her gaze lowering to the coffee table. Focused, she scooped the coffee cups into the wastebasket, then emptied its contents into the trash bag she had brought in. She felt his gaze on her, perhaps expecting more to the story, but she busied herself with the next task. Today was laden with enough complexities. Her history didn't need to be another.

Theo trailed her to the bathroom where she collected the trash. "Assuming you started at eighteen, that means..." His eyes twinkled, his expression one of mock concentration as if piecing together her age.

"Ten years. Ten years working at the resort." She'd better steer the conversation away from personal territories she'd rather avoid.

"Twenty-eight. Uh." He winked.

"How old are you?" She tied off the trash bag. "It's only fair."

"Nine years your senior." He looked taken aback, then grinned. "Still finding myself, I know."

"No judgments," she replied, feeling a vulnerability she didn't experience at work. "We all have a story." Then she snapped back to her professional demeanor. "We need to hustle. We've got a lot of rooms to cover."

"I hope not too many."

She handed him fresh towels, and her fingers brushed against his wrist and watch, the brief contact sending a surprising warmth through her. "You might want to pocket that watch."

"Oops." He raised his wrist, looking at his fancy timepiece, then unclasped it, and thrust it in his pants pocket.

As they went about cleaning the bathroom—Whitney scrubbing, Theo replacing towels—she found herself wondering about his story. Why would someone who could afford such a watch be working housekeeping, even temporarily?

"So, Whitney." Leaning against the bathroom counter, gaze keen on her, he broke her train of thought. "Is this the job you want to do for the rest of your life?"

"Not exactly housecleaning." She stepped back from the gleaming shower, inspecting it like a painter might consider a finished masterpiece.

"It looks immaculate." His compliment sounded genuine.

"Thanks. My dream job would still be in the hospitality industry, just at a managerial level." She smoothed out the shower curtain. "I was hoping to level up here at the resort, but the timing was never right."

"I'm sure you'll have more opportunities."

Back in the main room, they tackled making the beds. She almost had her bed made when a muffled sound emerged from Theo. She tucked in her last corner and turned. He stood wrestling with the fitted sheet, his expression a twist of frustration and utter confusion.

A chuckle escaped her. "Let me guess, you've *never* made a bed before, have you?"

He rubbed the back of his neck. "Not one that requires this level of... precision."

Shaking her head, still smiling, she took over to show him the proper technique. Once she finished, she pulled it all off and thrust it at him. "Your turn."

Watching him try to recreate her movements was like watching a toddler try to build a skyscraper with blocks. When he arranged the pillows as if he were building a fort, she burst into laughter, and he chuckled too.

"You're very meticulous." He shrugged. "I want to do a good job under your watch."

Warmth cascaded through her, his genuine compliment resonating, not merely passing through as fleeting words. "You're doing great so far," she encouraged. "So, what did you do before coming here?"

"A bit of customer service and sales." His attention seemed to waver when he reached for the spray from the cart. "Should I start spraying anything?"

Whether he was avoiding the question or eager to move on to the next task, she wasn't sure. But time was ticking.

"On to cleaning." She handed him a cloth. "You spray, then wipe. Easy, right?"

The scene that followed had her struggling to contain her laughter. Theo, armed with a spray bottle, drenched the nightstand, leaving it glistening as if caught in a downpour. A forgotten cloth dangled from his hand while he gazed at the miniature flood, bewilderment leaving his eyes wide.

"Less is more, Theo." She wagged a teasing finger at him.

His face turned upward, a smirk curving his features and a sparkle lighting his eyes. "Guess I went a *little* overboard, huh?"

He then fumbled before getting into a cleaning rhythm. What an enigma! For some reason, she found herself wanting to understand the why behind the man.

His blunders injected a dose of levity into her daily grind. "Okay, let's move along," she said when they were almost through with the next room.

Theo followed her to the bathroom, shooting a wary glance at the bottles of cleaning supplies lined on the cart. "What's next, boss?"

"Time for the grand finale—cleaning the toilet." She extended the toilet brush like an emcee offering a trophy.

His grimace was priceless. "The throne, eh? How regal."

Chuckling, she handed him gloves from the cart. "You'll want these for this part."

He snapped on the gloves with a touch of dramatic flair as if about to perform surgery. "Ready as I'll ever be."

Whitney started on the sink, leaving the "throne" for him. As she wiped down the faucet, she peeked at him, and his face contorted through multiple expressions—confusion, determination, disgust—while he navigated the unfamiliar task.

"Who knew cleaning a toilet could be so... complex?" he muttered, standing up to inspect his handiwork.

She took a quick look—immaculate. "Not bad."

He wiped perspiration from his brow as though he'd run a marathon, then let out a relieved laugh. "I survived."

"You sure did." A sense of camaraderie, unlike any she'd experienced with a coworker on their first day, warmed her. "Ready for the next room?"

Theo shot her a look of mock horror, which transformed into a genuine smile. "I guess so. But only if it gets me closer to your level of housekeeping mastery."

Airily, she waved a hand, then pushed the cart out of the room. "Oh, you've got a long way to go for that."

As she stopped by the ice machine for her usual handful of cubes to munch, she was tired, yes, and the ache in her muscles confirmed the day's labor. But a lightness buoyed her, an unanticipated joy from teaching him and sharing laughter amid the mundane tasks. The routine, long grown monotonous, seemed brighter, and she began to look forward not only to the next room but also to the next day.

Despite the soiled sheets and bathroom cleaning, some days on the job *could* turn out refreshing. And maybe tomorrow—and however many days Theo worked in housekeeping—would be more interesting than she'd ever imagined.

CHAPTER 4

Theo drew a deep breath, his fingers lingering, hesitant yet poised, over the laptop's power button. A mental tug-of-war unfolded between the urge to continue and the necessity to pause. A multitude of tasks demanded his attention beyond monitoring the stock value of TSF Media Holdings. With a resigned click, he pressed it down, the laptop offering its final hum before succumbing to silence. He encased it within its brown leather bag to secure it away in the cupboard locker.

His choice of a five-star hotel, over a modest one, was tactical, boasting unwavering Wi-Fi, a hushed environment, and a spacious realm to navigate virtual meetings. A glance at the digital clock spurred his urgency of time—it was seven. In an hour and a half, he'd be diving into the day's commitments at the resort.

In the vibrant rhythms of Brazil's nine a.m., the corporate symphony of Theo would be composing decisions, orchestrating approvals, and conducting meetings across the extensive scores of his media empire. He rose, stretching, feeling each vertebra pop back into a more comfortable alignment. His gaze wandered to the window beyond which Houston's morning rush was in full swing. Cars clustered in traffic, and people hustled, all in the warm, golden ovation of the early May sunshine.

Within his air-conditioned sanctuary, one could forget the city's scorching embrace.

Taking up the role at the resort presented a refreshing interlude. Busyness always offered solace from the echoing loneliness in his family's absence.

He strode back to the bed, deftly peeling off his current tee and replacing it with a crisp, blue one. His mind wandered back to yesterday as he'd cruised through hallways lined with cleaning carts and air tinged with the sharp scent of disinfectant. A current of gratitude flowed through him, stirred by Whitney's thoughtful suggestion to leave his grimy uniform at the resort for laundering.

No doubt, she was at work, already embracing the day's responsibilities. He'd requested to show up an hour later today, due to an "emergency." He cringed at the lie to Charlotte, but he'd needed a morning meeting with his media team executives to approve content right away. Such lies were an unfamiliar tune in his moral symphony, casting discordant notes of unease. What did God think of this situation?

Then there was Whitney, utterly captivating. With her loyalty and dedication to the resort, she might even have insights about his elusive uncle.

Four weeks. That should be enough time to evaluate the resort's viability.

Drawing in a breath, he straightened his shoulders against the gravity of multiple worlds he now straddled. More than evaluating the resort's future, he was seeking closure over a family member he never knew. His lawyer should soon find out more about this uncle, the brother of Theo's biological dad, whom Theo had also never met.

His phone's ringtone shattered the morning tranquility, and he grabbed it from the nightstand. His brother Wade's name lit up the screen.

"Did you catch the news about the Rockies' new manager?" Wade asked, his enthusiasm palpable once Theo answered.

"I haven't had much time for sports lately." Despite their busy schedules, sports remained a common ground for them. "What's the buzz?"

"The guy's got an impressive track record. There's talk about some big changes in strategy. Could be a game changer for the team." He rattled off the new manager's statistics and achievements, and Theo pressed his phone to his ear.

Then Wade's tone shifted to a teasing jab. "Tell me you swapped out the GLA for a Civic." Their closeness in ages—Theo had a few months' lead—and their shared interest in the media industry made for a real conversation between them. "If you're keeping a low profile, a Mercedes is not the way to go."

Theo wedged his phone between his ear and shoulder, simultaneously stuffing clothes into a dry-cleaning bag. He rolled his eyes, a silent acknowledgment of his brother's advice on changing rental cars. "Yes, Dad."

"But seriously, how did the first day go?" Wade snickered. "You didn't scare anyone with your boss-vibe attitude, did you?"

He snorted. "For your information, I cleaned rooms to perfection."

Wade's laughter boomed from the phone. "I can't imagine *you* doing housekeeping."

"Yeah, I'm also surprised I pulled it off." Whitney flitted across his mind. Her eyes, her laugh, her teasing had all become the day's highlight. But divulging that to Wade? No way. That was off-limits for now. "It's hard work, but it's not like I can't handle sweat."

"Is it story-worthy? You know, potential script material?" Wade asked, ever the screenwriter and producer.

"Unless you're planning a sequel to Cinderella"—Theo had to halt those creative gears turning in Wade's head—"it's not blockbuster material."

In the following pause, Theo could envision Wade's forehead furrowed in thought. "So, Dad and Mom have been—"

"Are they all right?" Theo's stomach knotted, and the usual fear lassoed him. How would he be if anything happened to his parents or any of his siblings? "I should've returned Mom's call last night."

He'd let one of his twice-a-week calls slip through the cracks. Haunted by the vivid shadows of separation anxiety from his childhood, he was granted the comforting bonus of extra weekly chats with his adoptive parents, primarily Mom. "As far as they know, I'm here to weigh the resort operations."

"Let's hope they don't pay you a visit before you reveal your identity." A serious undertone firmed Wade's voice.

Images of their sprawling family, the Stones in all their boisterous glory, flooded Theo's mind. "If Mom shows up with Dad and whoever, unannounced, can you imagine a surprise Stone family reunion here?" The dizzying thought sucked him into a delightful whirlpool of chaos and affection he wasn't prepared to navigate at River Oasis. "I'd be exposed in seconds."

"Speaking of the reunion, I wanted to clarify the dates. Was it the first or second week in June?"

"I can't believe you're only asking now." Theo was certain his assistant had sent out the email to his family at the beginning of the year. Yet, even he couldn't recall the exact dates without consulting his calendar. But their youngest sister was always one step ahead. "Ask Iris for specifics."

"Okay. But when can I have a script ready about your housekeeping adventures?"

"It's not happening." He checked his watch, but his wrist was bare. So he glanced at the clock, then sprang into action. "I've got to go. Can't afford to get fired on day two." That was a remote possibility, but the HR manager, who'd signed a nondisclosure agreement to keep his secret at River Oasis, would frown at tardiness.

His smile lingered, unchanged and familiar, the kind that always graced his features following conversations with any member of his family. Memories of his birth mom were faded, almost like an old photograph. He'd floated between foster homes in Colorado until he met Regina, his counselor-turned-mother, and Kyle, his adopted father. They'd adopted Theo and nine other kids, uniting them into a family. The biological child, a bonus to the family, flipped them from an even ten to eleven. Ten siblings drove him to the brink of insanity and filled his life with chaotic joy. Running an empire in Brazil seemed far, but besides the phone chats, he returned to the US every week to see his family.

As he headed out, he savored appreciation for his family. They were loud, they were messy, and they were his. For better or worse, he couldn't imagine a world without them.

***

The cluttered aftermath of a wild party spread out before Theo, a chaotic display of recklessness. As he and Whitney stepped into the room, Jake held the door open, his face contorting. "See for yourself."

Discarded food containers lay abandoned like wounded soldiers, empty bottles clustered like discarded weaponry, and the heavy stench of alcohol and sweat pervaded the air, marking the battleground.

"It's just a messy room. Nothing new." Whitney's eyes widened when they found the vile vomit near the bed.

With the smell so overwhelming, Theo's hand shot to his nose, his eyes watering. His grip found Whitney's hand, and he led her back to the hallway's sanity.

"I ain't touching that." Jake wrinkled his nose and swung the door shut behind them. From what Theo gathered yesterday during lunch break, Jake was a newbie, only on the job for a month.

"It's all right. I'll take this one," Whitney volunteered. "Jake, why don't you handle the room opposite. It shouldn't be a war zone there."

Jake muttered a raspy "thank you" and hurried down the hall as if granted parole.

Admiration swelled in Theo's chest, fanning the sparks of his attraction to Whitney. It wasn't just her competence—it was her selflessness. Her messy ponytail and the way it framed her face somehow rendered her even more stunning.

Her gaze met his, and he cleared his throat. Had she caught him staring a second too long at her? "That was a decent move."

She shrugged, her smile turning her eyes into something magical. "It's just a task like any other. Plus, Jake isn't great with... Well, stuff like this." She rubbed rising goose bumps on her forearms. "When I was training him on his first day, we encountered a similar mess, and he threw up. I had to clean up two messes instead of one."

Theo grimaced. His gaze darted down the long hallway, already dreading the disasters that might lurk behind each numbered door. "If that's the benchmark for today, it's gonna be a long one."

She raised her chin, challenge glinting in her brown eyes. "Why don't you clean the next room while I tackle this biohazard."

She started toward the door, but he tugged her arm to stop her. When she looked at his hand, then at him, the softness in her eyes made him realize how intimate the act was. So he pulled back his hand.

"We'll need masks and gloves." He swallowed, already envisioning the putrid terrain they'd be navigating.

Her eyebrows arched. "This is Jake's room. You don't have to—"

"If you're cleaning it, why not me?" He held her gaze, determined to see this through no matter what. The thought of her dealing with the mess alone was somehow worse than the thought of diving into a cesspool himself. "I won't enjoy it, but I won't let you do it alone."

Good thing, she was a pro at dealing with such catastrophes. She produced an arsenal of cleaning supplies with the efficiency and flair of a top executive orchestrating a flawless media campaign.

They flung the windows open and turned on the fans, and fresh air waged its battle against the putrid scent.

He then took on the gut-wrenching first step—wiping down the soiled area and depositing the waste into a heavy-duty trash bag. Whitney followed, navigating a scrub brush drenched in detergent and hot water. After exhaustive shampooing and generous amounts of disinfectant, the room smelled less like a frat party and more like a hospital.

If he ever entertained the idea of keeping the resort, the carpets in this room would be the first to go.

As they transitioned to another room, her movements slowed, and her breath came in short, rapid bursts. "Already worn out?" He couldn't blame her. She'd attacked the last room with the intensity of a seasoned warrior.

"I just need a moment." She pressed one hand to her chest and braced the other against the wall for support. On instinct to help, he took her elbow and led her to a chair in the sitting area.

"I've got this room," he said. After all, she trained him well.

With her chin propped on her hand and her elbow on the table, she quirked an eyebrow. "Really?"

"You're a good teacher. What can I say?" He fumbled for words, not about to admit his reason to help her today was far less about learning and much more about cherishing time spent together. "I come from a big family. I rarely have opportunities to do things solo."

She perked up. "How many siblings?"

"Ten." He ripped open a new linen package. Discussing his family might open him to questions he couldn't answer without blowing his cover. A change in subject was needed—quickly. "So, how do you handle rooms like that every day without getting burned out?"

Her eyes softened, her smile serene. "Passion." She paused for a deep breath. "When you're driven by a love for hospitality, you push through the hard parts." Her eyes flickered, almost as if debating whether to add what came next. "And being accountable to God. Doing my best because He expects nothing less."

His chest tightened. Every time he lied to her, he was lying to God. "I very much believe in God." He smoothed out the duvet as if the action could smooth out the disquiet rumbling within him. "Thanks to my parents."

Oops. Better steer away from dangerous personal territory—*again*. "So, are you happy working at the resort?"

She began capping the cleaning bottles, her actions methodical, but her expression distant. "It pays the bills." Theo could hear layers of untold stories in her voice, dreams deferred but not forgotten. Just like him, she had her reasons, her secrets—and the untold weight of them hung between them, as invisible as the disinfectant scent.

A deeper twinge tugged at him, a constant reminder he was playing a role while others, like Whitney, were living their reality. There were probably more employees like her who relied on their jobs at the resort to make ends meet.

Room complete, he followed her into the hall. He'd have to connect with more of the employees, perhaps during lunchtime chats. Learning their stories might help him see the larger picture of the lives entangled before he made any decisions.

"Where were you born, Theo?"

"Colorado." At least, in this, he could respond with honesty.

"I've heard great things about Colorado." She paused by the ice machine, shooting ice into her palm, then moved across the hall, and inserted the pass card into the next room's lock. When the lights flicked on, her gaze met his. "So, what made you leave Colorado for Houston?"

As she popped an ice chip into her mouth, his pulse quickened like a market reacting to a surprise announcement. "The same reason as you."

"I was born and raised here, by the way." Her words were calm, but her eyes were like laser beams, cutting through his veil of half-truths.

Dangerously close to being exposed—and terrified by that vulnerability—he walked past her into the room.

"Ever worked a gig like this before?"

"Yesterday and today." He slid open the drapes and then started stripping the linens from the bed, a diversion from her scrutiny.

"You've done pretty well in housekeeping." Her ice chips finished, she shook a finger at him, and a playful tone sneaked into her voice as she swiped her damp palm on her uniform. "I hope the next department you work in is a lot easier."

"I can handle it." Housekeeping, while physically grueling, paled in comparison to the mental acrobatics he was doing to keep his story straight. Whitney was smart—too smart. Continuing to spend time with her would be like playing with fire. His lies, even those of omission, were a flammable material that she could ignite with her probing questions.

"Are you planning to work in hospitality forever?" She paused from wiping down the nightstand.

Avoiding her gaze, he focused on tucking in the duvet. "Let's just say I'm in between things and need a change."

"We all have our reasons." Her hint of melancholy tugged at him.

Silence stretched out, almost palpable as they finished the room. He cringed at her drawn-out breaths, her appraising glances. Was she suspicious of him? If so, his operation could unravel sooner than he intended.

Right now, he couldn't afford the luxury of self-reflection or emotional entanglement. He needed to focus on learning the ropes while maintaining his cover. Even if, from their casual conversations while vacuuming, to the simple joy of sharing a meal, he found himself drawn to her. "I forgot to pack lunch again," he admitted, feeling foolish as they joined more employees under the shade of a tree in the picnic area. "I'm going to grab something from the restaurant. Can I get you anything?"

"Planning to splurge before your first paycheck, huh?" she teased, referring to the restaurant's extravagant prices.

He shook his head, smiling. "I saw the menu. It's a bit much, but this one time, I can manage."

"No need." She sat at the picnic table and unzipped her lunch box patterned in a cheerful green design. "I've got enough to share."

A sense of obligation stirred him. "I can't keep eating your lunch."

"I have extra grapes." She squished her face, and he found it difficult to refuse.

"All right," he conceded, sitting across from her. "But lunch is on me tomorrow."

"I don't know if I can trust you'll remember." She chuckled, pulling out two cheese sticks, a bag of sliced apples, and a couple of milk cartons.

Around them, the atmosphere was communal yet fragmented. Other employees sat at nearby tables, engaged in their own conversations.

She bowed her head and closed her eyes, indicating her silent prayer for the meal, and he did the same, thanking God for what he was about to eat. Then she tore her peanut butter and jelly sandwich in half, offering him one side.

It was a simple, familiar comfort, yet his heart swelled. She'd done the same yesterday.

"Thanks. You make a good PB&J."

She smiled, her eyes twinkling in the dappled sunlight as she crunched into an apple slice. "Is there another way to make a PB&J?"

"As long as you serve it with milk." He nudged a carton toward her. "Makes it like a gourmet meal."

She nodded, her smile warming him more than the humid air. Peanut butter and jelly had always been his favorite lunch in elementary school. "Glad you brought extra," he said, after a sip of his milk.

"I figured someone might forget lunch."

Had she known he'd forget his, or was this something she did often? Bringing extra lunch in case someone didn't have food? "Have they always left you guys to fend for yourselves, food-wise?"

"The resort never feeds us." Daniela, the hotel receptionist he'd met yesterday, slid in next to Whitney and forked at her salad.

"Unless you're working in the restaurant," Tina added from the next table over.

He stiffened. "It seems like it would be more convenient to feed the staff on-site."

Whitney half laughed. "It's not hard to pack a lunch."

"I'm with Theo on this," Daniela chimed in, her bangs falling over her face as she gestured with her fork. "You wouldn't believe the time it takes to whip up a salad!"

An older man from another table weighed in, "Well, with the way things are managed now, food should be the least of our concerns."

The comment prickled Theo's curiosity, but Daniela spoke again. "If you're going to be a floater, maybe put in a good word for us when you work at the restaurant."

"I'll see what I can do," he replied, already scheming a way to treat them all to lunch under the guise of it being a "chef's special."

As the lunch hour wound down, he gathered more stories, more glimpses into the lives dependent on River Oasis Resort, fueling his desire to contribute. So, when Charlotte asked Whitney to cover an evening restaurant shift after their housekeeping duties, he volunteered as well.

Frowning, Charlotte leaned against the laundry room's doorjamb. "We can't afford to pay extra."

"You don't have to pay me," he assured her. "Consider it restaurant training in case I get scheduled to work there sometime."

Whitney eyed him as she wiped her hands on her black pants, a mixture of surprise and appreciation there. In that fleeting moment, a commitment—not only to his undercover mission but also to the people who constituted the resort—strengthened him. He was part of this community, however temporarily, and that meant something.

***

The evening stretched on, each minute an eternity. He'd offered to help without understanding what a full shift in a restaurant entailed. He found brief respite when he exchanged weary smiles and small talk with Whitney. She looked drained, her eyes less sparkly, her movements lacking their usual grace.

"I need a moment to catch my breath." She sighed an hour into their shift, leaning against a refrigerator next to the counter. Pots clattered as the lanky chef stacked them.

Theo's gaze landed back to Whitney, and his lips tightened. The fluorescent kitchen lights cast a stark glow on her, accentuating clear signs of fatigue. "You're beat. Why don't you head home? I'll handle things here," he offered, forgetting his role as the supposed new guy, not the boss.

"You're not being paid to work, Theo." His name rolled off her tongue. "I'd be the one answering to Charlotte if you messed up."

His eyebrow arched, and he nudged her shoulder with his. "You don't trust my work ethic?"

She smiled, a tired but genuine expression that lightened his mood. "It's your first day in the restaurant."

"True, but it's not busy." He shifted his footing as the clatter behind them intensified.

"Weeknights are quiet," the chef chimed in, stuffing his uniform into a bag. "That's why I've been getting off at nine thirty lately."

"Aren't you supposed to close?" Theo's brows squeezed together.

"We serve whatever is left in the warmers if someone comes in late," Whitney explained, unfazed by the chef's premature departure. "Ever since the dining hours changed, we rarely have customers arriving past nine. That's why we only need one server for the evening shifts, except for Fridays and Saturdays."

So Whitney would've been the only server tonight if Theo hadn't shown up. Compelled to dig deeper, he nodded to the chef. From an earlier conversation, he'd learned the guy had been here for quite some time. "For the six years you've been here—"

"Seven," the chef corrected, slinging his backpack over his shoulder.

"—are you the only chef working nights?"

"There used to be three of us, but things have changed. Like every other department here, we're just running until the place shuts down."

That was saying something. Theo scratched his short beard, trying to puzzle out the resort. With the place cutting corners, losing its twenty-four-hour room service, and overworking its employees, no wonder it was slipping further from its five-star status every day.

His phone buzzed in his pocket, snapping him back to reality. A call from Gomez he couldn't ignore. He caught Whitney's eye. "Sorry, I have to take this."

She'd been watching him, but her expression was neither intrusive nor judgmental. She waved him off, and as he stepped out of the kitchen to take the call, he couldn't help but feel torn. There he was—a fake employee on an undercover mission, a series of deceptions for what he believed was a greater good. People like Whitney bore the brunt of poor management and unfortunate circumstances, yet they showed up every day with resilience. How could he reconcile his position with theirs, and what would his upcoming decision do to these people's lives?

CHAPTER 5

Whitney's hand tightened on the counter as she pushed herself to stand. Her breath came a little too quickly for comfort, and perspiration broke out on her forehead. It was disconcerting—she'd only been sitting for a few minutes. She'd been tempted to keep working, but the fear of collapsing, especially in front of Theo, had held her back. That would've been far more humiliating.

While Theo's phone call was none of her business, the frown creasing his brow as he spoke stirred curiosity within her. What had him so preoccupied? It better not be bad news. She'd seen enough of that to last a lifetime.

Reaching for a glass water pitcher, she moved out of the kitchen, her body screaming in subtle ways that she should call it a day. But she couldn't afford to. The restaurant's ambient lighting glowed on the three occupied tables, a sanctuary of sorts against the harsh realities outside its confines. From a central fountain, a marble maiden poured water from her pitcher, lights nestled among its spout turning the water to liquid gold until it splashed her bare feet. Beyond her, Theo's figure was visible in a more secluded area alongside the empty tables, outlined by the dim light. He seemed engulfed in his phone call, shoulders tense and face serious.

Breathing deeply, Whitney let the subdued sounds of evening diners—the murmur of conversation, the tinkle of glasses, the laughter of couples—soothe her. Still, each step across the marbled tiles felt like that statue wading through water, her energy waning. As she moved from table to table, refilling glasses and ensuring customers were satisfied, a mild, uncomfortable pressure throbbed in her chest. A sensation that went beyond mere fatigue, beyond something a good night's sleep could cure.

If only her problem was just a long, tiring day, and not a condition needing medical intervention—surgery she wasn't sure she'd be able to afford, let alone guarantee its success.

As she held the pitcher, her hand trembled. But she anchored her resolve, determined not to let her physical state control her movements. Surrender wasn't a choice. There were bills to pay, life required sustaining, and her body needed to endure just a while longer.

After ensuring none of the guests needed anything else, she returned to the kitchen and set the pitcher back in its place. She reached for the dish towel and returned to the dining area, sweeping across the tabletops, straightening the chairs, and making minor adjustments. As she lingered in the unoccupied section, her fingers brushed away unseen dust as if tidying the world could still her racing thoughts.

Hidden behind an ornamental plant, she couldn't help eyeing Theo where he stood by the picture window overlooking the gardens. The interplay of gentle golden indoor light and starker white outdoor illumination caught his features in an ethereal half-light. He looked so different now—not the man who'd shared lighthearted banter with her only hours ago. This man was a figure of authority, his posture rigid, his eyes laser-focused on something beyond the glass.

She strained her ears, even though she shouldn't, and his firm tone drew her in. "No, the analytics report isn't sufficient," he was saying, phone pressed to his ear. "I need more in-depth insight into the viewer trends, and the bounce rate is concerning."

The words were alien to her, but his tone was authoritative. This was a man accustomed to being obeyed, not a man who dabbled in menial tasks. She eyed his wrist, now naked of his luxurious watch, but even his shoes—though she wasn't one to recognize brand names—reminded her of the shopping app with brand-name shoes

Jada always perused. These disparate pieces of the Theo puzzle didn't fit together.

Lost in her observations, she felt the throb in her chest grow stronger as if scolding her for her prying. Her hand clamped over her chest, her breaths coming in shallow, clipped huffs.

With a mental shake, she expelled a slow breath. This was wrong. She had no business eavesdropping.

She sauntered back to the kitchen. The dirty dishes weren't going to wash themselves. With more staff layoffs, everyone was doing more than their job description these days. She gathered the used plates and glasses, her movements mechanical but precise as she rinsed them off and loaded them into the dishwasher. The morning chef shouldn't have to start his day cleaning overnight dishes.

She stopped short of reaching for another plate when the door swung open and Theo emerged. Elusive electricity zinged through her, and her heart pulsed in a different rhythm, one not associated with her usual chest discomfort. He smiled, and somehow, the world softened around the edges. That smile was too sincere to belong to a man harboring secrets.

His expressive brows arched. "Were you just doing dishes?"

Unable to muster words, her throat parched, she nodded.

"Isn't there someone who does dishes?"

"Things have changed." She sighed. So much decline. Here at the resort. At home with her mother. And now, even in her own body.

Theo picked up a hand towel from a hook and handed it to her. "You've done enough for today. I'll take care of the rest." He watched as she wiped her hands, then touched her back, aiding her to the cooler. "Sit. I'll take care of the customers."

She was too exhausted to argue, but his tenderness warmed her as he took over like a pro.

He quickly mastered the operation of the cash register, and together, they cherished a shared thrill each time a customer left a generous tip.

"Since it's your first night, you get to keep the tip," she insisted as they strolled through the shadowy empty halls after securing the restaurant for the night.

"No way." He shook his head, tugging his uniform shirt from his pants. "If anything, it's your money. I wasn't supposed to work."

They walked closer, their arms brushing against each other in the narrow hallway, and attraction bubbling. Her palm moist, she gripped her handbag straps.

"We'll figure out who gets what when the money comes through." He shifted his backpack on his shoulder as they reached the dimly lit employee parking lot.

"Taking the bus tonight?"

It made sense that he asked instead of offering her a ride. She'd declined his offer to drive her yesterday.

"I don't mind the bus." Usually. Tonight, the idea of waiting for public transportation in her exhaustion added another layer of misery.

He jiggled his keys in his palm, perhaps expecting her to turn him down. "I can give you a ride home?"

"I don't want to inconvenience you." That's why she hadn't accepted his offer to drive her yesterday. "I'm fine."

But she wasn't. And she wasn't a good liar. Her last words came out weak and unconvincing.

"Your mom must've taught you not to get in cars with strangers," he teased, his mouth quirking, his eyes twinkling in the lampposts' glow.

"She taught me not to talk to strangers." She stopped to catch her breath, the nostalgia of a past full of maternal wisdom wrapping around her. Those were the good old days when Mama was sober and free of addiction.

"You're okay?" He touched her shoulder, the metal key ring pressing into her skin even with the shirt between them.

She nodded. They were within reach of one of the three cars in the lot where his car should be. Weighing her options and her fatigue, she relented. "On second thought, I'll accept that ride. I have my pepper spray, you know."

"No kidding." He feigned a shiver, chuckling. "That's why I'm offering you a ride—you'll keep me safe."

Her stomach bubbled with genuine laughter, and the moment's pleasant companionship enveloped them.

"You had a long day today." He took her hand, his intention seeming more of concern rather than anything else, but his hand's warmth covering hers made her feel soft inside, the most authentic thing she'd experienced in a long time.

Why did she harbor this nagging sense that holding onto him wouldn't last, that their time together was fleeting?

***

The moment Whitney slid into the Civic's passenger seat, a fragrance that spoke more of luxury than housekeeping and manual labor enveloped her. It contrasted their earlier activities, a subtle reminder of the enigma that was Theo. A scent temporarily diffused by housecleaning products and food.

He asked for her address and plugged it into his phone before steering out of the parking lot. Their silence wasn't uncomfortable, but as they merged on the interstate, he broke it anyway. "So, how did you come to work at this specific resort?"

The question felt like an unspoken gesture of understanding. When was the last time anyone asked her such questions? "It was fancy, and they offered decent pay for a cleaner."

"Did you get into cleaning because it was the only job available or because you wanted to?"

"Availability was a factor," she admitted, her gaze shifting to the blur of headlights passing them and taillights leading them on.

"Why didn't you try applying in other departments?"

"I tried." A sigh escaped her. Even though she hadn't given up hope, it would take a while before she got a promotion. "There were always more qualified people. But honestly, I don't mind cleaning." Saying that was easier than admitting she never had the funds for training for a managerial position.

The conversation shifted. "Being at the resort for a decade, you must've known the owner well."

"He was a nice man. Just quiet and reserved."

"The owner or the manager?" Theo glanced at her sideways briefly. Why was he surprised?

"Mr. Lancaster, the owner and manager. He was hands-on, probably why the resort did so well." A melancholic warmth spread through her. "Rumor is that the place might be inherited by a distant relative who has no understanding of its value."

Theo drove in silence, navigating as his phone guided them to the exit. "Maybe the new owner won't know how to run a resort," he said, his tone tinged with an emotion she couldn't quite place. Was it concern or something else?

That mysterious phone call sure sounded like a business call. But no way was he related to the resort. It wasn't his fault that an aura about him made her think he was in a different class. Opting for a less direct approach, she asked, "Where did you work before this?"

When he didn't answer, she almost asked him again.

But then he exhaled. "All sorts of places. I'm new to the area here. River Oasis had an opening."

She opened her mouth to probe further, but the navigation system interrupted, indicating their arrival. The familiar mobile home community loomed ahead. Wanting to guard her privacy, she directed him to stop at the roadside before they entered the trailer park.

Theo parked and kept the car running. She unbuckled her seat belt, a sense of loss twinging her at the departure. Odd.

"Thank you for the ride."

"My pleasure." He unbuckled like the gentleman he was, and knowing what he was about to do, she reached and swung open the door herself.

"No need to open the door."

"Can I pick you up tomorrow morning?"

His question drifted when she saw a familiar figure. The offer hung in the air unanswered as her grip on the half-open car door tightened, a knot twisting up her stomach. Across the street, past the dilapidated Sunny Meadows sign missing its *S*s, her gaze locked onto a figure she knew all too well—Jada.

There she was, mingling on the fringes of a rough crowd. The group's raucous laughter and careless exchange of cigarettes and bottles contrasted with Jada's hesitant movements. At least her sister wasn't participating. Yet... why was Jada lingering there, and not at least near the faint glow of the convenience store where tattered posters advertised soda?

"Is it a yes?" Theo prodded.

"Yes." Whitney's mind was still tethered to her sister breaking the curfew rules and putting herself in danger. Her hand, hesitating on the car door, now moved with urgency. She stepped out and shut the door, only to pause when Theo called out from the lowered window. "Should I pick you up here on the sidewalk?"

Caught in the crosscurrent of her concerns for Jada and the need to respond to him, she shared her number. "Text me when you're close by, thanks." She might've mumbled another thanks for the ride, but all her attention remained across the street.

As she moved toward the community's entrance, she sensed Theo's questioning gaze on her. Each step forward felt heavier with the fearsome weight of responsibility. She glanced back once, catching Theo's hand in a parting wave, and offered a brief wave in return before bolstering her resolve.

Her pace quickened, driven by the urgent need to reach her sister, and her heart raced, anxiety and protective instincts intertwining.

Jada saw her coming and rushed toward her. "Whit, thank God you're home."

"Are you okay?" Whitney's voice teetered on the brink of breaking as she pulled Jada into an embrace. "You shouldn't be out here this late."

"It's Mama." Jada shivered, her arms wrapped tight around Whitney. "The Turners found her passed out in front of their place."

Whitney held her sister secure. The younger girl's sadness palpable, her emotions raw and unguarded under the dim security lights. "Oh, baby, Mama needs our help. And our prayers."

Jada stiffened, pushing away, and hugged her arms around her thin middle. "We miss Daddy too, but we don't go doing drugs."

Aching alongside her, Whitney touched her sister's jutted-out jaw. Mama would rather be high than sober to spend time in their company. "You should've called me instead of running out here."

Jada jerked back from Whitney's touch and nudged a pebble along with her sandal. "I'm out of call minutes."

The confession stirred a new concern. Jada shouldn't have run out of minutes, not so soon. They started walking, ignoring the leers and mumbles, the sharp, acrid scent of drugs.

"Who was that man?" Jada stopped.

"What man?"

"The one who dropped you off," Jada pressed, turning, and Whitney turned too just as Theo's car made a U-turn and drove off. He must've wanted to make sure she was okay before he left. Dismissing the sudden warmth over his reaction, she nudged Jada with her elbow. "How'd you even see it was a guy? It was dark."

"His lights turned on when you opened the door. Is he your boyfriend?"

She'd been harboring a few fantasies of him. How could she not? The gentleness in his actions, the strength of his presence, the friendliness of his teasing—it all swirled into a kaleidoscope of what-ifs.

"No," she said, despite the silent thrill the idea gave her. "He's just a coworker who offered me a ride."

"I thought I'd never live to see the day *you* got a boyfriend." Jada smirked as if she hadn't heard Whitney's denial.

"He's not my boyfriend." But Whitney's mind was in a whirl. Could she afford the luxury of a relationship with her mother and sister depending on her?

Especially a relationship with a man who seemed to be a puzzle with missing pieces. She'd seen two different sides of him tonight; The gentleman and kind diligent coworker and the hardcore businessman engrossed in a mysterious call.

As they walked, her thoughts drifted back to his car, the scent that wafted around him, the warmth in his eyes, the sincere way he'd asked if he could pick her up in the morning. For a fleeting moment, she allowed herself to consider the tantalizing possibility of "what could be."

But then reality settled back in as unforgiving and stark as ever. As they approached their dilapidated trailer, the lights from Theo's car faded like a distant memory, a faint glimmer from a world unattainable.

CHAPTER 6

Theo's hands tightened on the steering wheel as he drove the somewhat familiar road from last night, his heart radiating a warm glow. Whitney's hard work and exhaustion from yesterday had lingered in his mind, so it was the perfect opportunity to brighten her day as she had his.

He shook his head, a smile spreading across his face. The rich smells of six different hot beverages filled the car, making it feel like a little piece of home.

As he turned into the mobile home community, he could see the place better than last night. All homes were the same off-white color. Most displayed rust or chipped paint.

He parked on the roadside close to the entrance, as he had last night. The place seemed different now, quieter with the people who'd been wandering around gone. Random cars drove away, probably heading to work.

He turned on the music from his playlist, one of his favorite gospel songs to calm his nerves. He tapped on the steering wheel as he looked at the two drinks in the cup holders and the few he'd stashed in each cup holder in the back.

Did she drink tea or coffee? Or none? Too late to figure that out now.

Reaching for his phone, he thumbed the screen and typed a message to let her know he'd arrived. A response came right back.

Whitney: I'll be right out.

She'd been hesitant last night when he offered to pick her up, seeming distraught. Concerned about her, he'd waited to make sure she walked safely past the group. Only he'd seen her embrace a teenager before he drove away.

Hmm. Whatever that had been about, reminded him how little he knew about her. He wasn't even going to delve into why she didn't want him to know where she lived. He had her address and could look up her house on Google Maps if he wanted to, but there was no need.

She shouldn't be embarrassed by where she lived. The low-income housing wouldn't deter him or change his view of her. He'd seen plenty of people in similar circumstances, even sponsored and helped several in South and North America, but he'd also lived the same lifestyle before he was adopted.

Whitney approached in her uniform, her vibrant energy in stark contrast to her exhaustion last night. His heart gave an uncharacteristic lurch as a teenager strutted behind her, their resemblance unmistakable for sisters. He turned off the music, stepped out, and moved to the passenger side, intent on opening the door for her.

Before he could, she waved. "Good morning, Theo."

Her smile warmed him, sending flutters to his stomach. "Good morning."

What was with this pull of attraction? Most of his interactions with people outside his family were work-related. While he wanted to believe his connection with Whitney was professional, it felt different. Yes, something was brewing almost like a vacation from his usual life.

When they stopped in front of him, the petite teenager eyed him, and he took in her youthful style.

"This is my sister." Whitney hugged the girl to her side.

"Jada." The girl waved, her bright eyes curious.

"Nice to meet you, Jada." He nodded, an unexpected tenderness reminding him of his sisters. "I'm Theo."

"Cool." She adjusted the strap of her flashy backpack, her straightforward gaze exhibiting a confidence behind her nonchalance.

"Um." Whitney cleared her throat. "Would it be okay if we first drop Jada off at school? It won't be out of our way."

"Of course."

"I didn't get my homework done last night. Now, Whit thinks I gotta get to school over an hour early."

At Jada's complaint, Whitney gave her a nudge toward the car, and the sisters shared knowing smiles.

It appeared Whitney—or Whit, he rather preferred her sister's shortening of her name—had a strong influence on Jada's life. "Whit's idea is legit, don't you think?"

Jada rolled her eyes but swung the back door open and slid in without further argument.

Theo opened the front passenger door for Whitney, catching a delightful whiff of something coconut and floral as she slid into the car, her genuine smile offering her silent thanks. He closed the door, still absorbing the closeness of the moment. Her presence was starting to have a way of commandeering his feelings.

"Thank you for opening the door for me." She turned to him as he took his seat. "You didn't have to do that."

"I wanted to." An unusual connection sparked between them, and he struggled to breathe as he reached to tug at her seat belt, indicating she buckle in. "For your safety."

She smiled sheepishly before strapping it across her shoulder.

A companionable silence settled in as he started the engine, replaying the simple exchange, the way her eyes lit up, the way her hair smelled, the way his stomach lurched. Why did it feel like something important was happening?

As they drove, the first hues of sunrise painted the sky, and the promise of its coming beauty opened something inside him. Was he willing to explore if this new connection with Whitney promised to lead to something beautiful?

"Smells like cinnamon and chocolate in here," Jada said from the back.

Right. The drinks. He grinned at Whitney. "I got you some coffee. And tea." He tipped his chin to the two cups in the front cup holders. "Wasn't sure what you drank. So there's several options in the cup holders in the back too."

"She likes chai tea with whipped cream."

At her sister's words, Theo's eyes widened, and an unexpected thrill teased him. "Really?"

What were the odds they liked the same beverage? "I like whipped cream with mine too." Although he rarely indulged in it. "It's not a healthy drink to keep in my daily diet."

Whitney read the writing on one of the disposable cups she retrieved from the front cup holders. "There's chai tea right here. Thank you, Theo."

He braved a glance away from the road as she took a sip.

Her smile, her laugh, even her manner of sipping tea—everything about her drew him in. It was as if his car was the only one on the road. All the others were a blur.

"Can I have the caramel macchiato?" Jada piped up, and he glanced at Whitney, deferring to her opinion.

"Sure." Whitney laughed. "I hope there's not much caffeine in it. Otherwise, God bless your teachers today."

Jada rustled around. "What are you going to do with the rest of the drinks back here?"

"I'll let Whitney decide who she thinks deserves them at work." He'd bought the drinks for Whitney after all.

"Whit says you're still new in Houston." Jada's curiosity was evident, the shift of the conversation seeming more personal, yet that meant the sisters had talked about him. "Are you going to stay here forever?"

"Forever is a long time." He shifted his grip on the steering wheel, not wanting to delve into *that* conversation and reveal too much. "You girls live together?"

"Yeah." Whitney's response came so low he glanced at her, her lips pressing together in a sad line.

"We live with our mom too," Jada added. "Whit feeds us and pays the bills."

"Jada?" Whitney's voice was scolding.

"What did I say wrong? It's the truth, ain't it?"

Whitney sighed. "You shouldn't have *any* caffeine."

A heavy silence followed, unspoken questions and unacknowledged emotions weighing on it. His heart ached to know more, to understand what lay beneath the surface, but he held back, giving her space. After all, he had his secrets to keep.

The rest of the drive was quiet, the tension palpable, even as the blazing sunrise fulfilled its promised glory. Whitney gazed over the road whenever he glanced at her, not even acknowledging the beauty and hope before her, her mind elsewhere. His chest tightened.

They dropped Jada off next to a basketball court, and he rolled down the window as Whitney shouted a goodbye to the teen.

"Riding in the car sure beats the bus ride, thanks." Jada gave him a jaunty salute, then bent to peer into the side window. "Is it okay if I take another drink with me?"

"You're welcome to take—"

"No way," Whitney interjected, and her smile reemerged. "You see how much energy one cup of caramel macchiato gave her."

"I always have energy." Jada grinned, reached in, and snagged a cup, then wished her sister a good day and him better luck at the new job.

After she left, he drove them to the resort, the morning's revelations still hanging in the air, and he wanted to understand more, to know her better.

"Your sister is sweet," he said, meaning it but also needing to keep talking. Or he could play the music.

"Sometimes." She rolled her eyes, but a tender protectiveness belied the gesture. "She's a teenager, so there's always mood swings coming."

"She said you take care of your mom. Is she okay?"

"The thing is, she can be okay, but her choices..." Her eyes clouded over as if a shadow had passed across the sun, and the promise of a glorious sunrise, a new beginning, faded. "Lately, our bonding moments are just arguments."

She sighed and recounted their latest clash. "I only found her hidden drugs because my favorite cup broke." Her voice diminished as she reminisced about the cup, its motivational quote a daily source of inspiration.

He'd have to find her a replacement cup with a similar uplifting message. "It's nice that you take care of your family."

"I had to after Dad died." Her gaze shifted out the window, her body language closing off.

With his free hand, he reached to touch hers, a gentle gesture of comfort. "I'm sorry about your dad. What happened?"

"A tornado struck." She spoke so fast it almost startled him. Then she waved to the cup holder. "You just started a new job, and you bought all these expensive drinks."

His cheeks heated. He hadn't thought about maintaining his cover when he'd splurged. "I still have some savings from my previous job."

She blew out a breath. "That was very thoughtful of you, by the way."

"I was getting myself one anyway." He shrugged, that strange warmth invading his chest. He'd wanted to do something for her, anything to brighten her day. He pulled into the employee parking lot. "Do you know who you're going to give the rest of the beverages to?"

Her eyes sparkled as she listed off some names, most of which he couldn't remember. But he enjoyed listening to her, the cadence of her voice, the gleam of her eyes.

After she unbuckled, she surprised him by touching his arm. "I've been meaning to ask you. What were you doing that night I sprayed you? It was late, and you were wandering in the secluded part of the resort."

She was too inquisitive. "I like exploring." Yikes, the lies flowed so easily now. "I was staying there for the night, and I wanted to check out where I was going to work." Well, at least *some* of that was true.

She smiled, nodding along with his answer, and something in his chest loosened. "Well, then." She patted his arm and unbuckled her seat belt. "Ready for housecleaning?"

"As long as they don't move me around today." Whatever task he had today wouldn't likely include housekeeping. Which meant he wouldn't see her most of the day. The HR manager texted something about him working in maintenance.

As he helped her carry the drinks, he couldn't shake the suspicion that his lies were becoming the proverbial tangled web, one that could ensnare him at any moment. He didn't even want to imagine how Whitney would react if she found out he was lying to her.

But why did he care so much about her reaction?

That question he wasn't sure he was ready to answer yet. Still, the thought echoed in his mind as he followed her into the resort.

CHAPTER 7

The fresh coffee aroma blended with the grand lobby's inviting scents as Whitney stepped into her comforting haven, the source of her livelihood. Theo's presence was adding an intriguing new thread into her daily routine. There was something distinct about him, a depth underlying his acts of kindness. Somehow, she'd figure out this puzzle that was Theo. With her family in its current state, was she ready for whatever he was, whatever *they* could be, and whatever he might bring into her already complicated life?

The warm morning light cascaded through the vast windows, illuminating the marbled cream-colored tiles. Daniela stood behind the desk, savoring her coffee as if capturing each taste in her memory. The scent of coffee and the deep woodsy fragrance of polished mahogany enveloped them in a comforting bubble.

Daniela, eyes closed in delight after a sip of her white chocolate mocha, remarked, "Nothing beats a good coffee in the morning."

Whitney nodded, enjoying her chai tea. Their friendship had blossomed after Whitney began her job at the resort. The brief work interactions had become a cherished ritual, her only time away from her home responsibilities.

Setting her cup on the reception desk, Daniela nodded toward Theo, who was disappearing down the hallway. With a glint in her eye, she lilted in her Spanish accent. "Do you care to explain why he got you all these coffees?"

Heat crept up Whitney's neck. "Just like Theo said." She shrugged, recalling his offer to distribute the extra coffees she had suggested for the staff.

"A newbie buys you six fancy coffees, and you get to pick one?" Daniela's eyebrows shimmied, her grin widening. "Somebody"—she singsonged like a middle schooler—"*likes* you."

"Quiet!" Whitney hissed, casting anxious glances around the empty lobby. Good, no one heard. "Can you be *a bit* more discreet?"

Daniela's chuckle was *not* discreet. "So, spill." She nudged Whitney. "What's the deal?"

Edging closer and keeping her voice low, Whitney shared about last night's shift and Theo driving her home. She left out the distressing part about Mama's condition when they arrived.

Daniela tilted her head, her eyebrows shimmying again. "A ride, *six* coffees, and that lingering gaze during his farewell? Amiga, there's more to the story."

Whitney's heart fluttered. Was Daniela onto something? Was there more to Theo's acts of kindness?

But even if there was... Whitney sighed. So many obstacles remained in her way. Caught between the immediate needs of her family and the distant allure of something more, she imagined herself at a crossroads, and it was still too early to tell which path her heart was willing to take. Despite the roadblocks, a bubble of excitement betrayed a hidden longing for the thrill of a budding romance. "Jumping into a relationship isn't feasible right now."

"You could use a bit of romance to distract you from your busy life."

Whitney shrugged. "So, what's on your agenda this weekend?"

Daniela widened her eyes in mock horror, her hand dramatically flying to her chest. "Seriously? You've forgotten about our Sunday gig already?"

Whitney cringed. She'd requested *next* Saturday off for a catering gig assignment. "I thought the wedding was next week."

Daniela frowned and reached for her phone, scrolled through it, and slapped her forehead. "I can't believe I'd assumed it was this weekend."

"I'm glad it's you messing up this time." Whitney saluted her friend with her now-empty chai tea cup. At least, her busy life hadn't tampered with her mind. "Worse yet, you thought it was on a Sunday."

"You should invite Theo." Daniela shook a finger at Whitney. "I'm sure he could use the extra cash too."

"It might be too late for him to join." As the idea set her heart racing, Whitney's voice was less confident. Could she work at a wedding event with Theo? It would be like a field trip away from River Oasis. Warmth spread through her. After a few days of knowing him and working alongside him, so many unexpected emotions began to stir.

"It's not like he needs any training to clear the dishes from the tables." Daniela patted Whitney's arm. "If you're too shy, I'll ask him."

Whitney wet her lips, struggling to articulate her reasons against Theo joining them. But Daniela's knowing look stopped her short. Then someone approached to check out, Daniela slipped on her professional smile, and Whitney made her exit. They could chat more during lunch.

As she navigated the ornate lobby, replete with lush plants and elegant furnishings, her mind circled back to Theo. Was there a chance he was attracted to her?

She shook her head and pushed the thoughts away. Life had enough uncertainties without adding romance to the journey. Yet, as she stocked the cart with cleaning supplies, she entertained the thrilling prospect that maybe, just maybe, she was facing a crossroads, and perhaps she could step into the unknown and discover where it led.

***

Theo's absence made the following days longer and more tedious. How could Whitney miss him so much, given they'd only worked in housekeeping together for those two days? Except for the occasional days he worked in the restaurant.

While cleaning the rooms, she often glanced down from the balcony. Earlier today, her gaze found him by the pool, shoulders moving in laughter as he joked with Diego from maintenance. Now, she spotted him again, crouched by a fence, engrossed in a repair, the Texas sun casting a golden hue on his tan skin. Even from this distance, the furrow of concentration on his brow was evident, and she didn't need to be close to remember the soft brown of his eyes or the way curiosity lit them.

When lunchtime rolled around, Daniela approached the picnic table with bags of food, handing one to Whitney. "A gift from Theo. He said it was his turn to treat."

Whitney and Theo had been taking turns bringing lunch. While she brought PB&Js, he purchased their lunches.

With several others chatting around them and two employees standing aside smoking, Whitney and Daniela closed their eyes and silently prayed over their food.

Biting into the chicken sandwich, Whitney was met with a burst of flavors. Paired with the tangy freshness of lemonade, the meal was nothing short of a delightful change. The packaging didn't bear any familiar logos, and given its quality, it wasn't cheap. Did he have a lot of money saved up, or was he too lavish in his spending?

Daniela, seated at the picnic table alongside her, nudged Whitney with her shoulder. "You've been looking lost without Theo joining us for lunch."

Whitney shrugged, unable to deny she'd missed him. But no way would she admit how she'd been longing for even a simple mishap in a room that required her to make a maintenance call just so she could cross paths with him.

As the afternoon wore on with no sight of him, she made her way down to the pool area during her break, pausing by the ice machine for a handful to chew on. The sun had descended into the clouds, easing the heat, but the humidity hung thick still.

She spotted Theo and Diego in the shade of an oak outside the pool gate, lost in conversation while munching on packed lunches. Her steps slowed at a flutter of hesitation. Her nerves started pumping, and her bold decision to come here didn't seem like a smart strategy. What was the plan again? Okay, Diego was her friend and colleague, and she'd stopped by to say hello before. Whoa, were they conversing in Spanish? If so, Theo sounded fluent.

Diego, having noticed her approach, waved, his skin glistening and overly tanned. "Hey, Whitney!"

"Hey, Diego." What was with her voice? Nervous, she tucked her hands behind her back, determined to keep her focus trained on Diego, but through the corner of her eye, she could see Theo grinning at her. "I, um, thought I'd check how the new employee is holding up."

Diego chuckled and slapped Theo's shoulder. "Honestly? Feels like he's the teacher and I'm the rookie."

Her eyes betrayed her when her gaze flickered to Theo.

Mischief crinkled the corners of his eyes and mouth. "I've tinkered with a few repairs before." He gestured to the grassy patch beside him. "Care to join us for lunch?"

"I've had lunch already." But the warmth of his smile and the way her nerves danced out a jittery excitement in his presence, swayed her, and she settled onto the soft grass. The blades tickled her ankles as she stretched out her legs. She didn't have to worry about staining the dark scrub pants while she was cleaning after all.

Theo extended a bowl toward her. "Round two? Fresh fruit for dessert." The juicy berries and slices looked like cafeteria food, as did Diego's half-eaten wrap.

"I owe you one for the lunch delivery, by the way." She nodded to Theo. "Thank you for lunch."

"And you didn't think you could trust me to remember." He winked. "Seriously, though a few good tips yesterday made it easy to splurge."

"Y'know what this gourmet picnic is missing?" Diego spoke up. "Whitney's famous chocolate chip cookies. Those are always a game changer."

With an unmistakable twinkle in his eye, Theo said, "I'd love to try those someday." He skewered a strawberry with a toothpick and held it out to her, making it seem as though sharing food was their little routine.

Caught off guard, she chuckled before taking the offering, and conversation flowed. Diego recounted a day he'd subbed for housecleaning, leading to a soapy fiasco when he confused soap with floor cleaner and turned a room into a foam wonderland.

"Trust me. We've all had mishaps of some sort." Theo then regaled them with a story of getting locked out of his car during a downpour, keys mocking him from the driver's seat.

Whitney clutched her stomach as she laughed. She hadn't laughed this much in a while.

Then he pointed at her. "Come on. Everyone has a blunder to share. What's yours?"

She inhaled to ease her laughter and struggled to recall a lighthearted error amid her recent intense life challenges. "I don't think mine will beat yours and Diego's."

Steering the conversation back to work, she shared details about the upcoming weekend gig. "You're both welcome to join us." She tucked wayward curls behind her ears. "It's not a gold mine, but the pay's better than our regular housekeeping rate. We all could use some extra spending cash."

"Wish I could." Diego shrugged. "Gig somewhere else already."

Theo scratched at his jaw. "A wedding, you say? No interview required?"

"Straightforward gig." She nodded. "No background checks."

Feigning horror, Theo mockingly stroked his stubble. "But what if I'm a shady character? What happens if we work with questionable characters? Do you know these people?"

He was way too cautious. She snorted, stopping short of shoving his shoulder. "We'll be fine."

His thick eyebrows shot up. "You mean with your pepper spray?"

She buried her face in her hand. "I made a mistake and pepper sprayed you, but it doesn't mean everyone you encounter poses a threat."

He gave a dramatic sigh. "With your pepper spray, maybe we'll be safe."

"Wait." Diego bounced a finger between them. "You sprayed him?"

"Oh, she ambushed me all right." Theo's animated recounting of the pepper-spray incident had Diego doubled over with laughter, wiping away tears from his eyes. But Theo had avoided answering her about the upcoming gig. It didn't seem the money was holding him back. So, she let it drop.

As the day wound down, she transitioned to her evening restaurant shift, and Theo approached her. "I need to leave early today."

"See you tomorrow."

"I'll text you in a few." He left with his phone in hand as if he'd been in the middle of a call.

Later, while in the warm kitchen during the slow restaurant hours, the familiar chime of an incoming message rang from Whitney's phone. She pulled it out to read.

Theo: Hey, let me know when you're off. I'll drive you home.

Unable to contain a smile, she pressed a hand to her chest, touched by his offer. But he was already home, no need to inconvenience him.

Whitney: I appreciate it, but I'm good tonight. The bus is no bother.

Theo: If you're sure. By the way, I'd be up for that gig. Thanks for suggesting it.

Whitney: Great! I'll send you the application link when I get home.

Theo: Wait, I thought there were no interviews?

Whitney: Just a formality. They need your details for the paycheck.

Theo: Deal. But only if I get to be your chauffeur to the event.

Her cheeks heated. Was he flirting with her? Even if he was, Daniela was already her designated driver.

Whitney: Daniela's driving me. Rain check on that ride?

When he responded with a playful sad emoji, that uncontainable smile became a full-on grin, and a delightful flutter quivered in her stomach. Every interaction with Theo left her anticipating the next.

CHAPTER 8

The wedding unfolded on the vast grounds of a countryside estate repurposed as an event center. Though humidity blanketed the afternoon, a gentle breeze rustled through the trees lining the property, gifting Theo with a fleeting respite. He and Whitney stood side by side under the shade, their trays shimmering with champagne-filled crystal flutes.

Elegant white chairs dressed with lavender ribbons stretched out toward a beautifully draped arbor, wisteria shivering along the latticework. Beneath it, a couple exchanged their heartfelt vows. As the officiant declared them husband and wife, a surge of applause cascaded through the crowd. Accompanied by a string quartet, the couple's kiss displayed pure elation and elicited a poignant ache in Theo's chest.

Since when did he yearn for a moment like that? Always submerged in work, he'd never taken time to dream of such moments with that special someone.

"Tell me that's not the best smell in the world." Whitney's soft voice pulled him back. She was standing beside him, eyes closed, face turned up to catch the scent. "It's so delicate, but can you smell the wisteria?"

"Which ones are the wisteria again?" He nudged her, feigning ignorance.

Her eyes opened and twinkled as she gestured toward the blossoms. "All those, both darker purple ones on the fence and the paler almost milky-lavender ones on the arbor, are wisteria." Her shoulders sloped. "I hope to be surrounded by them when I die."

Something cold gripped him. Death was a reality he pretended didn't exist. Why in the world would she be thinking about *death*? "Surely you'd prefer them at a wedding."

Her gaze drifted toward the magnificent mansion beyond the altar. A shadow dimmed her eyes, and melancholy dipped her voice. "To dream of a wedding, one should at least have a boyfriend."

Wow! So she was single.

However, he couldn't yet pursue her, not without unveiling secrets he wasn't ready to share. But as their eyes met, the golden specks in her brown irises held him rapt, and awareness buzzed between them. They stood, bound in a world of their own. As the celebration echoed around him, his heart beat louder than the noise.

"What do you two think you're doing?" A sharp voice pierced their bubble.

Startled, he nearly lost his grip, causing the champagne tray to wobble. He steadied himself, only to find Karina glaring at him. The event manager's eyes, steely and unforgiving, sent shivers down his spine.

"Do I need to spell it out?" She waved one hand in the air, her tone disdaining.

"You instructed us to wait here," he replied, biting the inside of his cheek, unwilling to follow directions from someone so domineering. Man, he wanted to tell her to back off.

Her expression darkened even further. "There's a difference between waiting and slacking off." It seemed as though her tightly wound ponytail might snap from the sheer force of her anger.

Whitney tried to intervene. "We were just—"

An impatient gesture from Karina cut her off. "Pictures are about to start. Move!"

With that, Karina was off.

"I'm sorry about that," Whitney whispered to him, then hurried away with her tray, and he trailed, still fighting the urge to lash out at their boss.

Workers bustled around, shifting furniture beneath the expansive tent. Jazz melodies wafted from a music station, blending with the carefree laughter of children darting between grand oaks.

Navigating groups of guests immersed in chatter, Theo and Whitney passed champagne around. Some guests grabbed flutes with practiced ease, while others opted for hors d'oeuvres from fellow servers, all clad in crisp black-and-white uniforms.

By the mansion, a makeshift bar drew a lively crowd. Meanwhile, other guests, champagne in hand, relaxed on the manicured lawns, their attention captured by the wedding party striking poses for their photographer.

Theo made his way back into the estate's opulent interior, Whitney beside him, for more champagne. Daniela, with a practiced hand, filled each glass. "Theo. Whitney." She cast them each a knowing grin. "How are you liking the job so far?"

"It's not bad." He shrugged. Except for the bossy event manager.

Smirking, Daniela glanced between him and Whitney.

Whatever Whitney's friend was up to, Theo ignored her as he took his tray and waited for Whitney. Somehow, he savored Whitney's company. She was, of course, the reason he'd agreed to a gig, another job he shouldn't be adding to his long to-do list.

"I wonder why we're serving champagne outside when there's a bar set up right here," Whitney asked as they walked through the hallway.

"I thought the same thing." He stepped outside. "But it's a wedding, so—"

Was that a familiar face by the bar area? Yes, Juan Alves, a prominent journalist from Brazil. He'd interviewed Theo multiple times. Their eyes met, and Theo saw the dawning recognition.

Just great. His cover could get blown today. He needed to disappear. Fast.

He pivoted, almost causing Whitney to lose her tray. "I'm so sorry," he uttered hurriedly.

"Are you okay?" Her whisper pitched low, underplayed with worry as she eyed him.

He forced a breath. "I need a moment. Bathroom break."

Her gaze lingered, narrowing. "I'll cover for you. Just... be okay."

And there was that guilt gnawing at him again. She was concerned about him, thinking he was in pain or something. He whispered a hasty thanks as he started heading to the entrance, but his gaze darted to Juan, now weaving through the guests. The background noise seemed muted, his heart's rapid beat the only clear sound.

With every step, the pressing weight of his secret and the haunting echo of Whitney's concerned voice chased him. The clink of half-filled glasses on his tray resonated with his racing heart. Relief escaped in a rush as he reached the hallway, safe. He slowed his steps, uncertain whether to go to the back room or wander through the event center. Going to the kitchen was a better idea.

Footsteps pattered from behind. Then that voice, just as he was about to push through the kitchen door—

"Theo Stone?"

Theo ground his teeth. He might as well deal with Juan now, in Whitney's absence. He turned, masking his anxiety with a strained smile, and tried to keep his tone casual. "Juan. Let me set this tray down, and we can catch up."

Head cocked, Juan waved him off.

Theo pushed through the swinging kitchen doors.

Daniela looked up in surprise. "Why'd you bring that back?"

"Needed a bathroom break," he muttered, and maybe he should go to the bathroom, if only to keep that bit of truth intact.

Trays clinked, and chefs bustled around, prepping the next course. He took a deep breath, bracing himself for the coming conversation. Juan Alves wasn't just any journalist. He was a top-tier reporter. Their interactions had always been professional, but in this unexpected context, Theo wasn't sure where he stood.

Emerging from the kitchen, he steered Juan away from the main hallway, hoping to avoid running into Whitney or Karina. Once they passed the lobby and made their way to another hall, Juan asked, "*What* are you doing *here*?"

"Helping a friend." Theo pressed his back against a wall, his head brushing a framed photo. "It's a long story."

"This could make a juicy story, I bet." Juan squared his shoulders beneath his dark suit. His eyes glinted, the way they did when his journalistic instincts kicked in.

Theo glanced back at the activity in the opposite hall. The walls seemed to close in on him. If Whitney or Karina walked in and started questioning how he knew one of the event attendees—well, this wasn't just a simple wedding, but for someone influential or wealthy.

"You wouldn't want to make this a story." Theo's chest rose, then fell. What if Juan insisted on making a story out of this?

Juan raised an eyebrow, his hawkish gaze narrowing. "Is that a threat?"

Theo had no real issue with Juan, but some journalists would go to great lengths for a headline. "If you value your job"—he began, regretting his tone—"you'll act like you never saw me here."

Juan chuckled, but a tension strained the sound. So the guy grasped the gravity.

"So, why are you here?" Theo asked.

"My cousin's wedding—the actress."

"The one who filmed in Brazil last year?" Right, Juan had talked about her while chatting him up before an exclusive interview.

"The one and only."

Relief loosened the knot in Theo's chest. He slapped Juan's jacketed shoulder. "Have fun then."

"Wait, Stone." Still frowning, Juan caught Theo's wrist. "A media mogul moonlighting as a server? Surely, there are easier ways to help a friend."

"It's complicated," was all Theo could muster, casting a furtive glance down the hallway.

"She must be quite something, then." Juan's expression softened. "She doesn't know who you are, does she?"

"Not yet." Theo's voice rasped his throat, thick with the strain of withheld truth.

For a moment, Juan held on, perhaps debating pushing further. But then he exhaled and released his clutch. "All right. But when this is all over, you owe me an exclusive."

Theo chuckled. That was the best he could do. "Deal."

They shook hands before they walked back, his secret safe for now. Or so he thought until they approached the lobby at the same time as Whitney emerged from the other hallway with a tray of drinks.

"Good seeing you, Theo," Juan commented, not noticing Whitney standing there. Theo could only nod, his mind already racing for the right words should Whitney ask. Keeping up the charade was becoming increasingly tiresome.

CHAPTER 9

"Hey," Theo greeted Whitney, trying to sound casual, but his voice came out strained—guilty, even. An itch of nervousness tingled up his spine, and he gripped the back of his neck.

"The bathroom is over there." She nodded toward the lobby.

He looked in that direction, having no idea where the bathroom was. He hadn't thought of it since their arrival.

"Yeah." He rubbed his stubble, ducking his head from those captivating eyes now filled with—what? Confusion? Doubt? Definitely questions.

"What was that about?"

"He, um, ran into me on my way to..." The lie clogged his throat, and his gaze drifted to the massive chandelier.

"Is he who you were trying to avoid?"

So she'd figured out why he'd retreated.

"He's someone I worked with in the past." He took a step closer. Maybe he could steer them both back to their tasks and away from this conversation. Karina's arrival would be a relief, her scolding a welcome distraction from this awkward conversation.

He placed a gentle hand on the small of Whitney's back to lead her outside, and a comforting warmth spread up his arm, reminding him of how close they'd grown in such a short time.

"You've worked *with* him, not *for* him? Someone who looks... affluent. What kind of job?"

"Just because someone is related to the wealthy couple doesn't mean they're rich themselves," he snapped. *I promise I'll explain everything when the time's right.*

She halted, pulling away. Her brows scrunched together, and her head tipped at a curious angle. "Are you some kind of detective?"

His chest loosened up as he chuckled. "I've had a variety of jobs, but detective work? Far from it."

70

Her expression shifted, her face tightening. "I'll see you later."

He stood there as she turned, adjusted her tray, and strode away.

As the evening wore on, the rhythm of the event took over. Serving drinks and food, then clearing dirty dishes. Constant activity, punctuated by Karina's relentless commands. Until the sun sank beneath the horizon and Karina allowed a few of them a dinner break. He exhaled and rolled his neck, working the kinks out with relief, although he still sensed Whitney's questions.

Now, he stood by the bustling kitchen, waiting for his food. Whitney seemed absorbed in the mundane task of organizing the utensil boxes on a loaded and disorganized stainless steel shelf. She stood on tiptoes, arms stretched toward a higher shelf, fingertips grazing the steel wire, perhaps too hard. The boxes on the top teetered on the edge, looming above her like a suspended threat.

With a burst of urgency, he sidestepped the food table and closed the distance between them. His hand found the curve of her lower back and steered her away. The abrupt motion brought them close, their bodies melding in a brief collision as the boxes clattered to the floor.

The kitchen activity muted to a backdrop, overpowered by the intimate beating of his heart and hers in a synchronized rhythm. His arms encircled her, protecting and absorbing her into his presence. They stood entwined in a cocoon of shared breaths, matching the subtle rise and fall of each other's chests—a connection too palpable to ignore.

Whitney's eyes widened, a glint of surprise melting into vulnerability. His gaze flitted to her rounded lips. As he fought to keep his mind from conjuring what it would be like to kiss her, he couldn't help imagining a universe of unspoken words and tender understanding. The kitchen's warmth seemed to meld into the heat of their proximity, the mingling scents of spices weaving into a special, ephemeral connection.

"You're safe." At last, he breathed out, his whisper resonating in the space between them.

Her breath, sweet as the pastries on the kitchen counters, mingled with his, her face aglow with a vulnerable appreciation. "Thank you, Theo." Her words were a tender breeze in the heated room.

"Food's ready." The chef's announcement brought Theo back to reality, and he swallowed and untangled himself from her.

The world resumed its pace, and they moved toward a buffet setup—each carrying a tray to load up. Yet, in their shared silence, a powerful awareness simmered. He took slow, steadying breaths, feeling the depth of an unexplored ocean of emotions. He chose salmon and broccoli, while she selected diced sweet potatoes and chicken breast. Both selections were infused with the rich, mouthwatering aromas of garlic and other spices.

Steam rose on their plates as they settled into a room adjacent to the kitchen. He closed his eyes and said a quiet prayer over his food. When he opened them again, she was doing the same, her lips moving silently. Basking in the warmth of shared faith, he added a special thanks for this moment alone with her.

"Tell me more about your mom," he began, cutting into his salmon. He understood her mom's struggle with addiction, but he didn't know the extent. "Why isn't she able to work?"

Whitney sighed, her posture sagging. "After Dad passed, Mama turned to drugs and alcohol. They consume her now." She clasped her hands together on the table, food forgotten. "I poured so much money into rehab for her, only to realize she needs to want it for herself."

His heart throbbed as he imagined the weight of financial responsibilities on her shoulders. If only he could tell her it wasn't her job to shoulder all this, but he knew better. He would do the same for his family if the roles were reversed.

"I think Jada and I are such a burden to her that she drinks herself to intoxication to avoid us."

"I don't think so." He extended his hand across the table, gently covering hers. "You know she loves you guys." She was their mom, and while she had an addiction, any parent loved their kids no matter what—didn't they?

"I hope you're right." She eyed his hand on hers, so he slid it away. He'd felt the need to comfort, but he needed to do so without touching her.

As the conversation meandered toward brighter horizons, their hopes and dreams, the glow returned to her eyes. "I always thought I wanted to be a nurse, but now, I'm leaning toward the hospitality industry. Maybe one day I'll own a hotel or an inn." She scooped up a gooey spoonful of sweet potatoes. "What about you? If money weren't an issue, what would be your dream?"

He'd already achieved his professional dreams, but there was more to life than that. He forked a piece of fish, the edges crispy, the meat flaky. "I love spending time with my family." He preferred doing everything with his family if it came down to it, but he was an adult now. He'd wanted to prove he was capable of being far from home when he leapt at the business opportunity in Brazil. "Traveling, discovering exotic places. And hey"—he winked at her—"I might visit your hotel someday."

She chuckled, the sound pure and heartwarming. "Our dreams couldn't be more different."

"Opposites often complement each other." He lifted the fork of salmon to his mouth, picturing her in his life after his façade.

She nodded, then smiling, shared stories of her parents before her dad's passing. "So different, yet deeply in love." The atmosphere lightened, and the burdens of his secrets floated away, replaced by the joy of genuine connection.

Then Daniela walked in, plate in hand. "These events pay well, but with managers like Karina? Ugh." She flopped into a chair next to Whitney. "I was due for a break an hour ago."

"This job is hard," Theo said, wishing he'd demanded a break way earlier when the dance floor opened. "Ensure to demand your breaks next time."

"Daniela did the right thing." Whitney sliced her chicken, countering. "You can't talk back to your boss."

"That aside." Daniela flicked her wrist, the knife she held catching the light as it traced an arc in the air. "You wouldn't believe what happened during the shoe-removal ritual. This guy…"

She paused for dramatic effect, her eyes twinkling, and Theo's fork hovered midair.

"He ends up swapping shoes with someone else!" she burst out, her laughter punctuating her sentence. "Two left feet, mind you, and in mismatched colors—one neon green, the other burgundy!"

While Theo didn't find it humorous, Daniela's laughter made the incident funny, and he let himself laugh. Whitney laughed as well, the sound warming him to his core.

Then Karina strode in. "The men's restroom is messy." Her gaze pierced into Theo and Whitney. "Get up, now."

Theo narrowed his eyes at Karina. "Cleaning? We were hired to serve food, not scrub toilets."

Karina's face darkened a shade, her voice rising. "You'll do what you're told if you want to get paid tonight. Now, go."

Whitney, eyes wide, threw him a furtive glance. With her back turned to Karina, she mouthed, "We need this job."

We don't, the defiant voice in his head retorted. *I'll pay you enough to last a lifetime if you never work again.* Gesturing for Whitney to stay seated, he faced Karina. "We signed up for this event as servers, not janitors."

At Whitney clearing her throat, he caught her exasperated eye roll, but ignoring her, he lined out why they weren't going to do anything far removed from catering.

"Theo's right, actually," Daniela chimed in, and having her support emboldened him that he wasn't overreacting.

Karina's eyes flashed, and her foot tapped out a jittery rhythm on the tiled floor. "Is that so? Well, you can kiss your paycheck goodbye."

He scoffed. "As a five-star catering company, you'd deny employees their pay after working them hard all evening? I doubt it." Having researched the company online, he felt confident in his challenge. "I'm sure your superiors wouldn't be thrilled hearing about their company in the news for not paying their temps."

Karina's eyes lost their previous fire, her shoulders drooping as if an invisible weight settled on them. Gone was the air of command.

"We will fulfill our responsibilities as outlined in our contract," he said. That included various tasks, but not cleaning restrooms.

Staring him down, Karina relented. "Fine. Finish up and return to your stations. But don't let me catch you slacking again."

"Deal." The corners of his mouth lifted, relishing the small but significant victory.

Once Karina left, Whitney frowned at him. "That was brave. But what if the company never hires us again?"

"Theo, I have no idea what planet you're from." Daniela shook a finger at him. "We need those nerves in this job."

While he should bask in Daniela's praise, he wasn't sure what Whitney thought of his assertiveness. She kept looking at him with furrowed brows. "We'd best not bring you along next time. No one's gonna hire us with your fussiness."

But a hint of a smile curved her lips, and that was all he needed to get through the rest of their meal.

The evening wore on, the tasks becoming more demanding. Broken glasses needed cleaning, furniture moved and rearranged. Through the flurry, they shared fleeting glances, and he took solace in Whitney's presence, though his chest ached as her fatigue became evident in the way she dragged her steps. She still pressed on though, Karina's looming presence deterring any thoughts of taking a break.

Hours later, while loading equipment into the moving truck, Theo and another male coworker were up in the back, stacking the boxes of dirty plates and event items.

Whitney's hands shook as she passed a decorative lamp to him. Something seemed off with her.

"You need to take a break." He didn't care how late they stayed to load the van. It was already past midnight, another day anyway, but he'd rather she didn't overdo it.

"I'm fine." Her voice weak, she touched her forehead while walking back to the pile of items in the paved driveway. She'd needed breaks when they worked at Oasis, and she did all this to take care of her family. Who took care of her? She probably had another hour or two of working the moment she got home, rather than going to bed right away.

Theo accepted another set of items from an employee, but his gaze sought out Whitney every so often through the security lights illuminating the driveway.

She was carrying a decorative plant, walking toward the truck, when her feet swayed and she collapsed, the plant falling out of her hands.

His heart thudding, he jumped from the back of the truck, and his feet halted before he steadied himself to the ground. "Whitney!" he shouted, scrambling to her side.

Daniela ran to Whitney's side soon too, his fear mirrored in her eyes.

He checked her pulse. It was there. She was fine. More people surrounded them now. He ordered them to step back so they didn't crowd her. Plus, he needed to see her face, make sure nothing happened to her the moment he took his eyes off her.

Reaching for his phone from his pocket, he thrust it into Daniela's hand. "Call 911."

He then eased Whitney's head off the ground, ignoring the pavement's rough scratch against his fingers. Strands of her hair soft in his fingers, he cradled her head, trying to protect her. "She might have a concussion," he murmured probing the back of her head with a protective touch.

"No... 911," Whitney murmured. "Daniela! Don't call. I'm fine."

Daniela took the phone off her ear and pressed a button before kneeling.

Whitney pulled herself up. "Can you help me up, please? I need to help get the truck loaded."

"You do not." Theo looked her in the eye to assure her that. Not on his watch. "Your work is done for today."

"Theo is right." Daniela frowned. "Not sure what this is all about, but you passed out, Whitney."

Whitney nodded, and he looked between the two women, sensing something Whitney wanted to say or not. It seemed she knew why she'd passed out.

He was relieved about one thing as he helped her stand, their fingers intertwined. They didn't have to go to the hospital.

However, seeing her wince and stagger, he asked Daniela to take Whitney's other hand. Then he forced out a request he'd never expected to hear himself say. "Let me take you to the hospital."

"Theo, please." Whitney let out a shaky breath as he helped her lower herself to the stool propped against the side door to keep it open. "As long as you or Daniela can give me a ride home, I'll be okay."

"I'll drive her." After all, he needed to keep an eye on her and make sure she didn't pass out again or display any signs of a concussion.

"You guys should leave." Daniela waved them off. "I'll cover your tasks and bring your paychecks on Monday."

Right. They were supposed to be paid after loading the van and mopping the floors.

While he hated leaving Daniela to do their tasks, Whitney needed to get home and rest. He thanked Daniela and resolved to take Whitney home.

He was just a child when his mother passed away. Perhaps, if he'd been older at the time, he might have been more attentive, possibly trailing his mom around their apartment. Maybe then, he could have witnessed her collapse and called 911 sooner. Would that have changed that fateful day?

***

The drive to Whitney's mobile home unfolded in a quiet stillness. Theo preferred it as he maintained a vigilant watch over Whitney, attuned to any irregularities in her breathing or signs of discomfort. She had adjusted her seat to recline, her head resting against the headrest. The water he offered her earlier remained mostly untouched, resting in the cup holder between them. The rhythmic rise and fall of her chest suggested she might be asleep, though he couldn't be sure, nor could he be certain if that was wise with a possible concussion.

This time, instead of parking on the street as he did to pick her up and drop her off, he drove straight to her house, the address memorized from when he'd glanced over it on his phone.

The porch light cast a gentle glow on the dented Focus, likely her car that seemed out of commission. He parked behind it.

She shifted, her eyes opening. "Oh," she mumbled. "You know where I live?"

"From the first time I drove you home." In a protective rush, he exited the car and opened the passenger door to assist her out.

"Thanks for the ride." She ducked her head, her hands knotting into the sides of her uniform. "You saved me from boxes falling over me. Now... here."

"I want to make sure you're okay." He held onto her lower back to aid her toward the two steps to the door. Even this late, people loitered in her community, smoking, and whatnot. No wonder she carried pepper spray.

She patted her pockets, a frown forming. "My handbag." She gestured toward the car.

Right. He'd tossed it into the backseat. "I'll grab it."

She touched his arm. "I've troubled you enough."

Her reluctance to impose further only deepened his concern. How sad that she wasn't used to anyone helping her. He fetched her handbag and returned to find her resting her forehead against the door. His steps quiet, he paused behind her. "Has"—his throat closed—"this happened before?"

"I'll manage." She dodged his question. "It was just another long day."

He hovered. How could he respect her wishes while ensuring she was all right? "I don't feel comfortable leaving you like this." Not after her confession about her mom, who could be too incoherent to be of any help.

"I'm okay." She slid the handbag from his grip and managed a small smile while she fished for her keys. "Would you like something to drink?"

Her voice was almost lost in the dimness of the trailer as she pushed open the door.

"I should be the one getting you a drink. Do you have milk?"

"That's the one thing I always have." She stepped aside to allow him entry, the trailer's interior was faintly lit, barely enough to see. The air was heavy with a mix of odors—the sharp sting of alcohol unmistakable. From down the hallway, music played, its blaring beat incongruent with the somber mood. Whitney leaned against the door, her hand pressed to her forehead. "My house is not visitor-friendly."

She probably wasn't referring to the modesty of her home, but rather the current situation. He walked her to a chair, pretending not to notice the figure sprawled on the sofa under the dim light of a faded lamp. The woman, her breaths deep and her hair disheveled, seemed lost in a world of her own. This sight deepened his resolve to be there for Whitney, to ensure she wasn't facing her burdens alone.

"You don't have to stay."

Unfazed by her protests, he helped her settle into a nearby chair. Then, navigating the kitchen as if familiar, he located a mug, glad he'd ordered one to replace her broken one. He retrieved the milk from the fridge and warmed it in the microwave. His mind raced with thoughts of how he could offer more help, but for now, he settled for a gesture of kindness. He found the vanilla and sugar, added them to the milk, then returned with the steaming cup, and handed her the warm concoction.

"You know, I can manage fine on my own."

"I know. I've witnessed your efficiency and tireless work—not to mention your pepper-spray defense." He exhaled as the blaring music ceased. He stuffed his hands into his pockets, unsure if now was a good time to leave, especially with her mother unconscious on the sofa. "Still, any time I'm around, please don't hesitate to ask for my help if you need it."

A faint smile curved her lips as she sipped the milk. "Hmm, this is really good."

"My mom used to make it." Meaning Regina, the mother who raised him.

Whitney's saddened gaze flickered toward the woman on the sofa.

"Whit, you're home." Jada appeared in cartoon pajamas, then looked between them. "Hi, um, Theo."

"Hello, Jada." At least, she was awake and could keep an eye on Whitney. He didn't blame the girl for her inability to sleep until her sister got home.

"You're still up, I see." Whitney shook a finger at her sister, but the stern effect failed with her voice so soft.

Jada's frown expressed her concern when she narrowed her eyes and knelt in front of Whitney. "You look—Are you okay?"

"Theo and I worked hard today." Whitney reassured her sister, brushing Jada's braids back from her face and not mentioning her episode. "Nothing rest won't fix."

He moved closer and touched her arm, free to leave knowing she wouldn't be alone. "Promise me you'll take it easy tomorrow?"

"She's off work tomorrow." Jada blinked up at him. "I'll make sure she doesn't cook."

He nodded, his heart eased. With Whitney in caring hands, it was time to leave, but he'd carry the concern for her well-being with him. The lump in his throat grew as he took in the two siblings who only seemed to have each other. He struggled to swallow and spoke like cracked media waves. "Take care of yourself."

As he retreated, he could hear Whitney asking why Jada was still awake this late. The door swung shut. Even from a distance, he felt the weight of Whitney's struggles. She, too, had stories she hadn't yet shared. While he hadn't told her the real Theo, from today onward, he'd be a pillar of support, regardless of what the future held.

Back in the safety and cocoon of his hotel, a text notification startled him as he was settling into bed. It was from Whitney—at two a.m.? Had something happened?

Whitney: Jada and I are going to the beach tomorrow. Care to join?

The accompanying swimming emoji drew a smile from him.

Theo: You're supposed to rest.

Whitney: What better place to rest than the beach?

He chuckled at the umbrella and lounging emojis she added.

Theo: What time?

Whitney: After church, around one.

Theo: Need a ride?

Whitney: Was counting on you for that!

A smirk broke free at her playful use of emojis—hearts, flowers, beach balls.

Theo: Get some rest. I'll be there at one.

Whitney: See you.

Lying back, he felt a warmth spread through him. He had, perhaps, found a friend in Whitney, and he was more than willing to be there for her in every way he could. But what would happen when she found out who he really was?

CHAPTER 10

Whitney gazed at the mirror, studying the changes in her complexion. The golden beams of the afternoon sun filtered through her curtains, casting a warm hue on once-vibrant skin that seemed to have faded over the past three years. She adjusted the hem of her shorts, her fingers fiddling out her touch of unease. After the simplicity of her work uniform, casual wear felt cumbersome.

Her energy levels had resumed last night, and although Theo insisted she rest today, she had promised Jada a beach trip as a reward for an improved math grade. Whitney herself could benefit from a soothing escape to the shore.

The prudent choice after her recent episode would be to see a doctor, but with a looming surgery expense, every penny was precious. Neglecting her condition could escalate to heart failure, yet without insurance or a credit history, finding a facility with a heart surgeon willing to treat her seemed improbable.

She took a deep breath. It was no use letting circumstances beyond her grasp overwhelm her.

"Whit, you should wear this sundress." Jada's voice chimed from behind as she held out a one-shouldered pink floral sundress. "If you're getting a break from work uniforms, why not go for something cuter?"

Whitney cast an amused glance over her shoulder. Her fingers stilled on the waistband of the shorts she'd pulled over her navy swimsuit. "We're heading to the beach, not a runway."

Jada stepped up beside her, her reflection in the mirror showing the bright orange of her swimsuit beneath a breezy cover-up. "I get that. But you'd stand out in this dress. Besides"—she winked—"you never know who you might bump into at the beach."

Whitney chuckled. "I'm not on the lookout." Although she had to admit, Theo was the first man who'd piqued her interest in a long while—ever? After the length to which he'd gone to protect her yesterday, his kindness, and his way of looking at her, she was starting to believe he maybe liked her too.

"Is it wrong for me to want my sister to look her best?" Jada rested her head on Whitney's shoulder. "Especially if we run into some of my friends."

Rolling her eyes, Whitney tousled Jada's braids, their roughness slipping through her hands. "I've met all your friends, remember?"

Jada made a face, a teasing glint lighting her eyes in the mirror. "Not all of them."

"Oh? Like the boys you've conveniently forgotten to mention?" Whitney teased back, raising an eyebrow.

"Just wear the dress, Whit." Jada draped the dress over Whitney's shoulder. "It's yours anyway."

Whitney smirked, pulling the dress closer to inspect it. "Surprised you chose today of all days to return it."

"That's because today you have a reason to wear it. We're going to the beach!" Jada flounced to the bed, her energy infectious. "I've got our beach bag all packed. Made some peanut butter balls and sandwiches too."

Stepping out of her shorts, Whitney shook a finger at Jada. "Who are you, missy, and what have you done with my sister?" Whitney began to slip into the summer dress. "It's usually me waiting on you, not the other way around."

Jada picked up a body spray bottle from the dresser dividing their beds. Then a potent floral scent wafted through the room. "I wish Mama could come with us."

Whitney adjusted the fit of her dress, grateful for the turn of events today. "It's for the best that she's spending time with her friend today." Earlier, Whitney had managed to convince Mama to attend church, and there, they'd run into one of Mama's old friends, a lady who'd been trying to reconnect with Mama for ages. Whitney had nudged them into a plan to plant flowers at the gravesides of their husbands. "She mentioned she got plenty of flowers for George too."

Giving a twirl in her dress, Whitney appreciated how the elastic band accentuated her waist. Dressing up felt nice once in a while. Jada had been right.

As Whitney slid her feet into her flip-flops, a knock echoed from the door. "Mama's back already?"

"Hmm?" Jada, busy retrieving something from beneath her bed, spoke without looking up. "You wanna answer that?"

They seldom received unexpected visitors unless Jada had a new friend she hadn't yet told that they couldn't have visitors. Not because of Whitney, but because Jada was embarrassed. Unsure of when Mama might be "wasted" like Jada called it.

When Whitney swung the door open, her heart leaped into her throat. "Th–Theo?"

His amber-brown eyes sparkled under the afternoon sun as he held out a bouquet of red roses mixed with white baby's breath. "I tried for the wisteria, but the florist said cut ones are as fragile to transport as a crystal chandelier, so they seldom stock them. Glad to see you're up and about."

Their fingers grazed each other as she accepted the vase, sending a small jolt up her arm. He looked like he'd walked straight out of a beachwear magazine, though. His navy-blue shorts—could those be swim trunks?—combined with a breezy cotton button-down shirt and casual water shoes gave him a relaxed, summer-ready look.

"I also got this." He lifted a mug from his other hand.

Whitney balanced the vase in the crook of her arm to receive the mug. A rush of excitement surged through her as she noticed the intricate design—a delicate blue butterfly poised for flight. Her heart fluttered like those butterfly wings would as she read the quote—"Every day is a new chapter to write a better story."

He remembered the quote she'd only told him once?

"I'm sorry I never asked what picture you had with the quote on your previous mug."

"*How* did you remember the quote?"

"It had a good meaning." His casual shrug belied his thoughtful gesture. "My sister-in-law Joy told me a butterfly is a powerful symbol of transformation and new beginnings."

The meaning heightened Whitney's appreciation.

"I love it!" she gushed, hardly containing the joy radiating in her heart. If her hands weren't full, she'd hug him. Her old mug had a black-and-white photo of an open book. "This is better than my old cup."

"I'm glad you like it." He shifted his feet. "And thanks for inviting me."

"Invite?" She lifted the roses to her nose in an attempt to regain her composure. What did he mean about an invitation?

"Uh?" Frowning, he pulled out his phone and showed her a text loaded with emojis. "You invited me to the beach."

"Oh!" Only Jada flooded a message feed with those. How had her sister snagged her phone? Whitney chuckled. "You must think I'm crazy about emojis."

"Hi, Theo." Jada trotted up, beach bag in hand, a knowing grin in place. "Ready to head out?"

Theo rocked back on his heels and folded his arms, the muscles in his broad shoulders stretching his shirt taut. "Well, Jada," he drawled, a lilt to the words as he glanced between them. "I must say, I enjoyed all the emojis you sent last night."

"We needed a ride to the beach." Unabashed, Jada scooted around him. "Besides, it might help you get to know Houston a little better," she called over her shoulder, already making her way toward the car.

His shoulders inching up, his guilty gaze latched onto Whitney's. Then he ducked his head and ruffled his buzz cut. "Look, I can head back. You weren't expecting me."

"No, it's okay." The warmth of his nearness already seeped into her. She wasn't ready to give that up despite the surprise. His genuine concern was still seared into her memory. The way he'd saved her from the boxes about to fall on her yesterday—so many little things he'd done. "Thank you again for driving me home yesterday. Besides, you've got the wheels."

"With air conditioning." He pointed at her, smirking now. "And a cooler loaded with beach snacks."

"No way."

While he nodded, she placed the flowers on the counter and her new mug in the corner. It was too beautiful to be hidden in the cupboard just yet.

No one had ever bought her flowers, nor given her a thoughtful gift, which made Theo one of a kind. Was there any harm in enjoying these precious moments in his company?

But there was still a lingering fear that things between them couldn't last. He was too good to be true.

***

Whitney relaxed into the plush passenger seat, breathing in Theo's subtle yet alluring cologne. The radio crooned Christian melodies, creating a serene ambience, and the AC provided a welcome reprieve from the outdoor warmth, prepping them for the anticipated beach heat. She was looking forward to plunging into the cool ocean waters.

"Whit," Jada piped up from the back, her mischievous tone warning whatever was coming could be a problem. "Since you've got a boyfriend now, does that mean I can have one too?"

Theo chuckled. "So *that's* the reason behind today's invite?"

"Either way," Whitney responded, her tone light but firm, "we'll revisit *that* topic on your twentieth birthday."

"*That's* so not fair." Jada let out a dramatic sigh. "With the way you manage relationships, I'm not sure I should follow your relationship timeline."

Theo tilted his head to catch Jada's eye in the rearview before refocusing on the road. "How exactly does Whitney manage her relationships?"

"I've never seen her with a boyfriend... until you."

Great. Did Jada have to say that? A flush of heat rose in her neck. Afraid to even look at Theo, Whitney busied herself by pleating the soft, breezy pink fabric of her dress over her knee.

"Theo's just a friend." How could she ensure Theo didn't misinterpret her single status as something regrettable? After Dad's death, she'd shelved her romantic aspirations, focusing on her family's well-being.

Needing a distraction, she rolled down her window to let the warmth and unmistakable salty tang into the cool interior.

"So, Theo, do you like dolphins?" Thankfully, Jada offered a welcome topic change.

"Absolutely. They are remarkable."

"I did a school project on them last year."

Whitney glanced at her sister through the mirror above her, noticing Jada's beaming face.

"Oh? What kind of project was it?"

The easy rapport between Theo and Jada relaxed Whitney as they delved into a lively discussion on dolphins, marine ecosystems, and the wonder of oceanic life. A warm sentiment swelled within her. It wasn't just his evident knowledge or his eloquence but also his genuine attention to Jada, treating her thoughts and opinions with respect.

Once they arrived at the beach, they trekked along the sun-warmed sand. Jada, always spirited, sped off toward the water, twirling around in joyful anticipation.

Whitney leaned toward Theo, her words almost stolen by the coastal breeze. "Thank you for joining us."

"Should I be thanking you for the unintended invitation?" His olive skin was radiant beneath the sun as he balanced the folding beach umbrella in one hand and a basket, presumably filled with picnic treats, in the other. "Why didn't you invite your mom?"

"She had plans today." Whitney shifted the bag containing their towels as she shared about Mama's day out with an old friend.

"I'm glad she's spending some time with a friend." He set his load down, and she did the same. While he anchored the umbrella into the sand, providing them with shade, Jada's cheerful laughter rang out, merging the sea's restless whooshing and distant cheerful echoes from the people on the other end of the beach. For a Sunday, the place wasn't crowded at all. *What a perfect day! Thank You, Lord!*

Whitney arranged the blanket on the sand, letting him unload the picnic basket—store-bought fruits, perfectly sliced and arranged, and snacks, sealed and tidy. They settled side by side, watching Jada and the other beachgoers.

"You have a taste for the finer things, don't you?"

"We did have a good tip day yesterday." He grinned, shading his eyes to watch a sailboat gliding on the water. Daniela must have texted him about their pay as well. "So, other than beach trips, what do you two usually do for fun?"

"I'm mostly working. Then, on Sundays after church, I pretty much have to get laundry done or grocery shopping. I only planned today's beach outing because of a bargain with Jada."

"You're a stellar role model."

How nice to hear someone say so. Her chest expanded, and her stomach fluttered. "Thank you." She burrowed her flip-flop-clad feet into hot sand beside where she sat on the blanket and hugged her knees to her chest. "Tell me more about your family."

His eyes twinkled when he shared heartwarming stories of his large, adopted family and recounted the boys' many antics. "I'm still not over Wade pouring hot sauce into my mouth while I dozed off by the pool."

She could almost visualize the luxurious family home, complete with its backyard pool, a clear indication of his family's affluence. The stories sparked a desire to meet these extraordinary people. "Colorado isn't too far. Maybe they could visit you sometime."

Chuckling, he stretched out on the blanket. "Oh, trust me, they're a riot—boisterous and all."

"But they sound amazing." She folded her legs beneath her. The concept of a household bustling with siblings was alien, yet Theo's parents opened their hearts and home to ten adopted children. How touching! She was about to delve deeper into his past, perhaps inquire about his biological family, when Jada's voice called out.

"Hey, you two! Are you coming?"

Theo nodded, sprang to his feet, and offered a hand to help Whitney up. As he unbuttoned his shirt in preparation for a swim and reached for the sunscreen, she glimpsed his chiseled abs. For a fleeting moment, she lost herself in the sight, her heart skipping a beat. With his toned body a testament to his fitness dedication, she needed a conscious effort not to ogle him. The warmth of the day, coupled with his physical presence, left her overheated and breathless.

Noticing his struggle to reach the middle of his back, she found herself choking out the words. "I can, um, help with your back." Ugh, why did her voice have to betray her nervousness?

"Thanks." He sprayed his chest again before handing her the sunscreen.

She coughed, the spray catching in her throat, her hands trembling as she took the bottle. As she sprayed his back, her fingers tingled with the urge to explore the warmth of his skin. She scolded herself internally—such unpious thoughts for a Sunday! But then it had been a while since she'd been this close to a man, let alone a... boyfriend?

Setting down the spray, she peeled off her dress, revealing her swimwear underneath, kicked off her sandals, and followed him over sand so scorching she had to walk on tiptoes.

"Want a piggyback ride?" He quirked a grin at her.

She shook a finger at him, feeling playful and so free it was surreal. "I'll break your back."

"You want to test that theory?" He gave her a sideways glance, his water shoes crunching through the sand.

"Next time." She'd love nothing more than being carried by him as she breathed in his intoxicating scent.

"All right, then." He winked. "Race you to the water!"

"Nah. Don't feel like it."

"No challenges for you?"

"I'm not sure I want to challenge you." No way could she outrun him, so she had to act uninterested. As soon as he seemed to shift focus, she dashed ahead, a grin spreading across her face.

"Whit!" His laughter mingled with hers. Her name, shortened affectionately, warmed her heart. But her burst of energy didn't get her far. Theo's strong arms encircled her from behind, halting her sprint mere feet from the water's edge.

"Got you," he whispered, his breath dancing across her neck, sending shivers down her spine.

Then, with a burst of energy, he lifted her and tossed her into the water. "That's for trying to trick me," he called out, his voice blending with her splash into the water.

She blinked water from her eyes, then splashed him. Laughter bubbled in her stomach. "Payback, baby."

"Save some for me!" Jada hollered and splashed first Whitney, then Theo.

They joined hands, forming a chain, laughing and shrieking as they tried to dodge or leap over the oncoming waves. As the day progressed, they eventually settled on the sand. Warm grains stuck to their damp skin while they savored Theo's snacks and Jada's homemade peanut butter balls, the simple treats the epitome of a perfect beach day. Refreshed and refueled, they returned to the water for more fun. The sun descended when they left the beach, their bellies still filled with his snacks.

Not ready for this day to end, Whitney suggested they go for ice cream by the boardwalk. Then they strolled along the boardwalk, ice creams in hand, investigating the shops, conversing as if the people they walked past were a mere backdrop like the rumbling waves. Jada spoke about her love for journalism, an odd passion for someone who didn't like to read, but Theo engaged with genuine interest, encouraging her dreams.

Whitney nudged him. He'd barely eaten his ice cream. "Don't like ice cream?"

He squished his face. "It's the nuts. Not a fan of them on ice cream."

It was understandable that he hadn't anticipated the nuts; their presence wasn't hinted at in the dessert's name. "I can trade with you, but..." She gestured with her cone already partially tackled. "I can't claim it's a fair trade."

"Thanks." His fingers brushed hers in the exchange in a fleeting, yet electric, touch.

They continued meandering through the various shops, sharing stories about their most embarrassing fashion choices and laughing at some quirky merchandise. Brightly colored scarves fluttered in the evening breeze, while incense from a nearby stall wafted toward them.

He stopped at a stand displaying handcrafted jewelry under the warm hues of fairy lights. He purchased matching leather bracelets for the three of them, the antique silver beads in the center shimmering. "A memento." He held up the intricate pieces. "To remember today by."

Whitney didn't need a memento to remember this day. To remember Theo. How long was he going to stay and work at the resort before he tired of the minimal paycheck like all the others who'd left within weeks of accepting employment?

By the time they arrived home, night had fully set in. After Theo helped bring in their beach gear and said a cheerful farewell to Jada, Whitney accompanied him back to his car parked behind her dead one.

"Thank you," she whispered. It was the best day she'd had in a while.

"My pleasure." He leaned in and kissed her cheek. "I had a great time too. See you in the morning?"

She nodded, too hyped to talk, and a jolt jabbed her chest, both from excitement and her existing heart condition. His soft lips lingered on her skin, creating a sensation she hadn't felt in a while.

That familiar rush of warmth flooded her cheeks again, but this time, she welcomed it. Maybe, just maybe, this new dynamic wasn't such a bad thing. Regardless of what strange twist of fate had brought Theo here, it made her everyday routine anything but mundane.

She watched his car until it was out of sight, anticipation bubbling within her. The prospect of seeing him tomorrow made the night seem promising. How could she ever settle back into her regular life after he left?

CHAPTER 11

Over the next week, Whitney almost floated through each day on a cloud. Every morning, Theo picked her up, greeting her with a smile, a chai tea, and a pastry, and drove her to work. But he hadn't returned to his housekeeping role since his first two days at River Oasis.

Besides his different jobs at the resort, he was playing her chauffeur. As much as she appreciated the morning rides, she cherished the evening drives home the most as they talked and laughed about random things in their day. Plus, she didn't have to worry about missing the bus or sitting next to someone questionable.

Now, on Friday, almost a week since their beach escapade, Whitney finished her restaurant night shift and dropped by the hotel's front desk where he was working.

She found him standing behind the desk, engrossed in a phone call, his expression tight with concern.

Upon hearing her approach, he turned and ended the call with "I'll call you later," then set the phone on the counter. His focus shifted to her, his face brightening. "Ah, and here's the ray of sunshine in this corporate maze."

She smiled, taking in the quiet lobby before resting her hands on the counter. "Did everyone decide to take a day off, or did you scare them away with that intense phone stare?"

He leaned in. "Been counting every passing minute, hoping you'd pop by. How about a late dinner?"

How wonderful an evening out with him would be! But fatigue weighed on her. "You do realize it'll be midnight by the time you're off, right?"

He feigned exasperation and reached for her hand, sending a flurry of electric sensations through her. "All right, not a late-night dinner, but at least, we can make the best of our time here."

"It's a good plan." She'd rather wait with him until he got off. It was better than rushing for a lonely bus ride.

"Tell me the most daring thing you've ever done." His eyes lit up. "And don't spare any details."

She bit her lower lip as she searched her memory for something exciting. "Usually, Jada tackles enough danger for the two of us."

His eyebrow shot up. "Come on. You gotta have done something crazy."

"Okay. Here's one." She'd had some wild years—so far back though she could scarcely remember who that girl was. "In middle school, I once tried a rebellious hair dye that looked more like a cry for help than fashion."

He tugged a hunk of her hair still in its ponytail. "No way." His expression softened, His fingers shifted, drifting to the delicate wisps framing her face. With a tender touch, he tucked a few strands behind her ear, his voice a whisper. "I'd like to see that someday."

As his touch elicited delicious shivers, her gaze flickered to his mouth, her mind awhirl with possibilities for a kiss.

"Excuse me?"

At the brusque voice behind them, Whitney jerked away. Engrossed, she hadn't noticed the approaching guest.

"Apologies, sir." Theo cleared his throat, and his professional demeanor returned. "How may I assist you?"

"I just got a notification that I'm checked out tomorrow." The disgruntled guest began ranting about a reservation mishap, echoing complaints about the hotel's deteriorating standards.

Whitney shifted, busying herself with adjusting the flower arrangement on a nearby table, eavesdropping on Theo's calm, measured response and the subsequent mollifying of the aggrieved guest.

Soon, his fingers clicked on the keyboard, firing rapidly. "It looks like there's a double-booking. I'll get it adjusted."

"Every time I've come here lately there's been some issue! The dining room closes early. Don't even get me started on the menu."

"I apologize for the inconvenience." Theo's voice was firm yet empathetic. "To make it up to you, we'll offer you a complimentary seven-day stay, which you can use with family or friends. This will be a premium package."

Whitney straightened, her eyes widening. Premium packages included spa and golf. Charlotte would flip, and when the main manager got word of this...

"I'd suggest considering a visit in July or later." Theo continued. "The resort should have completed some planned renovations by then."

"Theo?" Whitney couldn't help but interject, trying to signal him.

He barely glanced her way, staying focused on the guest. The customer's frustration had, of course, transformed into delight at the generous offer.

"I'll have to confirm the details with my manager, but you can expect a voucher and an email outlining the specifics of this package tomorrow."

"You've just made a loyal customer out of me," the man enthused, shaking Theo's hand. Once the guest left, practically floating with happiness, Whitney strode back to the counter.

"What on earth did you just promise? Are you trying to get yourself fired?" She slapped the counter. Clearly, he didn't care about his job.

"I just retained a regular customer. Why would they fire me?" He smiled sheepishly. "He's a valued rewards member who visits often. Word-of-mouth from such guests is priceless."

"The resort is tight on funds as it is." Whitney touched his hand, hardly believing his composure. "Don't tell me you're this naive about business. They can't afford to raise anyone's salary or fill managerial positions. What gave you the idea they'd renovate?"

Theo walked around the counter, taking her hand. "I'll discuss it with the manager tomorrow. When they see the long-term value, they'll prioritize renovations to maintain customer satisfaction."

He went on, passionately talking about the significance of happy customers and strategic marketing for longevity. Where had he learned so much about marketing? Perhaps while he worked in sales three days ago?

Either way, he made her mind spin not just in a romantic way, but with his decisive authority.

She held up her free hand to stop his chattering. "Why aren't you in marketing?"

He chuckled, dropping her hand. "I'm enjoying experiencing all the resort has to offer. Every department teaches me something new."

"Well, someone's a fast learner." His ability to handle difficult situations with such poise left her reeling. She'd have to ask him later about his level of education, because again, what was he doing here—working as a floater? No doubt, he could be hired somewhere better.

***

One hour into her restaurant shift the next day, a rambunctious group ambled in. The four men exuded an air of camaraderie as they claimed a table for six, their laughter resounding through the room. With the hotel cutting out a greeter position, guests now chose their own spots.

She grabbed the menus and navigated past the marble statue of a woman pouring her endless supply of "wine." The evening sun streamed through the windows, bathing the room in a golden light that illuminated the damask white-linen tablecloths and made the filigree silverware glisten.

Only a few tables were occupied, and her colleague was already assisting one.

The group was noticeably affluent, their attire fancy, and their manner assured. Their interactions hinted at a deeper bond, like between friends or siblings as they teased one another one moment and then burst into laughter the next. As she approached, their conversations ceased, their attention shifting to her.

"Good afternoon," she greeted, introducing herself and distributing the menus. "Can I start you off with some drinks as you look through our menu?"

The one in a navy suit, whose watch probably cost several times more than her rent, scooted to the edge of his chair. "I can tell you're an excellent waitress." Despite his apologetic expression, she sensed the oncoming mischief. "But is there any chance Theo Stone could be our server?"

Theo was due in the restaurant as soon as he finished his stint as a caddy at the golf course.

"I'm certain he's working at the restaurant today." The gentleman in a maroon sports coat raised a hand, and as he flashed white teeth with his smile, he bore a striking resemblance to a Hollywood A-lister.

"I'll contact him right away." She nodded. Hadn't Theo been willing to go out of his way to keep pleasing their guests? Now more than ever, they'd better do what they could to keep River Oasis running.

"Thank you," they chorused, then ordered their drinks, requesting a span of luxury bottled waters, some of which the hotel didn't even stock.

The one with a Middle Eastern look rolled his eyes. "Honestly, tap water tastes the same."

The fourth gentleman, also in a designer suit, retorted, "Nothing wrong with indulging when you're out. It supports the business too."

"Any water will suffice," said the navy-suited one.

With their differing personas, their trimmed beards gave them a common look, like a team uniform.

As she moved away, snippets of their conversation followed her. "I can't wait to see the shock on his face," one said, and the others laughed.

Who were these well-dressed gentlemen, and what was their connection to Theo? Every new detail about him elevated the puzzle into a more complex 3-D creation, and Whitney found herself caught between fascination and caution. Could they be his siblings? No. These guys didn't look like the collective adoptive bunch he'd talked about fondly. While they seemed down to earth, they were too sophisticated for his company. But what was Theo's company like anyway?

CHAPTER 12

The afternoon sun cast long shadows beneath the swaying palm trees as Theo listened to the groundskeeper's grievances. He was already running behind on his next assignment, but giving an ear to the young man's complaints seemed essential at the moment.

"I honestly don't see the need to invest in this place." The young man's deep-set eyes betrayed his frustration. "I accepted this job in hopes of a promotion to a higher-paying position, but now, the place might shut down before I get a shot at that."

"Perhaps you should think about obtaining your GED first." Theo brushed a flimsy leaf from the restaurant uniform he'd changed into minutes ago. "It could be a stepping stone for you."

The young man's work ethic and current attitude wouldn't get him far in the professional world. Taking a deep breath, Theo added, "Focus on giving your current role your best."

The man gritted his teeth. "The moment I find a better job, I'm out."

"Constantly swapping jobs around doesn't reflect well on a resume."

"Theo?" A familiar, feminine voice called out, and he pivoted toward the club door. The sun accentuated the glow on Whitney's face, making her smile all the more radiant. His stomach fluttered, and warmth coursed through him. "You're coming?"

As she approached with a spring in her step, he clapped the young groundskeeper on the shoulder, gave him a polite nod, and a quick "catch up with you later" before excusing himself to join her.

"You missed me so much you had to come get me from work?" He spoke with a lightness he rarely had around female work colleagues.

Folding her hands in front of her, she smiled shyly. "Guests are asking for you, actually. Not just one. Several."

She started walking, and he fell in step.

"Guests? For me?" His forehead pinched as it creased with his frown.

She nodded. "Quite fancy ones. I'm beginning to wonder the caliber of company you keep." Stopping briefly, she deepened her frown and crossed her arms in mock judgment. "I mean, I've never even met any of your friends."

Sensing her suspicions again, he forced a chuckle and then used the nickname Jada called her. "You, Whit, are my friend."

"Whit, uh?" A teasing glint lit her eyes. "Am I in the right category for you?"

He touched her shoulder. "You're climbing to the top of my list."

As they resumed walking, his mind raced to the kind of guests he could have, but the only ones who would travel in a pack and knew his whereabouts were his brothers. "Can you describe them for me?"

Holding the door open for her as they entered the club, he listened intently.

"Four men. Some in sharp suits, fancy watches. They stand out in a good, wealthy kind of way," she described without missing a step, her heels clicking against the polished marble floor. "I tried to radio you, but—"

"I forgot to grab my radio after the break." Oops. "Thanks for seeking me out."

They maneuvered through the club, passing random guests immersed in chatter. When they turned to the long hallway that connected to the restaurant, the aroma of grilled steaks and roasted vegetables wafted out, mingling with the undertones of citrusy cologne from a passerby. The warm lighting overhead created a cozy ambience, casting a gentle glow on the wooden panels and plush furnishings.

As they entered the restaurant, Wade's boisterous laugh drowned the background music. It echoed through the space, emanating from a distant table by the window. With a strange mix of comfort and anxiety, Theo approached the group.

Whitney glanced at him. "You know those guys?"

Nate must have heard them approach. He turned, grinning. "Thanks, Whitney."

"And there's the man of the hour!" Logan grinned too.

Theo gripped the back of his neck, stopping within reach of the table and chuckling nervously as his brothers eyed him. "Well, life certainly has its moments of surprise."

He smiled at Whitney, who was standing alongside him, curiosity alight in her eyes. It was about time she got a peek into his world. Taking a deep breath, he announced, "Whitney, meet my brothers."

"Brothers?" Her eyes widened, and she leaned in to whisper just for him. "These glamorous individuals are your family?"

Guiding her closer to the table, he introduced each sibling. "This is Nate, Wade, Logan, Rohan."

Each offered Whitney a friendly handshake in turn.

"It's a pleasure to meet you all." She stepped back from the table and gripped her hands in front of her in a deferential posture. But her eyes sparkled, unabashed. "Where do you all live? How often do you see each other?"

"Ask away." Wade arched an eyebrow. His maroon coat gave him a more casual look than Logan and Rohan.

Whitney patted Theo's arm. "Theo has mentioned you all a few times, but he's been a bit tight-lipped about his own story."

"And hearing from these guys is not the best way to get facts about me." He guided her aside. "I'll join you in a few. We don't want Charlotte to notice our little reunion." The last thing he wanted was for his brothers to divulge more than necessary.

Since he'd unintentionally told a customer about the voucher for a free seven-day stay last night, trust from Whitney had been on a delicate thread. The inherent boss in him had taken the reins, forgetting his temporary position. He'd already changed his plans only to stay four weeks, but by the end of June, he'd reveal his undercover mission. However, his brothers might expose him before he had the chance.

Whitney departed, casting a final questioning glance at him and his brothers.

In the lush backdrop of immaculate seating, the situation felt tense, and the fountain's trickling offered the sole calming element.

"Really, Rohan?" Theo sank into the empty chair between Rohan and Wade. "A three-piece suit?" Hushing his voice, he focused on one of his younger brothers across the table. "Are you *trying* to blow my cover?"

"Logan and I had a business meeting when Wade called him." Rohan rubbed his forehead, his palm shadowing his brown skin as he explained how his joint textile business with Logan had summoned him from Dubai for investors in San Francisco. "Once I head back, you won't see me until the reunion."

Despite the joy of seeing his brothers, especially the seldom-seen Rohan, Theo folded his hands on the tablecloth. "This timing and location is *not* ideal."

"I was coming solo, but Logan wanted to tag along." Wade waved both his hands feigning innocence.

"And you, Nate?"

Nate spent most of his Saturdays at his races.

"No race for me today. And even though my better half isn't here"—Nate paused to pat the empty sixth chair beside him—"I'm here to discuss the wedding details."

"What happened to FaceTime or texting?" Theo spoke lightheartedly. "Plus, why do we need to discuss next spring's wedding *now*?"

"You wanted the reunion in Brazil." Nate tapped his stubbled chin. "Vee and I are moving our wedding to August."

"*This* August." Logan raised a finger in clarification. "Just in case you've forgotten his middle name."

"Mr. Impulsive. How can I forget?" Nate had named his race car Impulse, and it suited his rapid decision-making nature.

"The wedding's at The Peak." Wade brought his water to his mouth.

"Sounds reasonable." Spending time in their childhood home would be comforting, not just for Theo but also for most of his siblings. He drummed his hands on the table, the tablecloth jostling. "If we have a wedding to plan and a reunion, what's my role in the last-minute wedding?"

"Simple," Nate said across the table. "Just family and immediate friends. I want to keep this affair away from the media spotlight."

While Theo was all for the media, he, too, wouldn't want the entire world imposing on his wedding. That was if he ever got married someday. He frowned. Where had *that* thought come from? He'd never before considered a wedding of his own.

Whitney slipped back into his mind. Who was he kidding? They'd only just met, and once he finalized the resort's fate, she'd remain in Texas while he returned to Brazil.

"Are you still with us, man?" Wade jabbed Theo's arm.

"Nah, he's zoning out." Rohan smirked. "He doesn't want to think about his reunion preparations or the inevitable cooking he'll have to do, despite the chefs he's hired for the event."

"Okay, enough of that." Logan took over, silencing the others. "How's your undercover mission?"

The group leaned in.

"I have no time or desire to run another business." That had to be the right move. Still, Theo exhaled heavily. "You guys could've at least tried to blend in. Do you have any idea how hard I've worked to keep this a secret?"

"Come on." Nate chuckled. "Wasn't this thing for Wade's little drama?"

"And do I dare say, I sense a story?" Wade drummed his hands on the table, jostling silverware and sloshing their waters. "It seems a certain waitress is quite taken with our undercover brother."

"Don't even go there." Theo's cheeks heated. True, he and Whitney had some special moments. Also true, he found all sorts of excuses to touch her, flirt with her, and go as far as kissing her cheek. He shivered at the memory of the brief spontaneous moment. No way could he deny the attraction, but he sensed her doubts too. After today, he'd need to clear any more doubts she had of him first.

"Uh-oh. That took someone to memory lane." Logan's voice pulled Theo back to the present.

"And that look Whitney gave you?" Wade smirked and slung an arm around Theo. "There's a story there. Do tell."

Theo slapped Wade's hand away. Discussing his feelings for Whitney with his boisterous brothers was risky, worse if she overheard their conversation.

"She's quite the catch, Theo." Nate saluted him with his water glass, his confidence suggesting he'd already pieced together the budding relationship.

Theo groaned. "You guys are not making this easy. Your flashy arrival has already raised enough eyebrows."

Rohan smirked, straightening his tie with flair. "Undercover bosses on TV are one thing, but seeing one in person? I couldn't resist."

"He's really embraced the part." Wade caught Theo's chin and held it as if offering something on display. "Even got the I'm-overworked-and-underpaid look down to a *T*."

Rohan snorted his laughter, Logan shushed the table, and Theo jerked free and shot them a warning look as Whitney passed by, laden with a tray of dishes.

"We need to think of a strategy," Logan continued in a whisper, even when she moved further away. "Especially if we're going to help our brother secure a date for the reunion."

Theo pinched the bridge of his nose. "I just need tonight to go smoothly. So, just... act normal, will you? For once in your lives?"

The brothers exchanged glances, their promises unspoken. Sensing understanding in their silence, he switched the conversation and asked about their brother Owen's new real-estate business.

"He's still in training." Rohan shared Owen's first two months in Dubai. If there was a business Owen hadn't tried, then he hadn't heard of it yet.

"I hope he finds his groove there." Wade launched into a discussion about Nate's racing season. Nate's excitement was evident as he discussed his upcoming retirement. He couldn't wait to start a family with his fiancée without a pressing career starting next year.

Theo appreciated the distraction and at least none of his brothers intended to stay the night in Texas. Their company was always enjoyable, but right now, they posed a potential hazard to his undercover operation. The longer they lingered, the closer they'd inch to spilling secrets.

He finally served them dinner with Whitney's help taking their orders.

Later, when the restaurant lights dimmed and the last customer had left, he looked forward to driving Whitney home. As they strolled side by side, she nudged his arm with her shoulder. "You didn't tell me your brothers are wealthy."

"They're show-offs." Theo spoke with lightness at the memory of his brothers' sudden appearance. Affluence did, however, grace his family. Indeed, one of God's blessings. "But if you go on a date with me tomorrow, I promise to tell you all about them."

She halted, her gaze fixing on him, eyes luminous under the lamplight. "You know, I would've gone on a date with you, even if you hadn't promised to share about your family."

"In that case"—he teased, placing a gentle hand on her shoulder, feeling the warmth from her even through the fabric of her uniform blouse—"I won't tell you about them."

"That's not fair!" She swatted his hand away, snickering. "I want to know about your family."

As the shimmering lot lights revealed her sincerity, he wanted her to know everything about him, except for his lie for now. "All right. Tomorrow, then."

"Where would you like to go?" she asked.

"Let me surprise you. How about I pick you up at five?"

"Sounds like a plan."

CHAPTER 13

From the moment Theo arrived at Whitney's doorstep for their drive to the restaurant, she imagined she'd stepped straight into a fairy tale—every detail crafting the perfect first date. Except she shouldn't have worn heels that she hadn't worn since high school. She didn't remember the shoes hurting her ankles as badly as they did now.

"You look beautiful," he whispered once more, his eyes aglow as they neared the elegant wooden doors of the upscale downtown eatery.

She tried not to flinch when the shoe cut into her ankle.

The doors swung open, revealing a uniformed gentleman whose smile was as inviting as the ambience inside. A flush of warmth spread over Whitney, heightened by Theo's gentle touch guiding her by the lower back. Clasping her handbag straps on her shoulder, she tried to calm the excited nerves now dampening her palms. In contrast to her, Theo exuded an air of casual elegance in his blue dress shirt, jeans, and well-cut coat. When he leaned in, she caught a whiff of his cologne, a sophisticated scent she'd never find in the aisles of her usual stores.

A tantalizing blend of freshly baked bread and a hint of roasted garlic wafted in the air, making her stomach rumble. As they moved deeper into the room, the ambience shifted from classic elegance to modern chic. Tall candles in amber holders stood on pristine white tablecloths, while walls adorned with contemporary motifs in sunny oranges and yellows hinted at a more recent redesign.

A petite woman in her early twenties poised with grace greeted them and inquired about their reservation. As Theo shared his name, she picked up two menus and, with a gentle tip of her head, signaled them to follow. "This way, please."

They meandered past tables occupied by couples exuding sophistication and elegance. Even in her finest navy dress, Whitney ducked her head, feeling underdressed amid such opulence. They approached a secluded spot toward the back, the window beyond offering views of the city's twinkling lights. A solitary pendant light set a perfect mood, its gentle luminescence caressing rich wooden chairs and the gleaming silverware wrapped in napkins.

Depositing their menus, the woman hinted at their imminent service. "Your server will be with you momentarily."

No sooner had she spoken than a man, also midtwenties, approached with a warm, "Good evening."

Once the greeter had taken her leave, the server introduced himself and asked about their drink preferences. Whitney opted for water, scanning the menu in hopes of spotting a familiar soda. Yet, given the fanciness of the place, a soda might bear an exorbitant price tag.

Seeming to notice her hesitation, Theo ordered an Italian soda for her and water for himself.

The server, sensing their unfamiliarity with the menu, offered, "Might I recommend some of our specialties?" He then elaborated on their Italian offerings. "For the salad, you won't be disappointed in our insalata caprese, and for the soup, our wedding soup is always a favorite."

Whitney, overwhelmed by the choices and exotic names, leaned into Theo's culinary expertise. "Do you mind ordering for both of us?"

"You trust me that much?" The ambient light illuminated the twinkle in his eyes, and the tenderness in his gaze all but made her knees weak. Or maybe she could blame the shoes for her weak knees.

"I do trust you." What reason did she have not to?

Yet, for a fleeting moment, uncertainty clouded his features, making her second-guess her admission. Shifting to the server, Theo asked, "Can you give us a few minutes to look through the menu, please?"

The server retreated, promising to return soon with their drinks and freshly baked bread.

Theo put the menu in the center and explained the different dishes. All she knew about Italian was pasta, her favorite, which could be why he brought her here. He was that thoughtful.

"Not so into Italian?" No doubt he'd caught her puzzled expression.

"I love any kind of food I don't have to cook." She sank her teeth into her lower lip, embarrassed to admit she rarely ate out. "But this is a bit out of my usual dining experience." As in, not at all the fast food she'd expected.

His smile was understanding. "Any of the dishes I described sound good?"

"I like pasta... and chicken." She couldn't remember the name of the dish he'd described that was served with chicken, and did the meal come with three courses or not? "I'll let you order the rest for me."

Theo pointed to an item on the menu. "The petti di pollo al limone. You'll like it."

She leaned over to look where he was pointing, their hands brushing. The touch sent a little jolt of electricity through her body, just like any of his touches did. "That sounds lovely."

The server returned with a basket of bread, a water glass, and a pink drink that must be the Italian soda Theo ordered her.

"Are you ready to order?"

At her nod, Theo ordered their soup and main course.

"Excellent choices." The server scribbled down their orders.

After he left, Whitney leaned closer to Theo, the table edge cutting into her middle. "I would bite my tongue if I tried to say those dishes."

He chuckled, seeming too familiar with this sort of luxury.

"How did you hear about this place?" For someone new in town, he was fast to find a luxurious restaurant.

"This is Nate's newest restaurant." He unfolded his napkin and spread it on his lap. "He's a NASCAR racer, but he also owns a few restaurants across the country."

She couldn't remember which one was Nate. "Have you ever been to any of his races?"

Theo nodded. "I don't go as often as I should." He admitted his terror of watching his brother drive over two hundred miles per hour. He shivered as he talked about Nate's accident last year. "This is his final year. If you like, I can take you to one of his races this season."

"That would be nice." Was there even a race track in Texas that hosted NASCAR races? That was as far as she could travel. Missing more than a day of work was a luxury she couldn't afford.

She paused when Theo asked if she wanted to pray for their food. The intimate moment reminded her of the depth beneath his somewhat suave exterior. Reaching for the bread, she sliced it. She then smeared butter on the slice and handed the piece to Theo. "Tell me about your family."

He smiled and thanked her. "Every family has its quirks and imperfections." His smile softened, his gaze distant. "My family? They're far from perfect, but they mean the world to me."

"From our previous conversations and the way you carry yourself, it's clear they've done well for themselves. Besides Nate, what do the others do?" She took a bite of her bread.

"It's a big family. If I have to go through—"

"I have all the time." After all, he'd said he'd tell her all about his family during their date.

He ate his piece of bread, his chiseled jaw moving symmetrically, and she swallowed when his Adam's apple bobbed before he swallowed, then took a sip of his water.

"They're an ambitious lot." His chest puffed up a bit. "Eric set the bar high, always driven. When he felt it was time, he handed the reins to Logan." He explained Eric's foundation of the financial company Logan now helmed as CEO. "Rohan. Very health conscious, which contrasts with his love for exotic places. Now, he's making a name for himself in Dubai's elite Realty circles and, in collaboration with Logan, oversees a textile empire in India. Then there's Wade, who hates change. He's always been our storyteller. He's gone from bedtime stories to penning scripts for the big screen. And Owen? Well, he never stays in one place."

Her face split into a grin. "Your family sounds amazing."

"I hope, someday, you'll meet the rest of them." He held her gaze, and her heart fluttered.

"I'd love that." Ten of them, but he'd only talked about five. She leaned forward, wanting to know more, especially if she might meet them in person. "And the others?"

"I doubt you'd keep track of all of them. We might need another date to get through the list." He smirked, then paused, taking a sip of water. "My three sisters are the perfect blend to keep things exciting. Hailey is quiet, and Julia is a firecracker, which can be good but also intense."

He sank back in his seat and scratched his jaw. "Our little sister, Iris, is the only biological child and family bonus." A certain protectiveness hardened his face. "She's the glue in the family. Although, you wouldn't believe the scandal she caused—in a good way, of course—when she fell head over heels for the family chef. Great guy, but we gave him a hard time. They're married now, and they couldn't be better suited for each other."

"Now that's a love story I'd like to hear."

While this was her first date *ever* and her attraction to Theo was undeniable, did he find her attractive enough for marriage material?

Of course, that was dependent on assuming her medical condition didn't hinder her from pursuing such dreams.

Their soup arrived, steaming and sprinkled with cheese. She tested her soup, her spoon sinking past melted cheese, strings of it dripping as she tried to raise a bite. "How old were you when your mom died?"

He moved his spoon in the soup, and as he stirred up more steam, a shadow darkened his face. He frowned out the window, his reflection peering back surrounded by distant city lights. "Five."

Her heart squeezed. He'd been too young. "Do you know how she died?"

"I have this memory of being in the hospital." He shivered. "Oh... hospitals. I found out much later that she had a tear in her blood vessel. It happened so fast from what I've heard."

Whitney's heart constricted further. He hated hospitals, yet he'd been willing to drive her to one when she'd passed out? She reached out, placing a comforting hand on his. "I'm very sorry about your mom."

His gaze returned from the distant past, and his thumb rubbed the back of her hand. "Thank you." He let out a breath. "It was tough at first. I had a lot of questions, especially about my biological father I never knew. But my adoptive parents..." He talked about Regina who'd been his child counselor before she and her husband adopted him. "They've been my anchor. Their unwavering love showed me the true meaning of family."

The main course arrived, diverting their conversation from heavy topics. She admired the presentation of her chicken and pasta while Theo's eggplant parmigiana emitted a rich aroma.

As they delved into their food, he talked about his family's upcoming one-week reunion. "I'd like you to come with me. As my date."

Oh my! Meeting his expansive family would be both exhilarating and nerve-racking. "And this is in Colorado?"

"Actually. Brazil."

"South America?" She sliced her chicken. Her family background sure was different from his. "That sounds exotic."

"We're guaranteed beach-warm weather for the festivities."

"I can't afford to miss work. Or to leave Jada and Mama that long."

"Jada will be done with school by then." He forked his eggplant. "She and your mom can come with us. The more the merrier."

He continued all sorts of reasons why she needed a vacation from work and her usual responsibilities. Which all made sense.

"And no need to worry about flight tickets. Most of my brothers have jets, so we can utilize one of those."

She'd never flown before. Flying on a private jet sounded even more tempting. The fork clinked against the porcelain when she rested it on the plate. "When is this?"

"Second week of June."

In two weeks. Jada too, could use a real summer vacation. "A vacation will be nice."

"Then it's a deal."

She considered his words, touched by his sincerity. "All right. It's a deal."

That was an entirely new adventure. Her mind spun, processing the snippets of the trip, and her voice pitched higher in excitement. "So. Your family has their own jets?"

Theo chuckled. "Yes." His next words seemed calculated, as if afraid to say anything that she'd find alarming. "Some of my brothers have done well for themselves."

Did she dare let herself be a burden? She picked at her chicken, contemplating how to decline without hurting his feelings.

"Don't say you're backing out before we even hit the five-minute mark of our deal." Theo touched her hand on the table.

"I'm... humbled by the invitation. But won't it be weird for them, you bringing, well, a stranger to a family event?"

He covered her hand with his. "Whit, I wouldn't invite you if I didn't think it was right. And besides"—he patted her hand, his dimple more visible—"with the size of our family and dynamics, we're always introducing new friends. You'll fit right in."

His response was so sincere. Warmth flooded her, and she twisted her hand to squeeze his. "Okay, then. I've always wanted to fly someday."

"You won't regret it." His thumb brushed along the back of her hand. "And you've got to see my family's reunion tradition festivities."

She laughed, picturing a room full of his family ensconced in fun activities. "Now, that's something I can't miss."

The rest of the dinner went by in a blur, their conversation flowing. By the meal's end, she felt even closer to him, eager for their upcoming journey. After dessert, he suggested a walk to the garden.

"Let's digest the rich food a bit," he said as they stepped out of the back doors.

She winced at the pain her shoe caused on her ankle.

Theo's hand rushed to her lower back as if sensing how wobbly she was walking. "Are you okay?"

She nodded, hesitating to take a step and tempted to take off her shoes.

"I'll be right back." He patted her back and headed into the restaurant. He returned minutes later with a bag in one hand and a chair in the other.

"What's with—"

"Take a seat, please." He set down the chair and ushered her to sit.

Still confused, she flung her handbag on her shoulder and obeyed.

And he produced flip-flops from the bag. "They had some extras from their wedding-supply closet."

How did he know she was uncomfortable? He lowered himself to kneel. His fingertips tickled her ankle as he slid off her shoes, and the tingles shot through her. He replaced the heel with a flip-flop and did the same thing for her other foot. "There's no need for you to be uncomfortable."

Her throat tightened at his tender gesture. Struggling to say thank you, she only watched him slide the heels into the bag, then let him take her hand to help her stand.

Not only was he handsome and from a rich family but also extremely selfless. How could she resist falling in love with him?

***

Her hand still in his, she strolled alongside him into an enchanting garden behind the restaurant. Vibrant flowers, bursting with color and fragrance, lined the pathways. Twinkling fairy lights intertwined with the azalea branches, creating a canopy of stars and dreams. The melodic trickle of a nearby fountain provided a soothing background score, and a breeze sprinkled the air and their path with a swirl of blushing azalea petals.

They walked slowly, the pebbled pathway crunching beneath their steps, the distant hum of cars breaking the silence. The world outside faded away, leaving just the two of them in a tranquil oasis.

"I've never been anywhere like this before," she admitted, unable to contain her wonderment.

Theo gave her a sideways glance, his voice low and husky. "Then we'll have to change that."

A laugh escaped, and her whole body felt as relaxed as her casual flip-flops rather than the grueling and pretentious heels they'd left inside under the chair. "This is not the kind of place you want to come often." Far too expensive, even for him. Unless his parents gave him a handout.

She wanted this moment to last forever, for her to be taken care of and have someone fuss over her with little things like wearing heels that hurt her ankles. "I had a great time. With you."

Theo leaned in, his breath warm against her ear. "Every moment with you feels wonderful, Whit."

Her heart fluttered. "The feeling's mutual."

They reached a quiet spot by the fountain, the murmur of flowing water soothing. Silver rays from the moon cascaded down and rippled off the moving water, merging with the muted golden glows from the lampposts to illuminate the courtyard. A familiar aroma had her glancing around the vines over the gazebo behind the fountain. She inhaled. "Wisteria."

"I didn't mean to make you think of your death," he teased. "I hope the scent makes you think of living for a long time."

She chuckled. Wow, he even remembered her comment at the wedding. "I didn't mean what I said that day. In fact, I'd like a house with a porch trimmed with climbing wisteria vines. That's my kind of house, you know." Then she held up a finger. "But it wouldn't hurt to have nice flowers for my funeral too."

His elbow nudged her. "It's not funny."

Sensing his tinge of fear, she wanted to remind him that death was inevitable, but surely, he knew that since he'd lost his mom.

As they stood in front of the fountain, a distant guitar serenaded them. He turned to face her. His fingers traced her cheek, and she struggled for her next breath. "I don't want you to joke about death."

With his voice soft, the light illuminating his serious expression, she nodded. Then the world seemed to slow as he leaned closer, their breaths mingling, lips inches apart. Time seemed suspended in anticipation.

Oh no! She couldn't even remember how to kiss. What if he kissed her? It didn't matter though, she was breathing hard, already anticipating his lips on hers.

Then his phone rang. The jarring melody seemed out of place in their intimate moment but enough to have them tear apart.

"You should answer." Whitney tried to hide the disappointment in her voice as she nudged them back to reality.

"We're on a date. No phone calls," he whispered, wincing.

But as it rang again, she urged. "Please. It might be important."

He retrieved the phone from his coat pocket, his expression tightening as he read the caller ID. "I'll be quick." He assured her before he moved away for a semblance of privacy.

Alone by the fountain, she dipped her fingers into the cool water, distorting the ripples that reflected stars. She tried not to eavesdrop, but the snippets made it clear something was amiss.

"You've got to be kidding me!" His posture hunched, and his head shook. "It can't be."

The conversation didn't seem like good news.

"Look. I've got to go. I'll call you back." His footsteps sounded. Then his phone rang again, and his steps stopped. "Gomez? What's happening?"

Was that the same caller bearing bad news?

"Uh-huh." He drew out a loud breath. "Okay. Great. I'll see to it."

When he returned, a new gravity marked his demeanor, but instead of speaking, he wrapped an arm around her, pulled her close, and kissed her forehead.

The earlier happiness drowned, and concern dominated her heart. She lifted her fountain-wet fingers to his cheek, turning his face her way. "Is everything okay? That call...calls."

"I won't be at work tomorrow." He exhaled. "I have to travel. But I'll be back in two days."

Her eyebrows furrowed. "Is your family okay?"

He half smiled. "It's some other issues, although there's a family matter in there somehow."

If the call had nothing to do with a sick or injured family member, why wouldn't he tell her?

She crossed her arms. "Why are you working at River Oasis and not running a high-end office somewhere?"

He sure wasn't taking his job here seriously if he chose to take two days off like that.

He tucked a strand of hair behind her ear, his touch a whisper. "Can you trust me?"

"I want to." She'd trusted him so easily. But if she was a burden to Mama, her own flesh and blood, wouldn't she become a burden to him too? Was she already?

"Don't be upset." He waggled his brows, being all cute.

If he'd done that earlier, she would've laughed. Now, her heart was too unsettled. Adjusting her handbag strap, she said. "It's getting late. I have a long day at work tomorrow." *Some of us have to earn a living and have no siblings to bail us out of debt and bills.* Somehow, she held that thought silent.

He leaned in. His lips grazed her ear as he whispered, and her legs felt like jelly despite her mood. "I promise to tell you everything. After the reunion, okay?"

"As long as it has nothing to do with you robbing a bank or anything of the sort."

At his chuckle, she drew a deep breath and nodded, the promise of future revelations should bind them. Instead, her insecurities severed that connection.

Secrets. Did they involve a lie she'd have to hide for him like she'd tried to hide Mama's addictions from Jada?

CHAPTER 14

Inside TSF Media's Rio de Janeiro boardroom, every cough seemed to reverberate off the walls, and each tap on a laptop keyboard roared into the silence. The room, normally a hive of animated discussions and innovative strategies, was charged with urgency today because TSF Media's esteemed reputation was on the line.

"We're all aware of the gravity of the accusations Mendes leveled against us." Ricardo, the chief legal officer, cleared his throat. "This doesn't just threaten litigation. They're threatening the very foundation we've built."

Around the glass table, twelve faces remained tight-lipped, each executive and legal advisor staring at the high-resolution screen on the back wall. It displayed an email thread from Mendes Productions, a small media company. The subject line was demeaning enough: "Intellectual Property Infringement."

Litigation threats weren't unfamiliar territory for TSF Media. Over the years, many sought to profit by exploiting legal loopholes and slinging accusations.

"With all due respect, this is preposterous," Valentina, head of marketing, said.

"Our team brainstormed every aspect of our campaign. Any resemblance is—"

"Have we done a side-by-side analysis of the two campaigns?" Theo loosened his tie. It felt stifling after days of dressing informally at Oasis.

Valentina moved her mouse, and two distinct ads popped onto the screen. Several of the board released relieved sighs.

"Similar themes." Theo leaned forward, interlocking his fingers. He squinted to concentrate on the screen and not miss any detail. "But they're not identical. Far from it."

"Mendes is baiting us." Gomez spoke in a measured tone, forking his fingers through dark hair sprinkled with gray strands. "They're testing the waters to see if we'll waver."

"It's a flimsy claim, no doubt." Ricardo, TSF's legal brain, sat taller. "Mendes is using this to rattle us publicly. They want a seat at the negotiation table—with you specifically, Mr. Stone."

The room seemed to inhale and exhale as one entity, a palpable sense of agreement pulsing through the atmosphere.

"Then we'll give them their meeting." Theo decided, maintaining the firm approach he usually employed in such situations. "But strictly on our terms."

"I'll arrange the meeting." Ricardo nodded. "But be prepared—they may still push for some form of compensation."

"Let them." Theo tapped his chin as he considered the bigger picture. This was a minor obstacle in comparison to the challenges he'd navigated in the past. "If Mendes is looking for recognition and a collaborative dialogue, we'll offer them precisely that. But nothing—absolutely nothing—implies that we're at fault here."

Approving nods and murmuring agreements rose from his team, reinforcing their collective commitment. Yes, he could count on them to stand their ground. This company's integrity was not up for compromise.

As the meeting progressed into discussions of strategies and counterstrategies, Theo felt well prepared for tomorrow morning's meeting with Mendes—a man known for grasping at straws for compensation. They weren't even rivals, but that didn't stop the man from seeking any possible edge.

For the rest of the day, he hopped from meetings with content creators to discussions with data analysts, the pulse of his media empire beating in each interaction. Amid it all, he struggled to find time for one of his mundane but essential tasks—checking and responding to emails. He'd managed to carve out daily pockets for this at the hotel in Houston, but today, the hours slipped by too quickly.

The call about his biological father couldn't have arrived at an odder time than during his first date with Whitney. Before he could process the news about the now-deceased father he'd never known, Gomez called for Theo to return to headquarters. That demand reminded Theo he was far from suited for a romantic relationship.

Not only had the revelations from his biological father stirred long-dormant doubts in Theo, but he also realized he'd been rushing things with Whitney. Lies were a shaky foundation for any relationship. After the reunion, he'd set things straight and let her know about River Oasis Resort's fate. He didn't want any reminders of a father who'd never wanted him. The man had gone so far as to have his lawyer lie to Theo and claim he was Theo's uncle. Why?

No. He wanted nothing to do with that. He'd ensure generous severance packages for the staff since he wouldn't maintain the resort. He'd toyed with the idea of letting Whitney benefit from the sale, but managing a resort would overwhelm her with an unfair burden. And he'd learned, both from Nate and his own life experiences, never to hand out charity as a gesture of affection. He'd have to find a different way to show Whitney he cared, something more meaningful than a financial parachute.

Running a hand through his hair, he stared at his computer screen, his eyes locked onto an email that left him indecisive. Then a knock rapped on his half-open glass door, and Gomez leaned in.

"Stone, how about we grab dinner?" Gomez gestured to the door. "Catch up before you head back to the States?"

"Sounds great." Theo glanced out the window. The city lights had begun to sparkle as day transitioned into night. How had time flown by so quickly? With his mind bogged down by strategic plans and personal conundrums, a break was necessary, and nothing would be more welcome than a chance to step away from his desk and catch up with an old friend. "In about thirty minutes, okay?"

Gomez nodded, glancing at his wristwatch before he left.

As Theo was starting to compartmentalize his lingering concerns, particularly the perplexing email, another knock interrupted. This time, his assistant Frida, who'd been like a sister to him over the years.

"Would you like to join me and my family for dinner?" she offered. It wasn't every day that he was invited to family dinners, but given his recent absence from the office, his team must've missed him.

He chuckled at the coincidence. "I appreciate the offer, but I've just agreed to have dinner with Gomez. Rain check?"

"As long as you're being fed." Her Portuguese accent lilted.

Being fed wasn't the issue. Dinner would serve as a much-needed chance to set aside, even if temporarily, weighty matters. Otherwise, the unresolved email, his mission at Oasis, and this deepening relationship with Whitney occupied his thoughts more than he'd care to admit.

At the restaurant's rooftop patio twenty minutes later, the rich aroma of meat wafted through the night air, mingling with the vibrant strains of bossa nova music. Theo settled in, overlooking the city for a hearty meal of feijoada, a traditional Brazilian stew. Lights hung suspended over rough-hewn wooden tables, and the waiters' and patrons' steps padded along terra cotta tiles. The conversation evolved from business affairs to more personal topics. Gomez shared that their accountant's daughter had successfully undergone her recent surgery, and Theo resolved to reach out to Miranda soon.

"How's Carolina doing?" Theo asked, savoring the rich flavors of the black beans, pork, and sausages in the stew, accompanied by rice, fried plantains, and farofa.

"She's thriving in her new job." Gomez sank back in his seat, beaming as he spoke about his wife. "I can't tell you how much she appreciates a break from being a full-time mom. Toddlers are fun, but very busy little bodies."

"Work can be a sanctuary in its own way." Theo mixed the meat to blend with the beans in his stew. "It brings a different kind of fulfillment."

"Speaking of fulfillment." Head cocked to one side, Gomez studied Theo, and his discerning gaze seemed to probe through the flickering candlelight gracing each table. "Your long-term undercover mission? Getting out of routine—has it given you time to think about your future?"

"A future?" Theo reached for his glass and sipped his drink.

"I mean reconsidering your thoughts about a spouse."

The comment jolted Theo like the tangy Brazilian lemonade, sending a smooth rush down his throat. He'd told Gomez he didn't need a wife when Gomez tried to set him up with one of Gomez's cousins.

"Anyone interesting caught your eye? Someone worthy to be a wife?"

"Yeah, actually." Theo forked a fried plantain from the saucer and lifted it to his mouth. Its crispy texture and sweet taste provided a momentary distraction. With Whitney dominating his thoughts lately, maybe it was time to talk about it with someone outside his family. After all, telling his secrets to one family member meant telling the entire family. And he wasn't ready for that. "The real catch is she thinks I'm some poor guy working at the resort."

Gomez erupted in laughter, the sound, joyful and hearty, resonated over the music and the clinking dishes. "Well, that's one way to test if someone loves you for you and not your money."

"True." Theo took another sip of his drink, pure limeade, although surprisingly called lemonade, which didn't make sense.

Still, the drink's tangy sweetness nicely contrasted the heaviness of the stew and the complexity of his feelings. "If I reveal my true identity, I'm not sure she'll ever trust me again."

"Money isn't that bad." Gomez leaned back in his chair, hands laced in his lap, the leather creaking as he lifted the front legs off the patio tiles. "It's all about how and what you do with it."

Theo scooped another spoonful of stew, relishing the blend of flavors. Whitney's mother had already filled her with enough lies. She didn't need another source of deception. Plus, he had no idea how to handle whatever feelings he had for Whitney. "Relationships are complicated."

"No one says relationships are easy." Gomez dropped his chair back into position, picked up his spoon, and pointed it at Theo, his voice mellowing, eyes softening. "They take work. Be it family, friends, or romantic relationships, they're not that different when it comes to the effort required."

Perhaps he was right. But this was all too much to process. The knot tightened in Theo's chest, he needed a change of topic. "My family will be here in less than two weeks. I need to ensure everything's in order."

"You worry too much, Stone." Gomez tsked. "You own the resort, and it's always ready for you and your family. Like we discussed last month, Frida booked the caterers, and everything is set to go."

Theo needed some of Gomez's confidence. But life had taught him to expect the unexpected. So he'd better stay at the beach tonight and make sure the employees who tended to the property were aware of his family's arrival. "The pilots could get sick or something else—"

"On the bright side, your pilot's not sick today and ready to fly you to the island tonight." Gomez reached across the table and slapped Theo's shoulder, his action jostling Theo's bowl and splashing soup onto his woven place mat. "Life has its way of throwing curveballs, but the weeklong reunion will happen just as planned." Gomez then raised his lemonade glass for a toast. The crystal sparkled in the dim light, reflecting the ambience of their surroundings. "To future happiness and resolving complicated relationships."

Theo raised his glass in response, the clink echoing their sentiments. In that moment, encased in the fragrant aromas and enveloped by the lively music, he felt grateful for his friend and the weight of his responsibilities dissipated. Until later that night, as he settled on a lounger in the quietude of his beachfront home. Then he brooded over the unsettling call he'd received from his investigator. The spacious living room, usually a haven, seemed to close in on him. His fingers clenched, mirroring the tightness in his chest. Why had his biological father remained absent all these years? He could almost still hear the evasiveness in his biological mother's voice whenever the subject arose.

Recessed lighting cast shadows as elusive as his wavering thoughts. Beyond the wall of open windows, moonlight dappled the ocean's surface, and the sea's subtle scent intruded, mingling with the woody aroma of his walnut furniture. Other than the wash of the waves, all was silent. Maybe he should've stayed in his city penthouse where cars and noise could drown his thoughts, as opposed to the private island's pervasive solitude.

Whitney's image intruded. At her concern last time they spoke, he'd felt an overwhelming urge to share his freshly uncovered secret. But then Gomez called, and reality struck—Theo's father owned the resort where he'd met Whitney.

He eyed his phone, its screen as dark and inscrutable as his feelings. He could call her, but that would mean divulging his whereabouts and mission.

He let out a sigh and closed his eyes, reliving how he'd almost kissed her. He'd experienced something authentic and rare, something that couldn't be bought with wealth or elevated by status. Now, surrounded by tactile luxury and visual splendor, he grappled with a longing no material comfort could assuage.

Was this what being in love felt like? The constant ache to be near someone, the thoughts that strayed to them in quiet moments? He'd never missed someone who wasn't family like he now missed Whitney. Okay, it was a different feeling for Whitney, far different from his usual homesickness.

Theo's phone disrupted the heavy atmosphere. He snatched it from the table, Regina's contact flashing. His shoulders relaxed, and he raised his bare feet onto the ottoman before swiping to answer. "Hello, Mom."

"Hello, my darling," she cooed, her tone warm and soothing. "Have you decided what to do with the resort?"

"I'm thinking about selling it and perhaps donating to charity." His contributions usually went to heart-related charities in honor of his mother or to hospitals his brother Eric founded.

Mom was silent, the counselor she was no doubt mulling over Theo's words. "And you've prayed about it?"

"Actually..." He rubbed the bridge of his nose, relaying this would make her understand why selling the place made even more sense. "I found out my biological father owned the resort."

"No way." She gasped. "How did you find out?"

"My investigator."

"Are you doing all right?"

The heaviness settled back into his chest, as though humid air thickened further. "Knowing this helps with my decision about the resort."

"Why the rush?" Mom's voice carried a note of concern. "Let's take some time to pray about it. Don't stress over this new twist."

"I'm not stressing." Was he? Or was that a lie? His voice faltered. "I have you and Dad and our family." Many kids in his situation never got adopted. His throat closed over, and he swallowed hard to free the lump in his throat. "Thank you, Mom."

"Oh, darling." Her voice shook. "I can tell you're not fine."

Right. He cleared his throat. He wasn't the fearful five-year-old anymore, hence proving himself when he'd bought the company far from home. "Everything's good."

The pause stretched. Then, as if aware they needed a topic change, Mom said, "I heard you met someone at the resort."

"What?" His eyes widened. "Did Wade—"

"Sweetheart," she cut him off. "Your brothers got excited to see you with any hint of a relationship. These last weeks, you've gone days without calling your siblings—you even missed our weekly chats. When Whitney's name came up while I was talking to one of your brothers, I got to thinking maybe you've been emotionally occupied by her?"

Mom laughed, her voice bubbly. "So, what's she like? Will she be at the reunion?"

"I almost forgot you're a counselor, Mom." He chuckled, running a hand over his hair. He didn't want to fuel any false hopes, especially since he was still keeping the truth from Whitney. "Yes, she'll be at the reunion. But we're not...well, we're not anything official yet."

"Then make it something." Her tone shifted to an earnest gravity. "You have such a big heart. And you've always had enough love for your family. There's more than enough room in your heart for Whitney too."

Those words hit their mark. "Mom..." Whitney had indeed found a place in his heart that fateful day she'd pepper sprayed him.

"You've always been so family-centered, Theo. It's only natural that you hesitate to let others in. But perhaps it's time to consider making Whitney more than just a casual acquaintance." He sensed his mom holding back from comparing Whitney to previous fleeting relationships he'd let slip away.

Taking a deep breath, he reflected on what set Whitney apart. Putting her dreams on hold to take care of her mother and sister. "She's so selfless." His thoughts wandered to her beautiful smile, a special one for him alone.

"What else, sweetheart?" He could almost picture Mom, sitting on the sofa, chin resting on her hand, completely engrossed in their conversation.

"She's hardworking." He looked up to the ceiling, trying to capture all the qualities that made Whitney so special. "Kind, easily contented. She has a strong faith and doesn't complain, even when she has every reason to."

A brief silence enveloped them before Mom broke it with a soft chuckle. "I'm looking forward to meeting her. The last time you sounded this passionate was when you were buying your company."

He couldn't remember the extent of his excitement for his company, but this was indeed the first time he'd spoken so ardently about someone. He exhaled as the looming issues in their path crept up. "Whitney..."

"What's wrong?"

"She doesn't know I own the resort."

"Why don't you tell her? I doubt she'll go spreading your secrets to the other employees."

Now he was way unsure about this whole operation. Running a hand over his forehead, he asked one of the wisest people in the world, the most important woman in his life. "Should I have told her earlier?"

"Better late than never. Best she hears it from you rather than looking up your name on the internet and finding out."

First of all, Whitney didn't have time to peruse the internet, and second, she wasn't nosy. Besides Whitney and the HR manager, no one at the resort knew his last name. "I'll tell her. After the reunion."

In less than three weeks, she'd have all the answers. But would that answer his questions?

He sank back in his seat and crossed his ankles on the ottoman. "How's Dad?"

Mom talked about Dad's recent work trip to Thailand. Like Mom, Dad always worked hard. His role as a research analyst had him traveling often. When they were younger, he'd often tried to combine his work trips into family vacations, allowing for extra family time as they explored new places. Mom then changed the topic to Nate's wedding and her excitement that it would be in their childhood home at The Peak.

Then the conversation veered toward the immediate crisis that brought him back to Brazil, and she delved into all the details, not out of nosiness, but so she could cover every circumstance in her prayers—a practice she and his dad had instilled in Theo and his siblings.

"Oh dear." She sighed. "I hope it's not too serious."

"It's manageable."

"Well, it's significant enough to have you jetting off to Brazil last minute," she pointed out. "You may be too old to remember, but we've always turned to prayer for even the smallest concerns."

"Like the time I couldn't figure out how to skip a rock across the lake?" Theo recalled his ten-year-old self's frustration.

"Wow. You remember that?"

Vivid memories resurfaced, especially of that summer afternoon. In his childish frustration, he'd hurled giant rocks into the water, unable to master the simple skill his brothers had learned under their father's guidance. It took him three trips to the lake before he'd gotten it right. Mom had enveloped him in her arms, praying for God to grant him patience and a relaxed spirit so he could learn.

"There's hope for us all, then," he repeated the familiar comforting words she used with him often.

"Everything that matters to us—"

"—also matters to God," he completed the sentence for her, basking in a sense of completeness only a mother's love and age-old wisdom could bring.

As her prayer washed over him, the tension unraveled in his chest. She petitioned for divine guidance and favor for his upcoming meeting, peace about his biological father, and wisdom in both the resort decision and his relationship with Whitney.

He hung up, treasuring a resurfaced peace.

The next day's meeting proceeded more smoothly than he'd expected. With a composed confidence, he made a strong case for the graphic's originality, emphasizing its similarity to anything else wouldn't serve TSF Media either—especially given that it hadn't yet been released publicly. As Ricardo had warned, a request for compensation came up, but Theo remained unyielding yet diplomatic, stating that, unless Mendes Media was interested in being acquired by TSF, no monetary compensation would be on the table.

Now, with his CEO duties set aside, he sat in his office midmorning going over the event calendar Frida emailed. A charity event in early July and a media event his company sponsored in mid-July every year. As for the August events, he'd have to miss a couple for Nate's wedding.

A wedding made him think of his future. Such a commitment didn't seem as terrifying as it had three years ago. Maybe because in two and a half years he'd be forty?

His mother's words reverberated within him. He needed to be more intentional in contemplating the future of River Oasis. Selling it was an option, but how would he relay such a decision to the loyal staff? Yet, amid the swirling thoughts, sweet anticipation made all challenges seem surmountable: The thought of seeing Whitney again.

And one insight resonated above all else—he was ready for whatever the future would bring. At that instant, he knew he needed to head to Houston today, not tomorrow morning as planned.

He reached for his phone, which was integrated into his office setup, and pressed the speaker button to call his assistant.

"Yes, Mr. Stone?"

"Can you have Jovan prep the plane for this afternoon's departure? I want to land in Houston by eight p.m. local time."

"Of course, sir. I'll take care of it right away."

He disconnected with a sudden clarity. He was ready to explore a serious relationship, and Whitney was one woman he couldn't afford to let slip through his fingers.

CHAPTER 15

The morning, usually a herald of hope and fresh beginnings, did little to lift Whitney's heavy mood. Emotionally drained, she guided her frail-looking mother through sterile corridors under artificial lights and out the sliding doors.

The early breeze swept against her face. Its cooling touch lost on her, it only fanned the flames of her emotional firestorm. Running on empty and without a wink of sleep, she exhaled a shuddered breath. Her heart was still a discordant drum after the last hours, her raw emotions close to the surface.

The hospital's initial call had come around seven p.m., right in the middle of her restaurant shift, plunging her into a dizzying state. The ride there had been an agonizing blur, every red light and slowdown amplifying the telltale flutter in her chest, which hadn't ceased even now. Thank God Daniela had been off work and able to drive her, then stay with Jada so the child didn't have to witness Mama's unconscious form.

Mama was fine now, awake and alert, just frail. And only a profound gratitude penetrated Whitney's exhaustion. Those agonizing hours spent holding Mama's hand in prayer beside the hospital bed hadn't gone unanswered.

"Careful." Whitney cautioned, holding the crook of Mama's arm as they exited the hospital and navigated the sidewalk. A nurse wheeled an elderly man past them, his eyes distant, seeming lost in memories or perhaps just lost.

What she wanted to say to Mama weighed on her tongue, but what new words could she offer? What could she say to make Mama understand how tired Whitney was of this unending cycle?

Her gaze rested on the white Maxima among the handful of cars parked on the curb—the car the Uber driver had described in his text. With the driver's help, she settled Mama into the back seat.

Whitney took a moment to truly look at her mother. Her skin, once radiant, now seemed sallow, her eyes no longer glowing but dulled and distant.

Whitney's heart twisted into a painful knot.

"Mama, why?" The words spilled out as the car rolled into motion, blending into the backdrop of a Houston morning as bleak as Whitney felt. Clouds dominated the sky, casting a gray hue over the streets as if even the city shared her melancholy. "You said you were going to Bible study last night." She fought to keep her voice steady, but her emotions threatened to shatter her composure. "Why did you take so much?"

Mama turned her face toward the window, her gaze distant. "I don't wanna talk about it."

Inhaling deeply, Whitney tried to calm her racing heart, a struggle between her anger and the physical fatigue she felt. "Mama, every time you do this..." Her voice quivered as a lump formed in her throat. And yet here Mama sat in complete apathy toward the looming hospital bill, the ambulance ride, the draining emotional toll. "I don't know." Whitney pressed a hand to her chest as if she could hold her tattered heart together. "We're drowning in bills as it is. I'm trying to save up for..." She hesitated, swallowing hard, not daring to reveal her undisclosed health issues. "Things we need."

"I'm sorry, baby girl." Mama's voice wavered, a crack in her usual armor. When their gazes met, even if just for a fleeting moment, Whitney glimpsed unshed tears glistening in her mother's eyes. "I'll do my best. I promise."

Whitney nodded, drowning in hope, skepticism, and the endless yearning for something different. She'd heard her mother's promises before. Each time, she clung to the hope that "doing her best" would mean something real this time. Without that hope, what was the point of persevering?

"We have to make it through this," she murmured, the words more an inward affirmation than a reassurance for her mother. While she ached to believe in Mama's promise, her confidence wavered. The uncertainty loomed, making it difficult to trust that this cycle, once and for all, might finally end.

As they stepped out of the car, Whitney waved to Mrs. Williams, who was walking her yappy Chihuahua. Kids on bikes circled the cramped lanes between trailers, and the clatter of breakfast dishes escaped from open windows.

Sidestepping her parked car, she helped Mama shuffle toward their trailer. With Mama's steps uncertain, Whitney could only hope Mama would get enough rest today while Whitney was at work and Jada at school. Or so she thought—until blaring music greeted them as they stepped inside. Jada must've forgotten to turn off the radio.

"Would you like some breakfast?" Whitney offered Mama.

"I'll go right to bed, baby." Mama rubbed her tired eyes and shuffled off, so Whitney escorted her to the bedroom across from the room she shared with Jada. The music drowned the rest of Mama's words.

After getting Mama situated, Whitney strode to the closed door and swung it open. Her sister was sprawled on her back on the bed, eyes closed, headphones on. Heat surging through her, Whitney shut off the blasting radio before yanking the blankets off Jada. "What do you think you're doing?"

Jada blinked open her eyes. She didn't look like she had been asleep.

"Why aren't you at school?"

Jada pulled off her headphones and tossed them onto the bed. "I don't want to go to school." She crossed her arms defiantly to punctuate her statement.

Whitney exhaled a long breath, the heat threatening to boil over. "Well, I don't want to go to work either." God knew she needed sleep, but life didn't seem to care about her needs right now. "Life's funny that way. Sometimes we have to do things out of necessity."

"I don't need to do things out of necessity." Jada swung her long legs over the side of the bed. She was still dressed in the cutoff jean skirt and black short-sleeved top she had put on that morning for school. This was when Whitney checked in, sent Daniela home, and hurriedly got Jada onto the school bus before returning to the hospital for Mama. Apparently, Jada had tricked Whitney too. "If Mama does whatever she wants, then I'll do what I want."

Great. "Jada." Whitney ground her teeth, pressing cold fingers to her forehead as dizziness washed over her. "I'm exhausted. Save me the battle, okay? By the time I'm done changing into my uniform, you'd better be ready. We're leaving this house together, and I'm taking you to school."

She could barely speak past a weariness that went beyond physical exhaustion—the fatigue of shouldering too much for too long. But she couldn't afford to back down now, not when the threads of her family were fraying at the edges.

Jada's shoulders sagged, the defiance seeping out. "After what happened with Mama last night, you expect me to go to school and pretend everything's fine?"

Whitney looked into Jada's eyes, the sadness there cutting her to the core.

"She was wasted, wasn't she?"

The heat in her veins drained away, perhaps pushed out by the weight of Jada's question. It only intensified her urgency for daily prayers for Jada to steer clear of drugs and alcohol and for any future relationship to involve someone equally committed to abstaining. Whitney couldn't lie about Mama's hospitalization, but admitting the truth seemed equally impossible.

She sighed, sat beside Jada, and took her hand. "Sweetie, life doesn't stop, even when things get tough." She interlocked their fingers together as a symbol that she'd always be there for her sister. "Mama's back home, and she'll get better. You have to keep living your life."

Jada's raised brow spoke her doubt. Yes, Whitney knew it was wishful thinking too. But how could she not hold onto the hope that, one day, something would inspire Mama to turn her life around? "The best thing you can do is to trust that I'm always here for you."

Something softened in Jada when she rested her head on Whitney's shoulder. "I'm late. You'll have to come to school and sign in to explain why."

Thank God! Finally, something was going right this morning. Whitney wrapped her arm around her sister in a sideways hug. "We'd better get going then."

Choosing practicality over protocol, Whitney decided not to change into her work uniform. She stuffed it into her handbag so they could leave without delay. As she tried to smile at Jada, who seemed ready to head out the door, a momentary peace soothed her. Despite the challenges ahead, they'd face them together.

They arrived at the bus stop as one was pulling away. However, another was scheduled to arrive in fifteen minutes. They waited in silence, Whitney too spent to offer Jada any more comfort. At school, the secretary handed Whitney a form to fill out. She scribbled "family emergency" in the appropriate space, her pen tracing the words a bit more heavily than she intended.

Then Jada enveloped her in a hug and whispered "I love you" before darting off to join her classmates. Given that Jada risked the social peril of being seen hugging her sister in public, the sentiment was genuine. That hug fortified Whitney as she caught another bus to work, giving her the emotional sustenance to get through the day.

Skipping work was out of the question, especially after last night's hospital bill. As she sat on the bus, she fought off a yawn and tried to keep her eyes open. Her thoughts shifted to Theo and his upcoming family reunion. As tempting as it had been to imagine, taking an entire week off was unrealistic. The bills wouldn't pay themselves. Yet a faint smile crossed her lips as she reminisced about their date. For those few hours, he'd made her feel special, pushing her worries to the back of her mind.

The way he looked at her, the way he sensed her discomfort in heels, and the way he fetched her flip-flops was more than just thoughtful. He'd knelt to change her shoes, unbothered by the gross act of touching her feet. She'd rarely experienced that level of attentiveness and care. Could she mean so much to him that he'd go to such lengths to make her comfortable?

Tears misted her eyes, blurring the outline of the man dozing across from her. Her emotional state wasn't helping her stay focused, but thinking about Theo gave her a glimmer of hope in an otherwise overwhelming morning.

Had he tried to reach her last night? She hadn't even checked her phone. Sitting up straighter, she dug through her handbag, found the phone, and checked for missed calls or messages. The screen was void of any notifications. Emptiness deflated her stomach like the air being sucked out of a balloon.

Their date had ended abruptly after that urgent phone call he'd received, so she had no idea where things stood between them. But he hadn't shared what the emergency was. Surely, that showed his lack of trust and interest in her.

Shaking her head, she rubbed her temples. She couldn't afford to get lost in what-ifs. People depended on her. As tempting as it was to imagine a reprieve from her relentless reality, Jada needed her more than ever. And that was all the motivation Whitney needed to press on, one relentless day at a time.

***

"Whoa, girl, you look wiped."

Grateful, Whitney approached her friend in the lobby. Daniela had not only driven her to the hospital but also watched over Jada for several hours. Whitney managed a smile and a slight wave.

Daniela abandoned her post behind the counter and rushed over to envelop Whitney in a hug. "How are you feeling?"

Her friend meant Whitney's emotional state. She didn't know about Whitney's health. Holding Daniela, Whitney swallowed the clog in her throat. Her eyes stung, and her body shuddered. Words were too elusive, too inadequate. "Thank you," she managed, "for everything."

"Is your mom home?" Daniela took a step back, her eyes scanning Whitney's face.

Whitney nodded, then relayed the events that had led Mama to urgent care. "She'll be okay."

This time.

The words felt like another hollow promise, one she wasn't sure her mother could keep.

"Whitney." Daniela gripped Whitney's arms with a sensitivity that underscored the hard truth they both understood. "Your mom needs real help, and that's not something you can provide."

Whitney sighed. "I've tried getting her help before—"

"I know you have. What I'm saying is, don't throw any more money at this situation until she's ready for a change."

"I can't give up on her." Was her persistent hope a form of denial?

Her lips thinning, Daniela shook her head. "You need to rest. You look like you're about to collapse."

"Rest isn't an option right now." Whitney yawned involuntarily, feeling even more defensive.

Daniela wagged a finger at her. "Skip the restaurant tonight, go home after your cleaning shift, and sleep. Theo will cover for you."

Whitney wanted to argue, to say she had already committed to working the restaurant shift, which she had. While Theo and another employee could handle the shift... "He's not back yet."

"Not back?" Daniela frowned. "Did something happen during your date?"

A warm flush crept up the back of Whitney's neck. She *might* have been the catalyst for Theo's abrupt departure.

"He received an urgent call and had to leave town," she explained more to assure herself than Daniela. But the unsettling thought remained. Had she seemed clingy and driven him away? She gripped her stomach. Was he distancing himself because of her?

A customer walked in, the sound of his rolling luggage signaling his need for assistance. Taking it as an unspoken signal to leave, Whitney stepped back and gave Daniela a quick wave. "Catch you at lunch."

Her friend waved back, then pivoted toward the arriving guest.

As she trudged through her cleaning shift, Whitney's energy depleted with every passing hour. Cleaning up two rooms soiled with vomit only added to her exhaustion. When lunchtime rolled around, Daniela had an extended break and seemed to pick up on Whitney's flagging spirits. Without a word, she took it upon herself to clean two rooms from Whitney's assignment list. How could she ever repay such kindness?

Somehow, Whitney muscled through the rest of her cleaning shift and even fulfilled her commitment at the restaurant. With a tidal wave of exhaustion ready to crash over her, how much longer she could sustain this pace—physically and emotionally—and stand firm for the sake of those who relied on her?

The restaurant, mercifully calm that evening, offered a much-needed respite. Besides the other staff member, who was to end her schedule at eight thirty, Daniela had stuck around, as if sensing Whitney might keel over without extra support.

An hour before the shift's end, Whitney entered the kitchen, balancing a tray full of dirty dishes. Daniela's eyes widened as she approached and relieved her of the cumbersome tray. "Oh my, it just hit me—it's your birthday!"

Caught off guard, Whitney did a mental calculation. "What day was it, anyway?"

"What a lousy friend I am, forgetting your birthday like that." Daniela huffed, jamming her hands on her hips.

"It's fine, really. I forgot it myself."

"Go outside. Take a break." Daniela nudged her chin toward the exit. "Let's call it my belated birthday gift to you."

"It's okay. I—"

"Please." Daniela tilted her chin in a pleading gesture. "It'll ease my conscience, knowing I did something for your overlooked birthday."

Unable to argue and craving a moment just to breathe, Whitney thanked her friend.

What a peculiar way to celebrate a birthday—navigating family crises, juggling responsibilities, and waiting for a text that may or may not come. Her twenty-ninth had crept up on her, another year marked, not by achievements or joy but by increased strain and complications.

But at least, the night air was a balm as she stepped outside, a welcome reprieve from the stuffiness of her life. She settled onto a bench, the grass beneath her tingling with dew on her ankles. She pulled out her phone.

The screen lit up, casting a pale glow in her eyes. No new messages, certainly none from Theo. In the days since their date, the silence from his end had become deafening. Was he all right? What had been so urgent? She took a deep breath to steady herself, her finger hovering over the screen.

She began to type "hello, Theo" only to erase it. Her thumb hovered. She didn't want to seem needy or clingy. Yet, the need for some emotional support, a comforting word, or even a sign of life from Theo was becoming hard to ignore. Daniela was a lifeline, but even she had her limits and burdens to bear. And besides, Daniela already did so much, like watching over Jada during Mama's troubled episodes.

With resolve, Whitney's fingers danced over the screen again, and she typed out the words *I just wanted to see if you're okay.*

She paused. Could she press send? Would this message bring clarity or complications? Her thumb hovered over the send button, a trivial action that felt momentous.

Her finger was still hesitating there when the kitchen door behind her creaked open. She turned, her phone slipping from her grip and thudding on the grass as her eyes met his.

"Theo!" Breathless, she sprang to her feet, her knees weak, her intent to run toward him.

"Whit," he breathed out. In two long strides, he'd closed the distance between them, pulling her into an embrace so full of longing and relief it almost knocked the wind out of her.

"Whit," he repeated with an emotion she felt deep in her bones.

"You're back?" Warmth flooded her chest, filling the void his absence left. She hugged him tighter, breathing in his smell, a mix of cologne and sophistication, even in just a T-shirt and jeans. Allowing herself to teeter on the edge of vulnerability, she confessed, "You were missed."

"You were missed as well." He cupped her chin and leaned into her, and her heart quickened as his lips hovered close to hers. "I wanted to do this on our first date."

The warmth of his breath whispered over her skin, sending her heart into overdrive. Then his lips brushed against hers before he sealed them to hers. Something like a dam bursting rushed through her—each pent-up emotion, each unsaid word released from where she'd confined them, conveyed through the urgency of their first kiss. His beard was soft against her flesh, softer than she'd assumed, and kissing him felt so natural and familiar, as if she'd kissed him before. Not caring that she was doing this the wrong way, she moved her lips against his, again and again. Each kiss felt right because she sensed a warmth and promise in his lips. And, for a timeless moment, the world faded away.

His fingers worked through her hair, unraveling her bun, and her fingers gripped his T-shirt hem.

Her stresses—the endless juggling of work, family, and emotional exhaustion—melted, leaving just this, this raw and tender connection.

When he drew back and pressed his forehead to hers, they were both gasping for air. Then he laced his fingers with hers and led her back to the bench. She squeezed their interlaced fingers afraid to break even the smallest point of contact.

"Happy birthday," he whispered, his eyes twinkling even in the dim light.

"How did you—?"

"Daniela told me."

"What have you been doing? Where did you go?" Each word emerged as a placeholder for the worries she'd harbored during his absence. Maybe now he'd explain the abrupt call that ended their date.

"I thought about you. About us." He lifted their entwined hands and kissed her fingertips, igniting goose bumps across her arm.

"You... thought about us?" A wave of emotion, so strong it left her lightheaded, picked her up and nearly carried her away. "About what, exactly?"

"How I like you." He breathed a kiss against her cheek. "How I enjoy your company."

The doubt dissipated when he looked deep into her eyes as if seeking permission to enter her world, her struggles, her dreams, and her fears. "Tell me what you did while I was gone."

The openness in his eyes invited her to share, not just the events but the emotions, the fatigue, and the triumphs of her days without him. For the first time in what felt like forever, she felt truly seen, deeply loved, and fully protected.

Needing to know before she got all into this relationship, she asked an off question, a heavy concern and one of the top things on her list for a spouse. "Tell me you don't drink or do drugs."

"I don't." With his free hand, he brushed tendrils of hair from her forehead, his tender touch seeming to reach inside her and soothe her vulnerability. Then his voice dipped to a whisper heavy with shared understanding. "My brother Logan had a traumatic childhood that led our family to abstain from alcohol and coffee."

Warmth spread within her. "I wouldn't have guessed any of your brothers had trauma."

"You'd be surprised how many people carry burdens like that." His thumb caressed the back of her hand, and his gaze shifted to the palm trees swaying in the breeze. "Just two days ago, I got a call that my biological father, whom I thought was long gone, had been alive all these years."

"Oh no." She tightened her grip on his hand. "Was that the call you got during our date?"

He nodded. "So, what's going on with you?"

She bit her bottom lip, torn between probing further and respecting his need for privacy. Opting for the latter, she shifted the focus. "My mom..." Her voice caught in her throat. "She was in the hospital."

His eyes widened, and as he gasped, his palpable concern almost shook her. "Is she okay?"

Tears she'd been holding back broke free as she shared Mama's recent episode. "I'm hoping she'll still be home when I get there tonight." She could barely get the words out, the emotion overwhelming her.

He untangled their entwined hands and reached out, wiping away her tears with his thumb. He peered into her eyes, seemingly understanding how fragile the balance in her world could be. "How's Jada handling this?"

"We had a battle about going to school today, but it worked out."

He pulled her into his arms. "You're taking tomorrow off."

"I just told you I have unexpected medical bills to pay and—"

"Shh." His whisper hushed her, and his hand rubbing her back soothed her. "I'm covering your room-cleaning duties tomorrow, along with your restaurant shift. You'll get paid."

Her heart swelled. "I have to talk to—"

"I've got it." He cut her off. "I'll talk to Charlotte about covering your shift tomorrow. Don't worry about it."

While worry was often an unwelcome companion in Whitney's life, right now, it felt far away. She nodded, moved by his unwavering support. She wasn't sure how he'd persuade Charlotte to let her take the day off and still get paid, but he had a knack for commanding attention and getting results. How he'd managed to compensate a customer with a one-week stay without getting into trouble was a testament to that.

"I've scheduled an appointment for you, Jada, and your mom at eight tomorrow for your passports."

"How?" She shifted in his arms to meet his gaze. "You've been busy. Out of town."

"I made a call."

She'd been about to tell him she couldn't take a week off for his family reunion after the new medical bills. Instead, she found herself agreeing to the passport application. With his arms around her, contentment and love pushed aside her lingering doubts and worries. The fact that he included her mother, whom he'd never even met, added another layer of warmth to her already full heart.

For the first time in what felt like an eternity, she allowed herself to relish the happiness of the moment, deeply touched by his thoughtfulness, and a profound relief and love that seemed to promise a better tomorrow.

CHAPTER 16

"Mama, even if you don't plan to leave the country, it would be nice to get your passport while we have the chance," Whitney urged, adjusting her handbag straps as she stood near the brown sofa where her mother sat.

"I already have an ID." Mama waved her off and continued sipping her coffee as if to punctuate her indifference.

"If it's of any help, Jada and I aren't planning to go to Brazil either." Whitney tried to offer some solace because she was still figuring out how to tell Theo that she couldn't afford a week without pay.

"I'm going!" Jada chimed in, appearing in the doorway from the hall.

Whitney's forehead wrinkled as she eyed her sister. "Since when do you wear eye shadow?"

"Since today." Jada twirled to show off her snug black top. At least she'd gone with the dark color Whitney suggested based on instructions for passport photos. "It's not every day you get your passport photo taken."

Probably best not to inquire where her sister had found the eye shadow. Today was too good a day to deal with quibbles. Mama was looking well—no puffy eyes and her dark hair with hints of gray was neatly combed and gathered into a ponytail. She seemed sober and alert, a rare moment of stability. If only it would last!

That morning, Mama had made grits. They'd all prayed together before sitting down to eat breakfast, the atmosphere warm and relaxed. They'd even shared a few jokes and gentle teasing. Whitney had made fun of Jada's sudden obsession with international travel, given her notorious dislike of long car rides. Jada had shot back, saying Whitney couldn't even handle a roller coaster, let alone a

147

transcontinental flight. Mama had chimed in too, noting that both her daughters had inherited their low motion tolerance from her.

The banter felt so wonderfully normal. Whitney caught herself wishing such tranquility could last forever. After their recent challenges, this semblance of family unity displayed a significant victory. It was a moment to be savored, and for once, Whitney allowed herself to do just that.

"We'd better get going." Whitney bent to embrace her mom. As they hugged, a faint scent of alcohol mingled with her mom's subtle perfume, a reminder of the challenges they still faced. But for now, she savored a warm hug.

"So, when do I get to meet this, um, Thor, is it?" Despite the slight slurring of her words, Mama's eyes twinkled as Whitney separated from her embrace and Mama patted the cushion for Whitney to sit.

"His name is Theo," Whitney corrected and settled in. Was it possible Theo might soon be integrated into her family life? "We can arrange that."

Jada scooted closer, then plopped onto the couch beside Whitney, peering tentatively over Whitney's shoulder at Mama. "You're not coming with us?"

"No, baby," Mama replied, her voice a bit wistful.

"Whit, didn't the email say we have to bring a parent?" Jada raised her eyebrows. "I'm thirteen, and I need a parent to sign the papers."

"Oh." Whitney winced, having forgotten that detail in the rush of handling so many responsibilities. "Actually, you do need to come with us, Mama."

Mama sighed, her shoulders drooping as if she'd been asked to move mountains. "I'm not... going out in public like..."

"You'll be fine." Whitney rubbed her mother's arm. Mama had lost so much of her self-assuredness. "It's not a job interview or anything."

Mama hesitated, then nodded. "I'll go change."

"You look fine," Whitney began before casting a critical eye over Mama's sweatpants paired with a dark-purple long-sleeved blouse. "Okay, maybe just change the shirt to a darker color."

Mama left and returned shortly, in a black skirt and long-sleeved blouse, and Whitney's chest swelled as they all exited the door together. They were still a family—imperfect, but a family nonetheless. Jada started chatting away as Theo's car came into view.

"Can you believe Whit's boyfriend is working her shift today just so she could have a day off?"

"He sounds like a wonderful beau." Mama's husky voice carried a note of approval Whitney hadn't heard in a long time.

As they approached the car, Whitney hurried to open the passenger door for Mama.

"Mind if I sit in the back with Jada?" Mama asked.

With a nod, Whitney closed the front door and circled to the back. As she opened the rear door and returned to sit in the front, relief flooded her. Despite the hurdles, they were making progress toward reclaiming the close-knit family they used to be and maybe, just maybe, could be once more.

Securing her seat belt, Whitney glanced in the rearview mirror—a habit instilled by Theo, who never started the car until she was buckled in. In the mirror, she saw Jada's contented smile, and her mouth reflexively mirrored the expression.

"Feeling left out, in the front here," Whitney teased, echoing their easy banter earlier over breakfast.

"With me in the backseat, I'll be able to look at you as I talk without craning my neck." Humor warmed Mama's voice.

Whitney let out a slow breath. Maybe Mama was turning a corner. Maybe things were finally looking up. She pulled out her phone to check the directions to the clerk's office where Theo had arranged their passport appointment.

As she merged onto the Houston interstate, she took in the morning sun casting golden hues over the skyline. She turned on the radio but kept the volume low for conversation. A gospel song played, and she thought of Theo. Not only because his lingering scent filled the car but also because he'd be listening to this song if he were driving.

"As soon as we get home, I'm going to look up what Brazil looks like." Jada wiggled in her seat. "Theo must be from a rich family if they're having a reunion out of the country." She then launched into a detailed observation about the name-brand tennis shoes he'd worn.

"I hope I was clear that you're going to school after the passport office today." Whitney brought the conversation back to reality. She'd looked online last night. There was no way their passports would be ready in less than six days, despite his assurances about expediting them.

"In case we don't go on the trip, I don't want you—"

"I hope it works out for you to go on this trip," Mama interrupted. "It seems this man really cares for you. I'd call it love if I can meet him."

"He loves Whit, Mama," Jada chirped.

"Maybe," Whitney conceded, although, in her heart, she was sure about Theo's feelings. How could she not notice his kindness?

"He's working double or triple shifts for you to have this day off," Mama pointed out. "You're driving his car while he took the bus to work. No boyfriend ever did that for you."

"Whit's never *had* a boyfriend before."

Whitney had to smile because Jada was right. Her sister wouldn't remember Whitney's high school boyfriend. Besides, Whitney couldn't remember any acts of kindness he might have done. Theo had been in her life for such a short time, and already, he'd filled her with a nearly overwhelming happiness.

"He is really nice." she found herself admitting. He'd given her his car the night before, even calling his insurance to add her as a driver.

Oddly enough, he'd insisted on taking an Uber home, not wanting her to drop him off. Maybe he didn't want her to see the motel where he was staying, but that hardly mattered now. What mattered was this moment of her feeling wholly content with her family together.

For the rest of the twenty-minute drive, Jada chattered about Brazil and wanting to go shopping for the trip—something Whitney couldn't entertain. She still had to request time off work, and the mere thought unsettled her.

She tried to cherish the joy of the day, especially when Mama pointed out a café they drove past. They used to visit it on Sundays after church. Yet smiling at her in the rearview, Whitney witnessed a fleeting shadow cross Mama's face, likely triggered by memories of Dad.

The passport application process turned out to be straightforward. They even managed to persuade Mama to apply for a passport, which led to a comical moment when they reviewed their initial photos. Mama had blinked, Whitney sported a goofy grin, and Jada had erupted into laughter just as her picture was taken. They then went through a second round of photos, sharing chuckles over the amusing missteps.

To capitalize on the happy vibes, Whitney opted not to send Jada back to school. They went to the café for lunch. Finances were tight, especially with upcoming medical bills, but these moments with Mama in high spirits were too rare to pass up. Over pancakes, with the aroma of syrup filling the air, they laughed and revisited old memories.

"Do you remember the time we all went to the zoo, and Jada tried to feed the peacock?" Whitney started.

"Ha! Do I ever?" Jada snickered. "That nasty creature chased me halfway around the park!"

"And Whit, instead of helping, was busy capturing the moment on her phone." Mama giggled.

"Hey, that video is a classic family memory now!" Whitney defended, and they all laughed.

"It was one of Dad's favorite videos," Mama said, then ducked her head, rubbing at her eyes, and they fell into the silence of a shared sadness.

Regardless of the sad memories, it was indeed a good day. On a whim, Whitney suggested they stop by the library. They borrowed a family comedy movie, which they watched together on the sofa later that afternoon, laughing as if they didn't have a care in the world. Just for today, they could forget debts, health concerns, and work.

Later that night, close to nine, Whitney found herself thinking of Theo. He shouldn't have to take an Uber home after a long day of work, so she texted him.

Whitney: Did you survive the day?

She didn't expect a reply, given how busy he'd said he'd be. Yet, she texted again.

Whitney: Don't get an Uber. I'll pick you up.

Maybe tonight she'd discover where he lived, adding more pieces to the incomplete puzzle of who he was. She knew so little, and perhaps that's why she felt an insatiable curiosity to learn more about him, this compassionate man who entered her life and captivated her in ways she couldn't fully understand.

CHAPTER 17

Exhaustion hit harder when things were slow. While cleaning rooms earlier had been tiring, at least it hadn't been dull. Theo yawned as he dropped dirty plates into the sink.

The other server, whose name momentarily escaped him, leaned against the counter and dangled her washcloth on the hook. "Whitney is so lucky to have you cover her shift," she cooed, her gaze lingering on him a moment too long. She twirled a strand of blonde hair around her finger, her playful intensity making him uncomfortable.

"She's blessed to have good colleagues like you too," he replied diplomatically, reaching for the brush to scrub the grime from the plates.

"Trust me"—she arched an eyebrow—"if I could sit at home and be guaranteed a paycheck, that's what I'd do."

"Unfortunately, that's not how the real world works." He turned on the water to switch his focus to the dishes, grateful for his upbringing where work was seen as a blessing and not a chore. But he also knew the importance of balance—of not letting work consume your life.

His circle of loved ones consisted mainly of his family and some close work colleagues. Whenever he had free time, he spent it with them—golfing, discussing work or simple family matters. Romantic relationships hadn't occupied his mind or time until he met Whitney. The more time he spent with her, the more he wanted to know about her world and to have her know his world.

"Theo." His coworker's voice broke into his thoughts prompting him to shut off the faucet. She slung her purse over her shoulder, already moving toward the door. "I'm meeting up with some friends at a sports bar nearby. Care to join?"

"Sorry, I have to work." He kept his tone polite but firm. Even if he were free, bars weren't his scene, and his heart was already spoken for.

She paused at the door, her penciled brows lifting flirtatiously. "I could wait for you to finish up, you know."

"That's all right. I enjoy the quiet. Good night." With that, he turned the water back on and resumed his dishwashing, his movement a clear signal he was uninterested.

"Did the manager tell you Whitney usually closes up?" Her voice rose over the water, trying to keep the conversation going.

He nodded but kept his focus on his task. If Daniela hadn't blurted out that he was covering for Whitney—and that she was still getting paid—none of this awkwardness would be necessary.

He glanced at the stove clock before pulling the dishwasher open to load. Nine forty-five. He couldn't wait to be done for the day. He'd never liked doing dishes, even as a kid, and yet here he was, setting plates and silverware into a commercial dishwasher and feeling satisfied knowing Whitney could have a break.

In less than an hour, the restaurant would close, and he could breathe easily. He hadn't been saddled with multiple shifts today since he wasn't even supposed to be back until today. He'd approached the HR manager with a special request—a temporary replacement for Whitney for the next two weeks. Citing her long tenure at Oasis without ever taking time off, he insisted she deserved paid leave. Once he revealed his true identity after the family reunion, he'd surprise Whitney with a bonus. He'd see this through—along with the enhancements he had in mind for the resort before its upcoming sale.

After finishing the dishes and wiping down the counters, he walked over to the table where he'd left his phone. When he powered it, Whitney's contact lit the screen. Four texts from her.

Each word warmed him like a burst of sunshine that dispelled the drudgery of his day.

"I survived," he mumbled as he read Whitney's messages thanking him for her day off and letting him know she was waiting in the employee lot.

He opened the hotel app to cancel the ride he'd scheduled for himself, then turned his attention back to texting Whitney.

Theo: Hey, you.

Whit: Hey, yourself. You shouldn't text when you're at work.

Theo: Says the employee who has been bombarding me with all sorts of messages. Blowing up my phone, are you?

Whitney: I'm not at work.

Theo: Ten more minutes before closing. Can I log out now?

Whitney: You need to work until 10:30.

Theo: So boring.

He grinned at the winky-face emoji she sent. Soon, the final minutes of his shift passed, and he was logging out. His heart practically skipping, he made his way down the sidewalk toward the employee parking lot. Each step felt lighter than his heartbeat, filled with sweet anticipation. All the hours of exhausting routine tasks faded, eclipsed by the simple, pure joy of being near someone he was starting to care for deeply.

When he emerged into the parking lot, the Civic's driver's side door swung open, and Whitney stepped out. As he neared, she rushed to him, enveloping him in a warm embrace. His heart swelling, he breathed in the simple but intoxicating fragrance he was growing addicted to.

"Did you have a good day?" He leaned in to kiss her. His pulse quickened as their lips met, the world around them dissolving in that sweet, fleeting moment.

"The best day," she whispered, her lips still hovering close to his. "Mama had lunch with us."

When they separated, he let his fingers stray to her hair. "Do you want me to drive?"

"I hope you're hungry. I'll drive—you'll eat."

"How did you know I hadn't eaten?"

"Because whenever I'm busy, I forget to eat." The softness in her eyes warmed his heart.

He opened the driver's side door for her and took the passenger seat. She handed him a paper bag branded with a restaurant logo, and his stomach responded to the aroma of fried food.

"I thought you didn't buy takeout."

"Today is special. Money can't buy happiness."

Knowing her financial constraints made her gesture even more touching. "Thank you. You want some?"

"I'm not hungry."

Even as hungry as he was, he wasn't fond of eating in the car. "Can we sit on one of the benches near the picnic area at the far end of the hotel?"

"I'm ready to stay up all night," she chirped, stepping out of the car. "I've had my rest all day."

As they walked hand in hand along the path bordered by shrubs, she inquired about his day.

"I knew you worked hard, but I didn't fully grasp it until today. And I had Jake help with three rooms."

"How did you get him to take on my rooms?"

"I have my ways." He grinned, omitting how he'd bribed him with lunch.

Turning a corner, they encountered a night guard who greeted them in the same spot where she'd sprayed Theo in the eyes before.

"Did you bring us this way on purpose?" She swung their hands between them.

"I didn't tell you to spray me." He spoke through laughter.

"Did you complain to management and have them rehire security?" Her guileless eyes widened beneath the light. "I know you like to voice your complaints."

"I have no influence over that." He'd indeed pushed HR to make the hire, but his other business was footing the bill. "Maybe there are other people you've sprayed?"

Her laughter rang out, making him feel as though everything was right in the world. They reached one of the grassy areas and sat on the bench, his food separating them. He coaxed her into sharing the meal.

After a quick prayer over their food, she handed him a wipe from a packet she'd brought along.

"I was so hungry. I would've eaten without washing my hands," he admitted, even though he'd washed them back at the restaurant at the end of his shift.

As they shared that fleeting moment, enveloped by the aroma of fried delicacies and night-blooming flora, he felt an unparalleled connection with her. He let out a pent-up breath, irrevocably content where he was.

"Tell me more about your day." He bit into his chicken sandwich. The lamppost nearby cast its glow on her face, making her eyes glisten like never before.

"Thank you for today. I kept Jada home from school. Probably shouldn't have, but it felt like the right thing to do. Mama... she was different today, happier."

She beamed as she talked about the café they visited and the time spent with her family. Knowing he'd played a part in bringing her this happiness produced a sense of accomplishment he couldn't articulate.

"I doubt Mama will go to Brazil, and I don't even think Jada and I will make it."

"Why not?" He kept his voice even, despite the disappointment hollowing his core.

"Passports take forever these days, even when expedited—"

"Don't worry about the passports. I have connections that could speed up the process."

"Right, you have famous siblings. I almost forgot. So many connections!" She grabbed a fry from his bag. Then her shoulders sloped. "But that doesn't solve everything. I have to work."

"I talked to the manager about that." Not exactly but close enough.

"You mean Charlotte?"

"No, the main guy." When her eyes widened, he chuckled.

"You went straight to the top? I've only spoken to him maybe three times during my entire employment."

"If you want paid leave, it's best to speak to the person who can grant it." Though technically, he hadn't talked to the top boss. His HR manager acted on his behalf. "By the way, my mom's looking forward to meeting you."

"You told your mom about me?" Her face lit up even more, and the happiness radiating from her in waves crashed over him.

"I hope it's not too soon, but I figured—"

"I'm glad." She placed her hand tenderly on his knee. The sensation sent a comforting warmth through him. He told her about the reunion logistics. "Being my turn to organize means I have to whip up a meal of some sort."

"I can help you with that."

"I was counting on you before you knew it."

"Really?" She squeezed his knee, seeming giddy and no doubt looking forward to the trip. She kicked her sandaled feet on the grass. "Speaking of family, my mom wants to meet you too. Would you be able to join us for a late lunch or early dinner after church?"

"I'd like that." And he meant it. "I'd like that a lot."

He savored his sandwich while she regaled him with stories from her childhood and teen years. Apparently, she used to play volleyball, so he insisted that she'd have to be on his team for the reunion games. Their laughter harmonized with the ambient sounds of crickets as the night matured, lending a surreal quality to their intimate gathering. Time seemed to be of no consequence, and neither of them minded.

Eventually, he drove her home. After opening the passenger door to help her exit, he bade her good night with a tender kiss, and her lips tasted like a mingling of fries and mint.

"Pick you up in the morning?" he asked.

Before she could answer, he pressed his lips against hers. She gripped his collar, kissing him back. And the distant music from a nearby trailer faded into obscurity as she reciprocated his affection.

"In the morning," she affirmed almost breathlessly as they parted.

He escorted her to her door, only turning back to his car once he heard the lock click behind her. As he settled into the driver's seat, a profound contentment enveloped him. It had been an extraordinarily good day, and he had a feeling many more such days were on the horizon.

CHAPTER 18

Whitney gave the blinds another impatient nudge, awaiting Theo's arrival. With the air inside the trailer stagnant, she wished even a small gust of wind would alleviate the tension. Sunlight streamed in, warming the room but not her jangled nerves.

If Theo was as affluent as his brothers, how would he react to her humble surroundings? The last time he'd been here, it was at night in the dim light. Now, daylight revealed every nook in the house.

She envisioned him dressed in a suit and that lavish watch he'd worn when they'd met. Would he find her home's simple setting acceptable? Would the heartfelt warmth she and her family could offer be enough?

Shaking off these thoughts, she opened the oven, letting out a rush of the roast's savory aroma. Oh how that reminded her of the Sunday dinners Mama used to prepare! In fact, Mama had been the culinary architect of today's roast.

The trailer was as spotless as she, Jada, and Mama could make it. Jada had repeatedly polished the dining table, and Mama had attended to every corner, dusting each nook and cranny.

"Theo's not going to notice all this cleaning." Jada tossed a cleaning towel onto the table, dramatically groaning. "He'll be too busy swooning over you."

"Move that towel, please," Whitney instructed, her gaze settling on the still-bare tabletop. "It's missing something. Flowers would've been nice." She could have snipped a few wisteria blossoms from the vines at church. Soon, wisteria would be scarce.

Turning her attention to her appearance, she scrutinized her white skirt, its lavender flowers complemented by a matching lavender top. She'd fussed for hours in front of the mirror, initially braiding her hair only to undo it and revert to a ponytail. At Jada's

160

insistence, she decided to let her hair fall naturally, framing her face and free from any ties.

"I think he's here." Mama's taut voice floated in from the living room.

"Really?" Whitney's heart revved up. She leaned toward the window for another look. Theo, undeniably handsome, stood there holding two bouquets. His hand trembled as he shifted his weight from one foot to the other. Then he took a deep breath as if he, too, was nervous.

"He's here," she whispered, more to herself than to anyone else. Her pulse kept quickening.

This was it. She pivoted from the window, drew her own grounding breath, and approached the door where her family had already gathered. This was more than just opening a door—she was opening up her life, her imperfect home, to someone she had fallen for.

Her palms, damp with nervous excitement, gripped the doorknob. It felt cool and slippery, a stark contrast to her rising warmth. With a final deep breath, she turned the knob and swung open the door.

"Hell–lo," she stammered, clutching the doorknob.

His fragrance mixed with the scent of wisteria and roses. He raised the bouquets, showcasing a lone yellow rose in the reds.

"Hi there." He grinned, his appreciation taking her in. "You look lovely."

Too flustered to remember what she was wearing, she glanced down to see, and her fingers fumbled with her skirt. "Thank you."

"Something smells delicious in here."

"Hi, Theo."

"Jada." His gaze shifted past Whitney's shoulder, and Mama spoke from the background, asking if Whitney was going to invite the guest inside.

"Oh... sorry. Come in!" Whitney finally stepped aside.

As Theo passed her, he leaned in and planted a featherlight kiss on her cheek, sending a little thrill of giddiness through her. Then he handed her the wisteria and ushered her to step in first.

"Thank you so much." Touched by his thoughtfulness, she lifted the flowers to her nose and inhaled, savoring their scent. "They're my favorite."

"I know." His mouth curved into a knowing smile.

How touching that he'd remembered. Unlike the flowers he'd brought her last time, these weren't commercial, not like the elegant roses prepared in a vase, and the gesture felt even more heartfelt because of it. Unless the motel he stayed in had wisteria vines, he'd have to have asked for permission to pick this many.

"Welcome." Mama greeted as Theo stepped inside. "I'm Madonna."

"It's great to finally meet you, Madonna." Theo shook Mama's hand before passing her the red roses.

"My, aren't you a gentleman!" Mama exclaimed.

"And, oh"—he plucked the single yellow rose from the bunch and bent in a small bow as he offered it to Jada—"this is for you, young lady."

"No one's ever gotten me flowers before," Jada marveled.

When his gaze found Whitney's again, her heart swelled. "Thank you."

Perhaps the tenderness in her voice could convey more than words ever could. He couldn't possibly know how special this moment was to her whole family.

Guiding him to a seat at the dining table, Whitney took the flowers from everyone. There was only one vase, the one from the flowers he brought last time. So she placed Mama's and Jada's roses next to the jar candle on the counter. Then, for the wisteria, she filled the vase with water and set them in it. They were simple yet radiant, just like her feelings.

"How long have you lived here, Madonna?" Theo inquired, seeming comfortable as he rested his hands on the table.

"Going on nine or ten years." Mama winced, a slight shadow crossing her face. "Before that, we lived in Huntsville."

"Whit says it was a smaller town than here," Jada chimed in, seated next to Mama.

"Ah, country living. I can imagine the peace and quiet it offered." Theo's eyes twinkled.

"City's nice for a change of pace."

Whitney smiled at Mama's comment. Mama enjoyed the noise, rather than silence. It helped her not think about Dad perhaps. Whitney brought the food to the table, the chairs scuffing against the linoleum floor as they all shifted into the proper position to sit.

Not having a variety of drinks, she was relieved to recall he'd only drunk water at the restaurant they'd been to. With Jada's help, she placed a water pitcher and glasses on the table.

Theo and Mama both asked how they could help, but Whitney waved them off. "Just relax."

Pride warmed her as she looked at her assembled family and the man she'd come to care so much for this month. She slid into her seat next to Theo, and they all linked hands. With her fingers woven into his, she offered a heartfelt prayer for the meal and gave a silent thanks for the warm pulse of his hand against hers. As the family said a collective amen, he pumped her hand with gentle squeezes, and his eyes met hers with a playful wink. Then she served a generous portion of roast onto the first plate and placed it in front of Theo.

"Thank you." His gaze held hers in a moment charged with unspoken affection before she moved on to serve Mama and Jada, then helped herself.

"This looks so delicious," Theo declared, his fork parting the steam rising from his plate.

"Mama made it," Whitney bragged, grateful for her mother's culinary talents.

"Whitney helped," Mama added and exchanged a knowing look with Whitney.

The comforting clinking of forks on plates underplayed their chatter as Theo praised Mama's cooking skills. A shy smile lingered on Mama's face. He then turned to Jada. "So, what's your favorite subject in school?"

"Am I too old to say recess?" Jada joked.

"What she means is her favorite subject is the one she skips," Whitney quipped, though she was sure Jada had never skipped a class. Her report card certainly didn't suggest it.

As Whitney looked around, her heart swelled. Theo seemed to fit into their lives, even in the humble setting of their trailer.

"Thanks for the passports, by the way." Mama broke into the conversation, turning toward Theo. "I had no idea they could get here so fast."

"That's what express delivery is for." Jada bounced a bit in her seat.

"I was surprised too," Whitney admitted. At least that detail had been smooth.

"It's unfortunate Madonna can't join us." Theo put his fork down and faced Mama. "But there'll be more opportunities in the future."

Mama's gaze dimmed. "I'd like to go next time."

"So, what can I look forward to in South America?" Jada, full of youthful enthusiasm, changed the subject. "I've never even been on a vacation before, let alone outside the country."

She shoved her plate aside, elbows on the table, chin propped in her hand, as she peppered Theo with questions, leaving him hardly any time to answer.

Amid this, Whitney's gaze shifted to Mama. Mama seemed lost in thought as she ate. Her erratic behavior involving alcohol and drugs was a constant worry. After a difficult conversation the previous night, Whitney had secured Mama's permission to enlist Mama's close friend to check on her and keep her accountable.

As the dinner conversation flowed, Theo shared about his upbringing in Colorado.

"I'd like to try out for cross-country in the fall." Jada caught Whitney off guard.

"You'd be excellent at cross-country." Theo continued his conversation with Jada, sharing stories of his middle-school days in cross-country before switching to soccer in high school.

The conversation never seemed to falter, and soon, it was time for dessert. Whitney had prepared individual cups of chocolate mousse the night before. The simple, no-bake dessert had always been a family favorite.

As they relished the sweet ending to their meal, Whitney tried to set aside her persistent worry about Mama and savor this cozy moment surrounded by her favorite people in the world.

Theo lingered well after dinner, filling the room with easy laughter and lively conversation as they discussed the exciting plans. Mama's eyes widened, and Jada clapped when Whitney told them they'd be flying in one of Theo's family's private jets.

"A private jet?" Jada pivoted to him, grabbing his arm, and Theo, clearly embarrassed, squeezed the back of his neck.

Like the gentleman he was, he then insisted on helping with the dishes, and they even broke out their classic Monopoly game afterward. Theo was fiercely competitive, capturing Park Place, Boardwalk, and most of the utilities with a triumphant smile.

Eventually, he said his goodbyes to Mama and Jada, leaving Whitney to walk him to his car. Outside, the dull glow of porch lights mingled with the natural luminescence of the night sky. The crickets' harmonic chirping seemed loud tonight.

"So, when am I going to see where you live?" she asked as they reached his car.

"We've both been working such late hours, but just so you know, I'm still living in a hotel for now." He leaned against the car and looked at her intently.

"Oh."

"After the reunion, I'll get everything sorted." He reached out, his fingers caressing her cheeks, and goose bumps scattered over her arms. "There's still a lot I have to figure out."

She swallowed, wavering beneath his tender touch. "We all have things... to figure out."

"True." He then leaned in and kissed her, the contact sweet and lingering, making all the world's uncertainties fade away.

When the kiss ended, his forehead rested against hers. "If you haven't committed to tomorrow night's shift yet, can I take you out on a date?"

"I've already committed." If only she hadn't.

He mock-groaned. "Well then, how about a midnight outing, after your shift?"

She smiled, her heart fluttering. "Sounds great."

"Okay." He kissed her again tenderly, and a promise in his kiss spoke of things yet to come. As he drove off, she felt like she was standing on the brink of something wonderful.

CHAPTER 19

With a unique sense of fulfillment, Theo walked alongside Whitney through the moonlit gardens he'd taken her to. Every laugh, every shared smile, and every moment of silence between them filled a hollow space in him. He'd always leaned on his family for that sense of companionship, but Whitney was completing him in a new, unexpected way.

Bathed in magical moonlight and sweet floral scents, he ached to prolong the night, to stretch out these fleeting moments. So, he squeezed her hand and guided her to one of the plush seating arrangements.

"You have a penchant for luxury, don't you?" Her eyes gleamed as she sat.

"When you're new to Texas and browse for places open late, usually the fancy hotels show up on the list." He was partly bluffing. He hadn't done that research. But he wasn't bold enough to tell her this was his temporary home away from home.

She simply smiled, an inviting gesture that melted his insides. She patted her blue top, which she'd changed into post-work for their late-night outing. He, in turn, had swapped his work attire for a casual cotton button-down. Neither of them were overdressed, but enough for the atmosphere.

But here, under the watchful eye of the night sky, in a place devoid of other people, they existed in their own little world. A world where he felt a depth of affection and fulfillment he'd never thought possible.

Curiosity lit her eyes, dancing with the reflections of lights hanging like stars above them. "It was your turn to reveal something about yourself. Something no one else knows."

Stalling, he sat beside her and instead of answering her, he preferred to prolong the admission she'd made moments earlier. "I'm your first boyfriend?" He couldn't resist repeating it, reveling in the significance of being her first love.

"And why do you find that so amusing?" She jabbed his ribs.

Turning toward her, the chair's cushion yielding beneath him, he grinned. "Because I want to strive to be your first and your last." More than a lighthearted jest, the words revealed a deep-seated desire—to himself as much as to her.

"And you? Ever had a girlfriend before?"

Her question, a delicate one, probed his past with a simplicity that deserved honesty. He stroked his stubble and vaguely remembered his short-lived romantic relationships.

"I've had a couple." Women often pursued him, seeking relationships with a financially steady man. "But they were nothing serious. I've always been more consumed by life and family commitments." Lately, work to be precise.

As her brow furrowed, he reached for her hand. His touch seemed to be the simplest form of truth. "I wasn't ready for something serious back then. But with you"—he gestured between them—"even though it's not been too long, something about us feels right. And promising."

"You think so too?" Her hand tightened around his, a silent plea perhaps for a deeper glimpse into his soul.

"I do." He nodded, his voice a murmur against the night. When she asked him to share one thing about himself no one else knew, she brought him to a darker revelation. With a deep breath, he faced a truth he rarely acknowledged. "I hate hospitals."

And he'd never admitted it before.

She already knew of his mother's death, yet she delved deeper, her voice filled with empathy. "Is there any specific reason why?"

Memories enveloped him, a chilling mist as he recounted the stark moments of his childhood. "I was almost five, but I just remember waiting in the hospital, an aide at my side, while they tried to decide who would look after me until my mom got better."

He shivered as the memories came reluctantly, each one sharp and cold. The sterile smell, the indifferent buzz of overhead lights, the uncertainty...

He withdrew his hand, a subconscious retreat into the sanctuary of his own arms. "Just that memory." His voice lowered, his gaze drifting to the potted plant ahead as the image crowded his mind. Everyone was in limbo until his mother's fate was sealed. "Before anyone could decide who would take care of me for the night"—the words caught in his throat, grating like shards of glass—"she... was gone."

And now, he'd shared that with Whitney. Sitting there, under the lanterns' glow, amid the muted splendor of the night, he'd let her into a vulnerable corner of his soul. And somehow, that made the darkness less daunting.

He recounted several hospital visits, each one a reminder of that initial loss. It was as if he'd opened a box of memories best left sealed, each one another reason to avoid hospitals. "It doesn't feel like a place of healing for me." With her comforting hand on his shoulder, he recounted the story of the tragic loss his oldest brother, Eric, went through, and through the story, Whitney's touch was a balm, her hand squeezing his shoulder.

"His wife too?" she whispered a gasp.

Nodding, he braved a smile to indicate Eric's resilience was a stark contrast to the grim past. "God blessed him with a wonderful new wife, and now, they have eight incredible kids." The warmth of the testimony eased the harsh memories. "Believe it or not, no one in my family is aware of my anxiety about hospitals, not even my mother, a whiz in child psychology."

Her eyes widened. "How do you act when you're waiting in the hospital with your family?"

"I try to play the comedian." He confessed the tactic he used whenever a family member was admitted to the hospital. "By turning a blind eye to reality, I spare myself the torment of constant worry."

How ironic—prayer was his true refuge, yet humor was his shield.

Ready to shift the focus, he leaned in to kiss her ear, and she gasped before he whispered. "Your turn now."

She hesitated, arms crossed, her gaze drifting along the cobbled walkways. "How do I even top that?"

"This isn't about one-upping each other," he reassured her, more interested in her story. "Please, tell me everything."

The struggle was clear as Whitney fought to reveal another secret, her eyes avoiding his. "I..." She took a steadying breath. "I need to have a procedure."

"What?" His instinctive response sliced through the calm.

The volume of his voice didn't seem to shake her, didn't even draw her gaze. "I have an irregular heart murmur." She kept her tone level. "It's not a big deal, but the surgery is inevitable."

Her words did little to calm the storm brewing inside him.

"Anything that involves the heart is a big deal." He tried to grasp the gravity of what she'd told him. He usually made things happen. But this was different. This was personal, deeply so.

"We're going to the hospital tomorrow." His protective instincts flared as he reached for her hand as if he could transfer his strength to her. His mind raced back to the night she'd passed out, the times she'd worked hard and ran herself ragged. His heart sank, and he lifted their entwined hands to kiss the back of hers, needing her to take this seriously so she could agree to go to the hospital tomorrow—tonight even, if he were calling the shots.

"For someone afraid of hospitals, you're really pushing for it." She smiled faintly, deflecting his alarm. "It's not a big deal."

But he knew better—anything involving the heart was critical. Why did her mom let her go to work every day while she was sick?

"Does your family know?"

She shook her head, her chuckle light but edged with something else—a stubborn independence perhaps. "I thought we were sharing things nobody else knows."

He ran a hand over his hair, hoping doing so would diffuse his rising agitation. "And here you are, working tirelessly at the resort."

His resolve hardened—no way would he let her overexert herself now that he knew of her condition. Taking a deep breath, he forced himself to adopt a semblance of calm. "When is your surgery scheduled?"

"I'll set it up as soon as I have the money." She spoke so calmly, as if talking about an ordinary errand and not a matter of life and health.

"You haven't *booked* it yet?" He yanked his hand out of hers, not wanting her to sense the tension tightening his grip as concern hardened to frustration.

She fiddled with her bracelet identical to his—matching the ones he'd also picked up for Jada and himself during their beach outing.

"Calm down," she soothed then, her touch grounding him. "The doctor assured me it's a routine procedure."

Didn't she know doctors had to keep it positive for patients? Dread clawed coldness along his spine and dug into his chest. "We should go to the hospital tomorrow."

She met his gaze, her expression unreadable beneath the light. "You're not thinking of paying for it, are you?"

"Yes." He spoke without thinking, but he meant it. He'd do anything to ease her burden, but that was his CEO side talking—she was unaware of the life he led outside their bubble.

"You just started working, and you blow your money like crazy." She gestured to their serene surroundings, seemingly making her decision final. "Plus, we have a reunion coming up. Jada has big plans for the beach in Brazil. Another thing I don't want to do is be a burden to anyone. That's why I never told anybody about my health."

His heart ached to see her so stoic, so determined to shoulder her troubles alone. He would stand by her—no matter the cost or the secret lives they led—but he would *not* let her see herself as a burden. "Please, you can burden me any day."

"You mean you're okay with me being clingy?" Her voice held a new, lighter tone as she leaned into him, a stark contrast to the heavy air of concern moments ago.

"I love clingy." He kissed the top of her hair, savoring her conditioner's subtle scent. "I've been trying to distance myself from my family to build my independence. That's one reason I left for... here." He almost slipped up, revealing what he shouldn't just yet. "I was too attached to my family, but these last few weeks have been different."

"How so?" She nestled closer, her head resting on his chest.

"Being with you has been more exciting than my usual family banter." He rubbed her shoulder, basking in their intimacy.

"The feeling is mutual."

Their conversation flowed, revealing more intimate details about themselves. Grateful for this connection they were forming, he navigated the discussion, withholding the truth of his stay at this hotel, his secret mission, and the façade he intended to maintain for another two weeks.

He shifted, and an object in his pocket jabbed at him. He pulled out the small bag. "I have something for you." He kissed her lips before handing it over. "I didn't get anything for your birthday last week, but I hope you'll accept this gift."

Her eyes sparkled like the diamonds in the necklace she unwrapped. "Theo, it's beautiful. It's... expensive."

Before she could think of refusing, he took the necklace and stood to move behind her. His fingers betrayed a faint tremble. With deliberate gentleness, he swept her hair aside, his touch lingering momentarily against her skin. Then, with a careful, almost reverent motion, he draped the chain around her delicate neck. Her involuntary shiver heightened his awareness, and he found himself holding his breath while he secured the clasp.

Back in his seat, he clasped her hand. The affection in her eyes mirrored that in his heart. "You've become very important in my life. We've only known each other for a short while, and here I am, acting like a lovestruck teenager."

She ducked her head, her free hand fiddling with the necklace, her posture shy. "Makes two of us."

"You're probably aware that I like you. A lot." At least, he hoped she knew that. "I think you like me even more," he teased, eliciting a chuckle from her.

"Who's giving all the presents?" she quipped.

He touched her chin, raising her gaze to his. "Would you officially be my girlfriend?"

Her eyes twinkled, her lips curling into a happy smile. "I like you and you like me. I thought I was already your girlfriend. I didn't realize a proposal was involved."

"Like I said"—he cupped her face, his eyes lost in hers—"I want to be the best boyfriend you've ever had and, hopefully, your last."

"As long as I'm your last girlfriend, it works for me." She leaned in, his lips captured hers, and his fingers wove into her hair, soft like silk. It was a mingling of hearts, full and boundless as they sealed their newfound commitment with a kiss.

The woman in his arms was strong and independent, yet vulnerable in her own way. With each fleeting moment, he was tumbling further into the depths of his feelings for her, irrevocably committed, for better or for worse.

CHAPTER 20

Whitney had never experienced luxury in a car like the one she rode in now. The leather seats contoured to her body, and the spacious interior gave her room to breathe. To her right, Jada was sampling a variety of soft drinks from the minibar integrated into the rear console. The sleek, illuminated compartment made it easy to pick and choose from the assorted beverages. Theo, sitting between them, seemed at ease, as though cruising in this high-end vehicle was just another day for him.

"What else haven't I tried?" Jada mused, pulling out another bottle. With a satisfying pop, she opened it. "I love these Brazilian drinks."

"I'm glad you're enjoying them." Theo chuckled, reached for a bottle, and offered the Brazilian soda to Whitney. "Guaraná Antarctica."

"I'm so full, thank you." She patted her stomach. The ride from the private airstrip had been short—far too short to necessitate the buffet of snacks and drinks they'd already consumed on their flight from Houston. She looked through the rear windshield at the control tower surrounded by lush tropical vegetation. Theo had shared that the runway was expansive enough to accommodate three jets at once, each with room to spare.

"Your family owns this place?" Whitney asked, still coming to terms with his family wealth.

"It's a family property," he confirmed, then steered the conversation back to the present. "Would you like the window rolled down to better enjoy the view?"

"Of course," she was eager to absorb as much of the scenic beauty as she could.

With a subtle press of a button, he lowered both windows, and the sea breeze flooded the car's plush interior. The scent of salt water and fresh blossoms danced through the air, mingling in a way that tugged at her senses. Her gaze drifted to the stunning vistas. Luxury reigned from grand beachfront villas to elegant gazebos graced with flowing silk curtains.

"Wowsers!" Jada gasped, and Whitney turned. Her sister's eyes were wide as she gripped the window frame as if she might miss something. "Is that a private lagoon?"

Whitney followed her sister's gaze to the serene body of water encircled by pristine lawns and towering palm trees. Cascading infinity pools shimmered in the sunlight, lined by inviting cabanas that surely offered captivating ocean views.

"This is—"

"Amazing!" Jada finished Whitney's sentence, articulating the awe Whitney was too stunned to put into words. Jada had the better view, but even so, Whitney's side had its wonders.

"We're here," Theo announced.

The car came to a stop. Then her door swung open, and the driver greeted her, smiling. "Welcome to Brazil."

"Thank you, Arturo." She stepped out of the car. Theo followed. Then Jada leaped out with a squeal.

"Whoo-hoo!" Jada twirled, arms outstretched. "This is the best vacation *ever*!"

"We haven't even started the vacation yet," Theo teased, his eyes aglow.

Whitney approached the trunk to help their driver pull out the luggage, but Theo assured her Arturo had everything under control.

"I'll give you a tour of the house." Theo looped her hand through his arm, then led her and Jada toward a sprawling mansion framed by palm trees and overlooking the beach. A mix of classic elegance and modern opulence, it stood tall over the azure waters, its walls of windows offering stunning views.

As they walked through lavish hallways, they encountered some of the staff, and he introduced Jada and then Whitney—as his girlfriend. Blushing, she savored the affirmation.

Each worker they met greeted Theo with humble deference, their gazes meeting his in a manner that spoke of respect.

"Mr. Stone," one of the maids greeted, pausing with a duster and dipping her head.

"Olá, Rosa." Smiling warmly, he turned to Whitney. "Rosa takes exceptional care of the place."

Whitney hugged his arm tighter, holding on as if to contain her emotions—awe over the splendor, yet also wonderment over how well regarded he was by those who worked for his family.

Walking through the residence, he pointed out various rooms—each more stunning than the last. From a home theater equipped with the latest tech to a serene exercise studio overlooking a private garden, she was walking through the pages of a luxury living magazine.

"Everything is so—"

"Overwhelming?" He rubbed the back of his neck, eyeing her for confirmation.

She held up one hand. "In the best way possible."

He grinned. "I'm hoping sometime this week we can catch the sunset from the balcony."

"I can't wait."

"All the ladies and couples will be staying in the main house." He opened another spacious bedroom.

With Jada touching and admiring every vase and photo within her reach, Whitney was glad they'd arrived a day ahead of the rest of his family so they could swoon over everything and get settled.

Forty minutes later, after they changed into swimsuits and headed for the beach, Jada wandered along the shore, leaving Whitney and Theo to stroll.

Whitney's feet sank into the soft, white sand, the grains cool and yielding beneath her toes where the receding tide had dampened them. Theo's gentle hand found hers. "Thank you for coming," he whispered, then kissed her temple, warming her to her core.

"I'm not even sure what to say." This was like paradise. How she and Theo had come to know each other was a mystery. It was nothing short of a miracle that a man, whose family had roots deep in this slice of heaven, had crossed paths with her.

He swung their hands between them. "You can say something after our ride."

"Ride?" She slid free and wrapped her arms around herself. The boats bobbing at the pier beckoned with the promise of adventure, yet her inexperience with watercrafts tethered her to the shore.

He smirked, his amber-brown eyes sparkling their teasing challenge. "If I tell you all the details, I have a feeling you'll bolt."

"If Whit bolts, her loss." Jada turned around, rubbing her hands together as she moved toward them. "Where do you want us to go, Theo?"

"Come on, Whit." He grasped her hand and uncoiled her arm from around herself before giving her a slight tug.

With his eyes so full of gentle persuasion, who could resist? Besides, no way would she douse Jada's uncontainable excitement. So Whitney let him lead them to a sleek, private watercraft that looked like something out of a thriller movie. After the ride, she and Theo settled on the sandy shore, unconcerned with the granules clinging to their clothes. They lounged, side by side, gazes adrift toward Jada frolicking in the water. A playful sea breeze teased Whitney's hair, while the rhythmic lull of the surf, harmonizing with Jada's laughter, wrapped Whitney in the embrace of a perfect afternoon. She inhaled deeply, savoring the ocean's breath, as crisp and invigorating as the presence of the man beside her.

"I'm assuming your parents bought this place in honor of your Brazilian roots?" Whitney asked, wanting to understand more about the man she was falling for.

"You could say that." He nodded. "It's where I thought I could find some connection to my mother's life, to her culture. She didn't grow up in the financial luxuries I have, but I'm sure she loved her heritage."

"I have no doubt she did." She already adored his parents for making sure he knew his roots and helping him connect. Now, she was looking forward to meeting them for sure. "What time will your family be here tomorrow?"

"They might arrive at different times, but I'm guessing anytime from noon onward."

Right, his family was wealthy enough for his siblings to arrive in their private jets.

As they sat there, a server appeared with a snack tray and Brazilian sodas and Jada rushed back to their side. They each grabbed a drink, clinking their bottles together in a toast.

"Here's to unexpected journeys and undeniable paradise," Whitney said, gazing into his soft brown eyes.

"To finding unique shells," Jada said.

"And to discovering treasures where we least expect them," Theo added.

Whitney sipped her bubbly drink. She'd already found an even bigger treasure in the man beside her than this paradise around them.

***

An hour later, they retreated to the house. Though the residence was expansive enough to offer them separate bedrooms, Jada wanted to bunk with Whitney. Given the king-size bed in her assigned room, Whitney had no reservations about the arrangement.

"This trip is like a dream come true." Jada bubbled, flouncing around the spacious room, bending and looking under the bed as if searching for a treasure. "Can you believe we're going to the market tonight? I can't wait for dinner! Do you think we'll be eating Brazilian food?"

"You'd better find what to wear if we're going to dinner soon." Whitney assessed a frail top from her luggage. She could've used some new summer dresses, but that wasn't an option in her financial stand.

"I know what I'm going to wear." Jada reached for her luggage next to the expansive dresser and unzipped it. "I also know what you're going to wear."

They were discussing Whitney's outfit while sorting through their luggage when a knock brushed against the door.

Whitney moved to swing the door open.

One of the house staff, whose name escaped Whitney at the moment, extended a basket encased in lavender-tinted cellophane and adorned with a deeper purple bow. "This is for you," the woman said.

Whitney accepted the offering with a rush of affection.

"Mr. Stone wanted me to let you and your sister know that everything in the closet is for you to use."

"Wait!" Jada squealed. "We have things in the closet?"

Expressing her gratitude to the staff, Whitney stepped back into the room. She set the basket on the table by the sitting area. Jada was already digging through the walk-in closet, pulling out dresses on hangers, one after another.

Meanwhile, Whitney focused on the card from the basket, and its simple message—

Welcome to Brazil. Thanks for coming with me. I love you! ~ Theo

"He loves me," she whispered, pressing the card against her chest.

"Of course, he loves you." Jada, now preening before a full-length mirror, rolled her eyes. "Why else would he bring us here?"

By now, the floor—inlaid with an exquisite mosaic of tiles and glass—was awash in a sea of clothing. Whitney's phone chimed with a text, prompting her to walk over to a grand cherrywood dresser and unlock a message from Theo.

Theo: Ready for dinner?

Whitney: Thank you for the card and chocolates.

She hadn't even explored the closet's treasures yet, but she had more thank yous in store for him. As much as she often felt drained, he had a way of replenishing her spirits. Was love the missing ingredient her heart had been yearning for all along?

Theo: I wish I could do more.

Whitney: You don't have to do anything. You've already won my heart.

Theo: Have I now?

Whitney: More than you'll ever know.

Jada's chatter rose in high-pitched squeals about the fashion boutique in their room. Whitney nearly forgot they were in a bedroom, but imagined it a grand hotel boutique as she faced a closet full of flawlessly fitting clothes, sandals, and shoes. Should she even ask how he knew their size or when he'd gone shopping? He must've informed his parents of their sizes, then had their personal shopper take care of the rest.

"I still have no idea how Theo knew our shoe size." Whitney held a purple dress before her in the mirror, contemplating whether it was the right attire.

"I told him." Jada sidestepped Whitney to look in the mirror. "When he had dinner at our house, I told him we could use some shopping for the trip."

"What? Where was I?" This was unacceptable. Whitney folded her arms to remind her sister they didn't go all over asking for help.

Dismissing her, Jada snorted and handed over a green floral dress. "Thought this was all part of the trip package."

Great. Now what did Theo think of Whitney? A gold digger? Her heart unsettled, she stepped into the bathroom and changed. Good thing she and Jada were the same size in shoes and clothing.

Too bad Mama couldn't relax here with them, even if just for a moment. Whitney would have to text her after dinner, using Jada's Jitterbug phone they'd left with her for communication.

They joined Theo for a feast with an assortment of meats, vegetables, and impeccable service Whitney was unaccustomed to. Throughout the meal, he seemed at ease, as if this level of luxury was his daily norm.

After dinner, Arturo drove them across a scenic bridge that linked the private island to the mainland. Locals and tourists bustled through the night market, contributing to its energetic vibe. The air smelled of salt, spices, and grilled meat as Theo clasped Whitney's hand in his left and Jada's in his right, guiding them through the maze of stalls, each a colorful display of local crafts and produce. String lights overhead cast a warm glow over vibrant textiles and crafts.

With the cement streets solid beneath her sandals and the tropical air balmy against her skin, Whitney paused at a booth where a vendor was selling coconuts and handmade hats. "It's been a really good day."

"Go ahead, take whatever you want." Theo encouraged Jada who eyed one of the hats. "You too, Whit."

"You've already spent so much." Whitney ran her free hand down the breezy fabric of her dress. "I already have to apologize for all the clothes you bought."

"We usually buy clothes for the guests." He shrugged, then gestured to the stand. "As for these, the items are quite affordable compared to what we'd spend in the States."

The vendor behind the booth seemed eager for a sale, showing off one vibrant hat after another.

"Local businesses can use our support," Theo added, sounding very much like a concerned citizen.

That tugged at Whitney's heart and spurred her to choose one of the bright-colored hats. She tried it on and struck a pose, wagging her eyebrows. "How do I look?"

His eyes softened, his gaze almost too intense. "Beautiful."

"And me?" Jada slid on a pair of funky sunglasses.

"You look perfect," Whitney and Theo declared in unison.

"Gracias," the vendor said and Theo handed him local currency.

"How'd you get the money transferred so quickly?" Whitney inquired.

"We visit Brazil frequently." Theo's hand returned to the small of her back, guiding her on. "We always have some Brazilian reals around."

His hand rested gently on her back, radiating warmth, as they meandered together through the bustling market. The cheerful strumming of a guitar's strings wove through the air, mingling with bursts of laughter and the animated chatter of spirited haggling. Theo's hand left her back long enough for him to drop money into the guitarist's basket. She shivered at the sudden chill, missing his touch already. Then his hand returned, and she tilted her head, taking it all in, even the faint lapping of water at the nearby shore. Had she ever—even in childhood—been this content before Theo came into her life?

"So, what do you think of your first day in Brazil?" He leaned in, his breath warming her ear while he broke their companionable silence.

"It's been amazing." She breathed in deep, her chest and heart too full as she tried to take it all in, holding it all in, for the darker days ahead. "It's my best experience—*ever*."

His hands came up to cup her face, his thumbs stroking her cheeks, his gaze probing her soul. "*You're* the best."

That night, she went to bed elated and liberated, wishing this slice of paradise could last forever. If Theo's family were as real as he was, then everything would be more than all right.

CHAPTER 21

An abundance of activities whisked them up the next day. Workers bustled around the island, erecting activity tents and laying out tables in various nooks. Whitney observed as they peppered Theo with queries during breakfast, seeking his nod on the setups sprawling across the grounds. He displayed a surprising fluency in Spanish and Portuguese, as he'd clarified when she'd assumed it was all Spanish he spoke to the workers who didn't speak English.

With breakfast plates cleared, he winked at Jada. "How about we talk your sister into parasailing with us?"

Whitney cocked her head. "Parasailing? What's that like?"

"It's like flying." A wide grin spread out his lips and made his trimmed beard ripple. "You're tethered to a parachute, which is pulled by a boat, lifting you into the sky. You'll love it!"

"That sounds awesome!" Jada clapped, springing to her feet. "Let's go!"

"Tagging along with you two." Whitney shook her head, her resolve waning when Theo stood, taking her hand in his. "I have no idea what else you're about to get me into."

"It will be fun. I promise." He winked. No doubt she'd enjoy anything as long as he was leading the fun.

Several minutes later, her heart was in her throat when they reached the parasailing station where the equipment and the boat were ready. Theo helped her and Jada with the harnesses, ensuring everything was safe and secure.

"Ready for the flight of your life?" he asked, his excitement abating her fears.

"Ready!" Jada shouted.

"Let's do it." Whitney responded more to get this done with than from the sheer excitement. She tried to focus on the beauty as

185

they took to the skies in their harnesses and the world shrank away, leaving only the vastness of the ocean and the freedom of the air.

The morning sun bathed the beach in an awakening glow, and its golden sheen rippled over the restless waves. The air was fragrant with the scent of salt, and the rhythmic sound of the surf provided a serene backdrop. Amidst this tranquil scene, Jada's excited shrieks mingled with the calls of gulls as they soared overhead.

No longer fearful, Whitney spread her arms, the parachute billowing above and the endless ocean sparkling below. The wind rushed against her face, and the thrilling flying sensation buoyed her heart.

"This is amazing!" she shouted.

After their heads were no longer in the clouds and their feet found the familiarity of solid ground, they sat under a cabana and indulged in an array of snacks. Theo, ever the architect of surprises, hinted at another mystery activity.

Jada chose to stay behind with one of the workers to learn how to set up a beach carnival game with a tropical twist. But Whitney, caught between the joy of flight and the anticipation of the unknown, couldn't help but agree to Theo's next adventure.

"Ready for another surprise?" He took her hand, his amber-brown eyes aglow as he led her outside, then asked one of the workers if they had a bandanna.

"There's a few in the game room." The woman bowed and offered to fetch one.

"Do I even want to know what you intend to use the bandanna for?" Whitney asked.

"No." He shook his head, his smirk bringing out his dimple. Whatever he was up to had her anticipating.

Outside the cabana, she took in the endless turquoise waters that stretched out to meet the sky. Exotic flowers spread a sweet fragrance in the fresh sea air. Palm trees swayed, their broad leaves rustling a calming melody that made the atmosphere even more enchanting.

The worker returned holding a broad red bandanna. With a nod and a smile, Theo thanked her, and once she left, he refocused on Whitney.

The white cotton shirt he'd paired with dark shorts billowed with the breeze, and he looked every bit the charming companion. His eyes twinkled, and his grin widened as he unfolded the bandanna. He held the fabric out, spreading it wide, then jiggled it. "Do you trust me?"

A warm rush of affection coursed through her. "I do."

His continuous support and love had made him her rock, her knight, turning uncertainties into discoveries.

As he blindfolded her, excitement fluttered alongside the slightest apprehension. With his warm breath fogging over her, and his subtle cologne surrounding her, the moment turned so intensely intimate she could scarcely breathe.

"There." He secured the bandanna. Tingles shot through her body at the brush of his hands through her hair. "Now, let me guide you." He grasped her arm and guided her as they began to move.

The ocean's endless washing of the sand became more pronounced while they walked, and the grains gave way beneath her ankle strap flats. The sun's warmth kissed her skin, and the breeze played with her hair. His reassuring presence made each step easier, turning the unknown into an adventure.

"Ready for the surprise?" His whisper warmed her ear, and she shivered. Had she ever felt so alive?

"What's the surprise?" She asked, the growing curiosity bursting free as playful shrubs brushed against her hands and seemed to whisper clues.

"It's not a surprise if I tell you." He laughed as he guided her. The path beneath them shifted from the murmur of waves to the sigh of rustling foliage. "Careful," he warned at intervals, his protective presence comforting. As they moved, the brush of leaves and shrubs against her arms wove a tactile melody. Twigs crunched beneath her shoes as the rainforest's very essence seemed to reach out.

"Ta-da!" He broke nature's silence, lifted the bandanna, and revealed a scene carved by adventurers' hands. A sheer cliff emerged from the rainforest, a zip line waiting for an adrenaline junky to take on the performance.

Theo greeted a man standing nearby, clearly an instructor, who welcomed them with an assortment of harnesses.

"No, no, no." Her hand instinctively pressed to her stomach as a flutter of nervous excitement took hold within. Her steps hesitated, then involuntarily retreated in a dance of reluctance. The cliff, the zip line, and the rainforest alongside the ocean's endless canvas all left her in a dizzying swirl. Her body was suddenly set in a fluctuating rhythm of fear, excitement, and awe. "Theo, you're insane if you think I'm doing that."

Leaning in, he brushed his lips against her cheek in a reassuring kiss. "You just soared across the sea with such grace." His whisper floated on the warm tropical air, infusing her with a sense of ease. "Zip-lining will be a leisurely stroll in comparison."

A laugh burst loose, the residual excitement of parasailing's thrill. The initial fear had melted away into exhilaration. "Maybe," she conceded, still hesitant, her nerves fluttering.

Theo's eyes, warm amber pools of encouragement, probed hers. "Do you trust me?" He clasped her hands, then squeezed them as his words squeezed encouragement into her heart. "I know you can do this, and I'll be right there with you."

His confidence didn't make it easy to protest, so despite the tight knot in her throat, she found herself nodding. He kissed her temple and whispered, "I love you, Whitney Reed."

She swallowed at his genuineness, her trepidation dissolving. "Promise you'll take care of my mom and Jada if anything happens to me."

Theo's shoulders shook as his rich laughter rang out to mingle with the rustling trees. "You're not going to die today. But let's ask for some divine backup, shall we?" He pointed skyward, his usual humor laced with faith.

"You go first." She said, a smile oddly tugging at her lips despite the nerves.

With a nod, he stepped into his harness, then extended a hand toward her. "Come on, love. We've got this."

Her hands trembled, but the guide's patient demeanor and Theo's unwavering support bolstered her courage.

"Has anyone ever fallen out of these?"

"Yes." Theo snickered. "But it won't be you."

"What if—?"

"What if you just relax?" As he secured her buckle, his breath on her neck soothed her fears.

When had she let her fears slip away like she did with him? His voice, always so soft yet insistent, urged her toward the edge of adventure, and oh how she needed this!

She slapped his shoulder. "This is like a dare thing I never agreed to, you know."

"You agreed to it when you pepper sprayed me that night."

Hands on her hips, she opened her mouth in mock horror. "So, this is, what, *payback*?"

"Not exactly, but now that you mention it." He shook a finger at her. Then the teasing mischievous light in his eyes faded, eclipsed by something so intense it took her breath. "You should know I'd die before I let anything happen to you."

Somehow, she just knew everything was going to work out. With her heart beating hard in her chest, she fiddled with the harness straps, their snug grip offering a silent promise of safety. Leaning close to Theo, she listened to the guide's instructions, her nerves tight as coiled springs.

"You ready?" Theo asked, his voice a buoyant note in the sea of her anxiety, his hand on her shoulder her gentle anchor.

"I'll never be fully ready."

"Let's do it!" With a boldness born of the moment, Theo leaped, his body cutting through the open air. The valley swallowed his figure, his laughter a vibrant trail that beckoned her to follow. Her heart raced, each beat a drumroll of fear and excitement. She whispered a prayer into the wind and entrusted their fates to God's hands. Then, with a breath caught between terror and elation, she let herself fall, soaring after Theo on wings she never knew she had.

Whitney's landing was not just a return to solid ground but a touchdown into a new realm of feeling.

"I love you so much!" she cried out, her arms finding their home around Theo's sturdy frame. His laugh echoed her joy as he enveloped her, a fortress against the world. In his arms, amid the wild beauty of their adventure, an overwhelming surge of love and trust spurred her on. They were safe, together, and nothing else mattered.

"I knew you'd love it!" He gripped her tight, spinning her around so fast her feet left the earth again. Then he set her down, his lips capturing hers in a kiss that tasted of salt, sun, and sweet soda. Her heart swelled in her chest, threatening to outgrow the bonds of her rib cage. Her knees trembled ever so slightly caught between the zip line induced adrenaline and the electric proximity of him. This muddled sensation lingered as they began their walk back, leaving her unsure of when exactly this exhilarating tumult had begun.

"What's the next adventure?" Whitney swung their clasped hands between them, her voice floating with the high of adrenaline and new experiences.

"And look who's adventurous now?" His chuckle was a warm caress against the cool ocean breeze. His teasing glance sparked a light in her chest, a continuous joyous flame.

The air around them was alive with the children's high-pitched excitement, the steady bass of the ocean waves, and the harmonious chatter of Theo's family. Her heart pounded in response — Theo's family was already here?

Apprehension crept in, but it dissipated when Theo brought their joined hands to his lips, kissing her fingers. His gaze met hers, a silent reassurance passing between them.

"My family will love you," he murmured, apparently aware of her sudden concern.

With that, she allowed herself to lean into the certainty of his love. After all, it was Theo she was in love with.

***

The air hummed with the cheerful chaos of a family gathering as they approached the kitchen under a canopy of palm trees. The fronds rustled in the sea breeze, and something sizzled in the background.

A woman with short brown hair sprinkled with gray at the edges, approached, her eyes as warm as her smile when she called Theo.

"Mom." Theo waved.

But, before he could greet his mom, three preschoolers charged him, tangling their arms around his legs. "Uncle Theo!"

"Sorry," he whispered to Whitney, releasing her hand to give attention to the littles.

"My goodness, you must be Whitney." The woman pulled Whitney into a hug that felt like homecoming and smelled like jasmine. She eased back, still holding Whitney's shoulders. She carried the aura of sophistication, matching her fancy floral perfume.

"I'm Regina, Theo's mom. He's had nothing but good things to say about you."

"Nice to meet you." Whitney's cheeks heated as she tucked windblown wisps of hair behind her ears. After parasailing and zip-lining, she must be a frazzled mess, yet this woman greeted her as if they'd known each other forever.

"And this is Theo's dad." Regina edged aside enough to push forward the man. His silver hair spoke of wisdom, and his blue eyes sparkled with the same kindness Whitney had grown to love in Theo.

"Kyle." The man reached over and offered a firm yet inviting handshake.

The kids provided a constant background of laughter and shouts as they chased each other around the spacious outdoor kitchen. The scent of roasting meat mingled with the sweet tang of citrus blooms that drifted in from the garden.

"How are you liking Brazil so far?" Kyle inquired, eyes crinkling at the corners.

"It's more beautiful than I'd expected." Whitney scanned the area and found Jada engaged in a lively game of table soccer with three kids close to her age.

"We've already met Jada," Regina chimed in, noting Whitney's glance. "She seems to get along with Eric's older kids." She tipped her chin toward the scene next to a tent where the game unfolded, boosted by the vibrant energy of childhood.

"She sure is." Whitney's heart swelled to see Jada so happily integrated.

"How was your flight?" Whitney asked, and Regina talked about her grandchildren's escapades on the flight over.

Amid discussions of their respective journeys, the background was filled with the harmonious cacophony of children's voices, the clinking of kitchenware, and the occasional bark of laughter from

Theo and the man he was standing with. Absorbed in her engaging conversation with his parents, Whitney hadn't even noticed Theo drifting away from her side.

"We'd love to have you join us for Theo's brother's wedding in Colorado," Regina was saying.

"If I can get off work." Whitney doubted she'd take off any more days after the two weeks she had off. "I'd like to come." Of course, she'd only go if Theo invited her, but he hadn't asked her, though he'd spoken of Nate's upcoming wedding.

"We have plenty of room for you to stay," Kyle said, and again, Whitney sensed the couple's warmth. Little wonder they were capable of bringing a bunch of kids to one home and making them a family.

Now and then, her gaze drifted to Theo, on the other side of the kitchen—a vibrant hub of activity with its rustic wood counters and thatched roof.

Cooking stations were set up on sand-smoothed wood, and a chef manned pans at a stone oven. Overhead, strings of lights waited for the evening to weave their magic. Theo, seeming to be the attentive uncle, balanced a toddler on his hip and split his focus between the child's glee and a conversation with the man who was trying to corral two more little ones. He sent a glance Whitney's way, his eyes crinkling with unspoken conversations.

"I'm sure you haven't met Eric," Regina said, perhaps noting Whitney's glance tethered to her son. With a gentle nudge, she edged her across the stony path toward the activity.

Theo's gaze lingered on Whitney, his affection weakening her knees. When they reached him, he breathed out her name as he balanced his niece, then ruffled the child's glossy curls. "This is Violet."

A familial warmth seemed to envelop Whitney.

Violet wiggled out of Theo's arms and darted to Kyle, who took her with open arms.

"Eric." The man extended his hand, his hazel eyes mirroring the warmth Whitney had started to associate with Theo's family. Theo had spoken of his big brother with such admiration. Now, the hero from those stories and descriptions was standing before her.

She clasped his hand. "I was starting to think you were a figment of Theo's imagination."

"I assure you." Theo smiled. "Everything she's heard from me is all good things."

"No family secrets, I see?" she teased, relaxing. Were big families like this, talking about everything freely?

"It gets tricky keeping secrets in a big family." Regina patted Theo's shoulder. They exchanged a look, a mother and son's silent conversation that needed no words, leaving Whitney with a smile of her own. In their interaction, in the ease of their laughter, she saw the roots of his warmth—a mirror into the heart of the family she may someday step into.

Regina and Kyle took the toddlers and excused themselves. The children, a whirlwind of energy and giggles, led their grandparents off. In their wake, a new presence arrived, her entrance marked by the vibrant yellow dress—a striking contrast against the soft palette of the beach.

"That's my wife, Joy." Eric beamed as the woman paused to talk to Kyle and Regina. She seemed a magnet for the children's adoration, her affection for them evident as she spared a moment for each toddler tugging for her attention. With gentle kisses and whispers to each, she convinced them to stay with their grandparents before she walked over.

"Hello." Joy's voice was like a warm breeze, her radiant smile and light brown skin a reflection of the tropical richness around them. "Whitney, right?"

Whitney nodded and put out her hand, but Joy's approach to Whitney was unguarded, her embrace enveloping. The hug welcomed Whitney into the fold without reservation. "I'm sorry." Joy stepped back. "I get carried away with hugs."

"I love hugs too." Accustomed to the rarity of such affection, Whitney took comfort in its sincerity.

"You're from Houston, right?" Joy seemed to catch herself. A hand flew to her mouth, her next words muffled. "Oh dear, I'm not being too nosy, I hope?"

"Very nosy I must say." Eric's eyes twinkled.

Joy smiled at her husband. "Staying in our cozy little town means Eric and I are always a tad behind the latest news." She clasped Whitney's hands. "But one thing we never miss is the news of another Stone sibling heading down the aisle!"

"Joy, sweetheart." Eric huffed out a low breath. "Please don't make our guest uncomfortable."

Undeterred, Joy pumped Whitney's hands. "I'm not making her uncomfortable. I'm just so excited to get to know her!" She exclaimed. "Do you, by any chance, play volleyball?"

Before Whitney could reply, Theo's hand stole one of hers from Joy, an unspoken declaration of unity. "She's on my team, and just so you know, she's a high school champ, no less."

"Eric and I are going to be on your team. Remember we choose teams." Joy jabbed him with an index finger.

"No thank you," Theo teased. "We need the best players on the team—not newbies."

"We'll see about that on the court, won't we?" Eric's competitiveness apparently flared up in the friendliest of ways.

Whitney chuckled at their easy banter. She was about to embark on a week filled with laughter, competition, and the Stone family's warm embrace.

When the sun dipped lower, casting a golden sheen over the beach, Whitney and Theo nestled into a cozy cabana to plan their contribution to the reunion feast. "Let's make kolaches." Whitney suggested her family classic they hadn't cooked in a while. "They're easy to make, and they'll stand out."

Seated across from her, he arched a brow. "Kolaches, huh? I'm game if you lead the charge. We just need to make sure the chefs have the ingredients."

"They're simple enough." She told him the ingredients, already picturing the delight on his relatives' faces as they bit into the savory pastries.

She scrolled through the digital spreadsheet on his iPad, reviewing the myriad of activities lined up. "I'm impressed with your meticulous planning."

"Well, I had a bit of help." He flashed a sly smile. She rarely utilized the internet, but it could come in handy with some planning of her own.

As the afternoon waned into a balmy evening, his family arrived in waves, each member introduced to Whitney with a warmth that made her heart swell. Jada was conspicuously absent, wholly absorbed in newfound playmates. Soon, dusk settled, and the bonfire gathered everyone together, casting a warm glow across their faces. Each one introduced to Whitney became threads in the intricate web of connections she hoped to maintain. She listened and engaged, eager to remember and become part of this animated group Theo called family.

In their company, she felt the pulse of life's celebrations. Every person added their unique hue to the family's rich tapestry—some boisterous, a few reserved, but all played a part in the evening's joy. The air buzzed with lively chatter and infectious laughter, the sound carrying far into the night sky.

It was a delightful whirlwind, a warm embrace she was wholeheartedly drawn to. But could she ever weave herself into their lives? Or was this experience just a memorable vacation, a sidestep from reality for her?

CHAPTER 22

Theo settled into the outdoor beach kitchen, a lively hub of family banter beneath the morning sun. A smattering of tables hosted over sixty relatives and friends, the group intimate by their standards where reunions swelled to eighty or a hundred people.

"The schedule says we have swimming today," Iris remarked, the morning light casting a gentle glow on the blonde highlights in her hair as she stirred her bowl of granola and yogurt.

The ocean's scent, stronger at low tide, lingered with the aroma of hot chocolate and flavored teas.

"There's also paddleball and bocce ball," Sabastian chimed in, his voice competing with the clattering pots and pans where the chefs stayed busy.

"Theo and I are teaching you all to make kolaches," Whitney spoke beside him. The fact that he had a girlfriend in the presence of his family was awe-inspiring.

"What's kolaches?" Owen raised a hand to shield his eyes from the rising sun.

"It's a family favorite." Whitney detailed the process of making kolaches, a pastry filled with sausages.

Owen's response was a soft chuckle. "I still can't believe..." he began, a glint in his eye as he raised his mug of hot chocolate. He paused midsentence, leaving his thought unspoken.

Theo exhaled, grateful Owen had halted before revealing details of his past employment at TSF Media.

"Anyway," Owen continued, "I only left for Dubai less than a year ago, and here's my brother in a relationship."

"Have you ever considered that your constant presence around Theo and the others might have made it difficult for them to find romance?" Julia chimed in. It was always hard to know when she was teasing or serious with her remarks. Unfortunately, Julia seemed unaware of the full extent of Theo's undercover mission at the resort and the secrecy it entailed.

"No one's impeding anyone's dating life." Iris scooted forward. "Today's perfect for a hike, and tomorrow's higher temperatures will be more suitable for swimming. I vote we change the itinerary."

Theo touched Whitney's arm, unsure whether she liked hiking. "What do you think of the switch, Whit?"

She laid her fork against her half-eaten pancake—a mirror to the one on Theo's plate. "I'm up for anything. If I survived parasailing and zip-lining yesterday, I can handle a hike."

"That's my girl," he murmured, pride coursing through him as he reached for her hand.

"You guys went zip-lining yesterday?" Julia piped up, her envious tone catching him by surprise.

"Of course, everyone can do as they please, Julia," Iris said. "We've planned group activities, but everyone is welcome to use their free time however they wish."

Shifting the conversation away from any brewing argument—after all, no one could instigate family drama like Julia could—Theo cleared his throat and nodded to Owen. "So, how's the new real-estate venture going?"

"Well, Rohan thinks I have a lot to learn, of course." Owen, always quick to jump into new business ventures, was also quick to respond. He nodded toward the table across the kitchen where Rohan sat in deep discussion with their other siblings. Theo's gaze drifted toward Jada, fully engaged and laughing with his nephews about her age. Her joy was heartwarming.

The morning unfolded into a series of hikes, split into two groups for variety. The family photographer, capturing candid moments, promised a treasure trove of memories for their annual family photo book. Theo would have to request an additional copy for Whitney as a keepsake.

After a lighter hike suitable for the kids, Eric and Joy led the younger ones home, leaving the rest of the adults to embark on a more challenging trail, an intense journey of discovery—some siblings even ventured into bouldering. Theo, walking alongside Whitney, enjoyed her wonder at each new vista, particularly at the majestic waterfalls that punctuated their path through the hills and valleys.

As dusk gave way to nightfall, the family regrouped for an early dinner. Tables flowed with culinary delights, each dish seasoned and cooked to perfection. The lanterns illuminated a glow over his family, as their stories melded into a cherished memory.

The rich flavors on his tongue intertwined seamlessly with animated conversations, recounting the day's escapades. Two tables away, Whitney laughed with Joy, Serafina, and Vanessa. Whatever Nate's fiancée was saying seemed to have most of the people at her table laughing.

As the stars began to sprinkle the night sky, the tables were cleared to create space for breakfast preparation. Strings of warm yellow lights crisscrossing the ceiling combined with the radiance of lanterns to provide an inviting ambience—perfect for their task of premaking kolaches for the following day. Family members joined them, each contributing to the preparation amid laughter and banter.

The kitchen brimmed with the kind of chaos only a family can create. Flour dusted every surface, including the little ones who giggled as they attempted to shape the dough with their clumsy fingers. Whitney stood at the center of it all, skillfully molding the kolaches while laughing with his family.

"Hey, no fair! You've got Whitney and Vanessa on your team. They're practically pros," Logan grumbled, attempting to roll out dough that snapped back at him.

Whitney looked up, a twinkle in her eye. "You think this is my secret weapon? Wait until you taste my secret ingredient."

Julia, leaning against the counter with a raised eyebrow, chimed in. "Out here in Brazil, Theo's convinced he's above the laws of culinary physics. Next thing you know, he'll be serving us dessert for breakfast!"

Theo smirked, his mother capturing his attention as she confiscated a butter knife from Eric's toddler before any kitchen catastrophes could occur. "It's all about the family magic," he said with a mock-serious nod. "Besides, who says dessert for breakfast isn't a tradition worth starting?"

Laughter erupted, accompanied by the occasional clang of a dropped utensil or an "oops!" as another sausage escaped. The room was warm, not only from the ovens but also from the closeness of shared work and joy.

After they finished the kolaches, the kitchen's hum subsided, replaced by the crackling from the bonfire. One by one, family members drifted toward the flames, leaving Theo and Whitney alone amid their baking bonanza.

He leaned against the rough-hewn wooden counter, contentment expanding his chest. His cheeks hurt from smiling as Whitney wiped a streak of flour from her cheek. "Tonight was a huge success." He stepped behind her, and she shivered at his nearness, which pleased him that his proximity affected her. He lifted her ponytail off her neck and breathed against the rich skin on her nape. Even if she'd been doing activities with his family, they hadn't had much time to themselves. "Tonight was wonderful."

"Except for our casualty sausages and flour fiasco."

"A small price to pay for memories, right?" He kissed her cheek, and she sucked in a breath. Then he spun her around so he could take in her beauty. "I'm really glad you're here, Whit."

With his thumb, he brushed a stray lock of hair behind her ear. He hadn't imagined having a girlfriend by the reunion. "This—all of this—wouldn't be the same without you."

She wrapped her arms around his waist, her eyes alight as she looked at him with so much love his stomach fluttered. "I wouldn't feel so happy right now—without you."

At her genuine confession, he couldn't contain himself. He cupped her face between his palms, tipping her lips toward his.

"I've wanted to do this all day." He struggled to breathe as he dipped down and her eyes fluttered closed.

A surge of emotions cascaded through him when their lips met. The kitchen's warmth, suffused with the day's joy, seemed concentrated in the tender sweetness of their kiss. The murmur of his family's voices receded to a distant echo, overshadowed by the thrumming of his heart against hers. He breathed her in, savoring a profound connection that transcended the moment. Bathed in the soft radiance of the lights, he found himself wishing this precious, perfect moment could stretch into eternity.

But reality's shadow loomed — thoughts of her impending procedure and his looming confession threatened to intrude. Determinedly, he pushed them to the back of his mind, focusing instead on etching this moment into memory.

***

Over the next two days, the shoreline served as a backdrop to continuous adventures. Mornings commenced with a collective prayer to set the tone for the day, followed by a hearty breakfast to fuel them for the activities ahead. From the revving thrill of ATV engines to the rhythmic paddling of kayaks and the whir of mountain bikes through trails, their days were a cascade of adrenaline and camaraderie. Theo's evenings were more relaxing, like last night's dinner, which had been hosted on a yacht, bobbing on the tranquil sea.

Amid it all, Whitney integrated into his family dynamics. Uninhibited and spirited, she dove into each experience with an infectious laugh, endearing herself to everyone.

Now, as they stood on the sun-kissed sand in the middle of their fourth day, Theo couldn't suppress his goofy smile. He batted the volleyball toward Julia, who popped it up for Whitney. With an athletic spring, Whitney slammed it over the net, scoring another point and prompting groans from the opposing side.

Those on the sidelines erupted in support, their claps and cheers resonating with the waves crashing nearby.

"Good job, sweets!" Theo wrapped her in an embrace and added a kiss on her hair, but the ongoing game interrupted the tender moment as the volleyball arced back over the net.

On the court with him, Whitney, Julia, Vanessa, Joy, and Logan stood poised to win.

"We're not done yet!" Julia cut through their celebration as she sprinted to keep the game alive. The ball, sent soaring across the net by Owen, was skillfully intercepted by Vanessa, Nate's fiancée. She launched into a dive, her form echoing the seagulls' graceful arcs above them, and with a flick borne of sheer will, sent it hurtling back over the net.

The crowd went wild, Nate's voice booming as he chanted Vanessa's name, affection and pride pulsing through his tone and beaming in his broad smile.

Laughter, competitiveness, and the affirmation of kinship resounded over the beach, bringing back sweet memories of times spent with his family.

"We're winning by ten," Julia bellowed as Whitney prepared for a serve.

Her stance focused and her eyes narrowed, Whitney measured the distance, the sun casting a halo around her athletic silhouette. She launched the ball into the air, her hand connecting with it in a perfect arc and sending it soaring high and fast over the net.

"No mercy!" Julia performed a spontaneous victory dance, her feet kicking up white sand. "Prepare for defeat!"

"It's not fair when Whitney played volleyball in high school," Iris called out in mock protest, her attempt to return the ball thwarted as it thudded into the net and dropped back, sand clinging to its surface.

Theo couldn't complain, not when Whitney's volleyball skills were shining through every movement. Each spike she delivered was met with an explosive burst of sand as she leaped, her hand hurtling the ball over with a precision that left their opponents scrambling. Her blocks displayed a deft combination of timing and power, often sending the ball spinning away at unexpected angles, and her saves—diving with the grace of a seabird, arms outstretched—were a spectacle that drew cheers from their team and appreciative claps from the elders watching from the sidelines.

Amid lively chatter and the soothing melody of waves, the group broke for intermission. Servers glided through the crowd and offered refreshments that sparkled under the sun's gentle caress. The ocean's hues, a stunning swirl of blues and greens, provided a mesmerizing backdrop.

"So, Whitney." Julia looped an arm over Whitney's shoulders. "I don't get why you only played in high school. You could've gotten a free-ride college scholarship to play."

Whitney shifted, standing beside Theo, her grip tightening around the soda bottle. "I'm not that good."

Sensing her discomfort, Theo lifted his water bottle, gesturing toward her to affirm her talent. "You're outshining all of us!"

It was the truth.

"Maybe I got a bit too competitive." Whitney raised her bottle in a return toast, her smile sheepish. "I'll try to tone it down a notch."

"Don't you dare." Julia cuffed her and added a half-serious glare. "I've got enough challenges in my career. Let me have my victories on the sand."

Laughter bubbled up around them, and the game picked up again. Theo and Whitney stayed on the sideline with the observers to let others take their turn on the court.

Julia leaned in closer, her voice a nostalgic murmur over the distant cheers. "This reunion's been a blast, Theo. Really, you outdid yourself."

"That coming from you means I deserve a medal." He smirked, basking in the rare compliment from his sister.

"Remember the first year we did the reunion? The game we played at the Peak?" Her eyes sparkled.

"Vaguely." He furrowed his brow, his attention drifting to the ongoing match.

"You brought all those stiff executives from work." Julia's nose scrunched. "They turned our family game into a team-building workshop. What a bunch of losers!"

He fought the urge to correct Julia that losers weren't executives. Instead, he caught Whitney's gaze, ensuring she didn't read much into the word. Then he sent Julia a silent plea to tread lightly, but she was already stomping forward, her laughter carrying toward Whitney. He tracked her movement, positioning himself as a subtle buffer in case the conversation veered too close to sensitive topics.

"If it weren't for you," Julia addressed Whitney, "I'm sure Theo wouldn't have pulled off organizing these activities."

Whitney gave his hand a reassuring squeeze. "Theo did all this planning."

Julia snorted, crossed her arms, and raised her eyebrows. "Of course he planned it all. By cheating!" She stepped in front of them.

"I should've known better than to think the wealthiest man in South America would spare time to plan everything!"

A knot tightened in his stomach. Julia's outburst, teetering on the brink of revealing his secret, twisted up things inside him. His sister's face flushed, her words spilling out faster than she could think. "To say—"

"Julia!" His admonishment rang sharp, a rare slip from his composed demeanor.

A blush scorched his sister's cheeks. "I'd better not be tasked with organizing a reunion soon. If I'm gonna compete, how am I to—"

"Shut up, Julia!" His voice cracked with urgency. Untangling his hand from Whitney's, he tossed his water bottle on the sand before reaching for Julia's hand. Perhaps he could communicate with her somehow. Maybe he didn't know his sister so well, but he dared not let her loose lips spill one more clue to reveal his real world.

"I'm just saying—"

Wade stepped in, grabbed Julia, and whisked her away, leaving a palpable tension.

A bead of sweat trailed down Theo's back despite the light shirt he wore over his shorts. With his heart thudding against his ribs, he turned to Whitney, facing her furrowed brows and questioning eyes.

"Sorry." He cleared his throat. His shoulders, so strong and firm, now sagged under the moment. "My sister... she has a temper and, um, can be a bit unpredictable."

Family murmurs reminded him he was now the center of attention, and a profound vulnerability wobbled through his middle and loosened his knees. How fragile this balance of his two worlds! How easily it could all come crashing down!

Whitney seemed to be processing, no doubt still shocked.

Please say something.

He offered her a wistful half smile, the ocean breeze suddenly sharp against his skin.

She handed her half-finished soda to one of the workers passing by collecting trash. When her gaze rose to meet Theo's again, something guarded it, and she folded her arms over her chest, creating a barrier between her and the world. Her gaze flitted to where his family surrounded Julia, offering silent reprimands or whatever. Then, as if seeking something familiar and safe, her gaze landed on Jada and the children, their laughter and focus on building a sandcastle a stark contrast to the adult complexities.

"You..." Her voice wobbled. "Is Julia correct?" That vulnerable tremor in her voice cut through him more sharply than any accusation could. "You... live here? Is all of this"—she gestured at the expansive beach property—"yours or your family's?"

His throat tightened, a physical manifestation of the walls closing in. He ducked his head, rubbed the back of his neck, and frowned at the grains of sand clinging to his skin. "Everything that's mine belongs to the family too."

The inadequate words fell into the space between them, too vague to suffice. No, he couldn't delay telling the truth any longer.

The volleyball game now seemed worlds away. His siblings' glances, once cheerful and conspiratorial, now carried concern. Whitney's piercing gaze, once warm and filled with laughter, now bored into him with an intensity of dawning betrayal. His heart beat faster. This confrontation was far from the careful revelation he'd planned.

"Is it true?" she whispered, her eyes big, her voice small. "You're a South American... billionaire?"

His jaw clenched, an involuntary reaction to the corner he'd planted himself in. "I wouldn't say billionaire." He struggled to keep his voice steady. He was one of the wealthiest men in the world, but he was still the same person from humble beginnings. With serendipity, his business ventures and unforeseen success spiraled from what started as a simple investment during a family trip. "God opened a door unexpectedly, one I didn't—still don't—feel I deserved."

He exhaled, each breath an effort to steady himself. "Let's talk, okay?" He reached out, not to grasp her hand but to offer it as a choice. With a nod toward a quieter stretch of sand, away from prying eyes and ears, he invited her to join him. It was time to peel back the layers of half-truths and unveil his raw, unvarnished reality.

As they stood down the shore, even the soothing waves couldn't soften his words. He let out a sigh, the grains of sand beneath his feet mocking him with their simplicity. "I started out small." The truth flowed out like the tide. "I was attached to my family, and I thought starting something far from home would provide the independence I needed."

Her brows knitted together. "And the resort?" She waved him up and down. "This whole... persona?"

He swallowed hard, the admission sticking in his throat. "Less than four months ago, I inherited a resort from an uncle, who turned out to be my father. My initial plan was to sell it, but..."

His gaze on the seagulls, he shared his siblings' advice that he go undercover. He wouldn't be in this debacle if he'd ignored his siblings. "Now it all seems pointless."

A heavy silence enveloped them. "So, you came to Oasis to prepare it to..." Her voice wavered, a tremble betraying the turmoil beneath her calm exterior. She swallowed hard and pushed one more word out. "Sell?"

Theo nodded, his lips pressed into a thin line, his heart heavy with the undeniable reality.

"I can't believe this." Her frustration evident, she brushed a hand through her hair, breaking the tight bun.

"I intended to tell you." Man, if only he could escape the mess! "I wanted to keep things simple between us. With you, I'm just Theo, not 'the mogul.' I was afraid of losing that... you."

"You think I care about your money? It's the lies, Theo." She waved both hands. "How do you expect me to trust you?"

"You're upset learning I have money—"

"That's *not* it!" she snapped, pointing an accusing finger. "You *lied* to me, Theo."

"Just like you kept your health concerns from your family?" He retaliated, a burst of defensiveness bursting free. "We all have secrets."

Hadn't she said as much the first day he worked at the resort under her supervision?

"But I didn't hide the truth from you."

She was right. His resolve wavered with the rise and fall of his chest. He'd had no right to attempt to drag her down with him. "I'm sorry." His voice broke, a crack in the façade he'd maintained. "I never expected to fall for you. But I did, and it changed everything."

Now, the thought of not having her in his life made him tremble.

He closed the distance, needing to hold her hand as he explained everything she needed to know, but tears streamed down her cheeks, the silent accusation, piercing him more deeply than any words could. As she pulled away from his attempted embrace, the distance between them felt like a chasm.

"How do I know what's real?" Her voice cracked too. "You're an actor..."

She went on, but his focus blurred at her accusation of him lying about his feelings for her.

"You know that's not true." He stepped closer, touched her shoulder, and attempted to comfort her by pulling her into an embrace, but she scooted back again, jerking free.

"I'll be fine." She created a distance that felt more permanent than temporary. "I need some time. To think... Jada and I should go home."

"Of course." He couldn't argue. "When would you like to leave?"

"Today if possible." She pressed her lips together, making it seem final between them.

"I'll... make the arrangements." His murmur barely rose over the crashing waves. He hadn't seen this coming.

Her footsteps receded, taking with them the warmth and light of the connection they'd shared. "I'm sorry," he whispered into the void she left, his apology as lost as he felt. The echo of the ocean was no longer soothing, but a reminder of the vast emptiness spreading out before him. Each step Whitney took forward created a gap he needed to bridge. But, how?

CHAPTER 23

Whitney fixed her gaze on her soggy cereal, a melancholic fog clouding her thoughts as Jada's complaints bounced around the cramped kitchen. The spoon in her hand cut lazy circles through the milk, each swirl a reminder of the chaos swirling inside her.

"What do I do all day?" Jada continued grumbling, casting a sulky glance across the table.

"Read a book." Whitney shrugged, her voice a distant echo, detached and hollow. The past days hung over her like the heavy Houston humidity, oppressive and unrelenting. She glanced at the clock. Only seven fifteen, and already the trailer felt like a greenhouse, stifling her breaths. "You and Mama should spend some time together."

"I have plans today," Mama said. Apparently, their sudden return had interrupted whatever plans their mother had. "Staying out late tonight."

Jada's eye roll was theatrical. "I could've been building sandcastles on the beach, but no, you had to go and mess it all up."

"Don't." The milk dripped from the spoon when Whitney pointed it at Jada, a silent plea for her sister to understand, to see beyond her disappointment. Her patience was threadbare, fraying at the edges. "Everything's not about you." Whitney's voice rose over the hum of the old refrigerator. "I had to do what's best for us."

Jada huffed, folded her arms, and narrowed her eyes. "You think running away from Theo is what's best?"

Whitney's heart ached at the mention of him. The mug he'd gifted her was at the center of the table, with the now-cold tea she hadn't touched. She'd backed off coffee after learning why Theo and his family didn't drink it.

She pushed from the chair, seeking some ice cubes to chew on as memories struck again—his face, his apologies, his sincerity. All of it haunted her. "There's a lot I need to figure out."

Jada's expression softened, sympathy breaking through. "It's just the beach. Theo would've brought me back later."

"I know." Whitney offered a weary smile, and with that, her thoughts drifted to the echo of the waves and the man she left on that distant shore.

Seventy-two hours ago, she'd gone from being on the beach, basking in the joy of volleyball and the warmth of Theo's love while Jada mingled with his family—to it all evaporating in a haze.

Jada had balked at their hurried departure and pleaded to Theo so she could stay with his family. Theo, his voice strained with emotion, had stood firm. "Whit needs someone to take care of her. Will you take care of her for me, please?"

Those words, filled with sincere concern, now haunted Whitney, stirring a rising guilt.

"Why did you all have to rush back so soon?" Mama's question lingered, a repeat of her inquiry from yesterday to which Whitney hadn't fully responded.

Jada reached across the table for Whitney's phone. "Theo's a billionaire," she said, sounding eager to explore more about him, but Whitney retrieved the phone, not keen on revisiting the billionaire list that placed Theo among the top ten wealthiest individuals globally. Last night, she'd delved into the internet, following the trail Jada blazed on their trip home that uncovered the extent of his influence and wealth as a media mogul.

"He's always been good to us." Jada dropped her chin into her hand, sighing out her admiration. "Remember how he took over your hotel cleaning while you rested?"

Mama lifted her coffee in a mock toast meant to be soothing. "What's wrong with a beau with money?"

Couldn't they understand? It wasn't about wealth. The comfort he'd provided, once tangible and true, now felt like another layer in his deceit.

"He lied." She'd had enough lies in her life. She couldn't handle more.

Jada tipped her head sideways, her cheek bunching up as she braced her jaw in her hand instead of her chin. "Mama's not always truthful either, but you never hold it against her."

The words stung, but Whitney couldn't deny them. She'd hoped Theo was different—she'd *needed* him to be different.

She rubbed her forehead, her mind swirling with the urgency of finding a new job. It had been a while since she crafted a résumé. Now, Theo was selling the resort. It made sense. After all, he was preoccupied with his business in South America, and his family ties to the resort were based on a lie. It must've hurt to realize his dad disguised himself as an uncle in the will.

Everywhere Whitney turned, deception lurked.

Her energy ebbed from her. The resort's potential sale left her adrift in a confusing uncertainty. Now more than ever, returning to work seemed like a lifeline.

Just yesterday, after landing, she'd called Charlotte to let her know she was ending her break early. In hindsight, Theo's cryptic calls and suggestions at the resort now made perfect sense.

She eyed the mug, a delicate blue butterfly poised for flight. *Every day is a new chapter to write a better story.*

Even today, the quote motivated her. Maybe it was time to write a better story, even if it would be a while before she topped a life with Theo in it.

With resolve, she stood up, leaving her cereal half-eaten.

"I need to head to work." She passed her phone to Jada. "Why don't you call a friend and go out." It was a small gesture, an attempt to mend a summer frayed by unexpected turns. Her hand on Mama's shoulder, she inquired, "What are your plans today?"

Mama's face brightened. "I'm going to a book club with a friend, and then I have a free counseling class at the recreation center. I'll be home by seven." Whitney's heart lifted at the mention of counseling. Maybe, just maybe, things were starting to turn around for their family.

The bus ride to work was a silent journey, her mind replaying the days Theo drove her and how they talked and laughed about all sorts of things. She somehow understood now the loneliness Mama felt after Dad's death. Theo wasn't dead, but he wasn't in her life anymore, which left a gaping hole in her heart.

Struggling to push his memory aside, she banished his image with a shake of her head as she stepped off the bus. Minutes later, she entered the lobby and headed toward a familiar face. Seeing Daniela at her post behind the counter offered a small but significant comfort, a glimmer of normalcy.

"Whitney!" Daniela stepped around the counter and rushed over, her heels clicking against the marble before she pulled Whitney into a tight embrace. "I thought you had two weeks off!" Daniela gripped Whitney's shoulders and lurched back to take a better look at her. "Did anything happen?"

"A few things came up," Whitney murmured. Not wanting to delve into the details, she rummaged through her handbag and displayed a colorful, beaded bracelet in the vibrant colors of the Brazilian flag. "I thought you'd like it."

"I love it." Daniela's eyes lit up as she admired the intricate design. Then she slid the bracelet onto her wrist. "Thank you!"

When Whitney only nodded, Daniela frowned and linked their arms. She then hauled Whitney toward a corner lounger and plopped down with her. "Okay, spill. What happened between you and Theo? The chemistry's been undeniable, but something's up."

Whitney ducked her head, her fingers playing with a stray thread on her uniform. Their relationship had all been a façade. She shivered.

Daniela would find out Theo was no longer in Whitney's life. "Theo and I..." She swallowed hard, searching for the right words. "He wasn't honest with me."

"Theo lied?" Daniela gasped, her grip tightening on Whitney's arm. "About what?"

"He has more money than he let on." No reason to go into the details of his disguise. "He's not just..." Whitney couldn't reveal any clues that would give Theo's identity away. Why were things so complex? "With everything going on in my life, I can't handle a relationship right now."

"So, he's from a wealthy family. You said his brothers are well-off." Daniela loosened her grip and smoothed out the wrinkles she'd created on Whitney's sleeve—if only she could so easily smooth out the wrinkles Theo created in her life! "I always got this vibe from him, like he was *so* out of place here. Is it related?"

Theo was a billionaire! Whitney still couldn't believe it. Nothing wrong with wealth, but the lie! She couldn't live with more lies in her life. "Let's just say his family is wealthy. Very wealthy."

Tsking, Daniela hugged Whitney and pressed their cheeks together. "Don't let financial differences come between you. If Theo loves you, which I believe he does, those things won't matter. Besides, he might help you with your mom's recent hospital bill."

"I don't want Theo shouldering my problems." He'd already done so by coming to her rescue at work.

Daniela gave Whitney a knowing look, her lips parted as if about to speak. Then the click of shoes on tile signaled a guest approaching.

"I'll see you at lunch, okay?" Whitney stood, grateful for the interruption, a momentary reprieve.

"Deal." Daniela winked, then hurried to the guest as Whitney headed toward her real task.

Amid the dreariness of the day, a weight pressed on her chest as her thoughts drifted back to Theo. Every scrubbed toilet and cleaned room only reminded her of the billionaire who'd worked alongside her, never once complaining or revealing his true identity... The irony wasn't lost on her—she'd invited someone of his status into her humble trailer for dinner.

Jada's voice echoed in screeching chastisement: *"But he worked for you all day while you stayed home for a break."*

Whitney cleaned the bathroom tile, trying to scrub away not only the grime but also her turmoil.

How could she have been so blind, not to see the kindness and sincerity behind Theo's actions? Brazil's lush landscapes and sparkling beaches seemed like a world away, replaced by a growing sense of dread. If only she'd not overreacted, she'd still be up to some new adventure with him.

The worst part that day was her shift in the restaurant. Everywhere she looked, she saw glimpses of Theo in the kitchen, at the tables, by the fountain. With her so exhausted, emotionally and physically by the end of her shift, the bus ride home felt longer than usual. Her longing for Theo deepened with each passing minute. She'd been fine without him two months ago, and now he'd taken a piece of her heart with him.

Her heart heavy with the decision to call him, to talk things through, she unlocked the door. The house was engulfed in darkness. Without thinking to turn on the light, she stumbled over a form lying on the floor. "Mama?" she called out, alcohol fumes souring her nostrils. Despair bubbled up, overwhelming her as she screamed into the void of her dark living room again, but blaring music from the bedroom she shared with Jada drowned out her cries.

Her anger erupted when she shook her mother awake, but Mama was too far gone in her stupor to respond. Whitney's heart sank further. Jada had probably been left alone for hours. Before she'd left for work, Whitney had confirmed Jada's outing with a friend and her friend's mom promised to drop her back by seven thirty after Mama returned. Whitney should've known better. Mama wouldn't keep her word. Groaning, she shuffled to Jada's bedroom.

Panic replaced her frustrated heartbreak when she stumbled into their shared bedroom, bright with neon lights from the strobe light on the dresser.

Her erratic heart started thudding, and a rush of heat surged through her body. Through the dizzying lights, she staggered toward Jada's bed to turn off the musical assault, but dizziness swept over her. Her hands went limp, and her purse thumped to the floor.

"Dizzy," she muttered, the room spinning as she fumbled to reach the bed.

"Whit?" Jada's voice was faint, muffled by the music.

Whitney tried to steady herself, but darkness washed over her, a curtain closing over Jada's alarmed shout as everything faded into nothingness. The thud of hitting the floor echoed in her fading consciousness.

***

Whitney lay there, her gaze fixated on the sterile white ceiling, the heart monitor beeping out a constant reminder of her fragile state. Jada's presence, her worried face etched with deep lines, was a small comfort in the uncertainty.

"You scared me, Whit." Jada's voice shook, her eyes glistening as she rose from her chair and moved to kneel beside the bed. "Your heart... Doc said you need a valve replacement. He also said blood isn't flowing in the right direction in your heart."

Whitney pressed her lips together, swallowing the emotion lodged in her throat.

Jada seemed to have come to the truth. "You *knew* you had a heart problem?"

Whitney remained silent.

"Why didn't you say anything?"

"It's not a big deal." Whitney's voice croaked. She sure hoped it wasn't complicated, but what else could she tell Jada? Whitney reached out, brushing a tear from her sister's cheek. "I don't want you to worry." Needing to change the subject, she asked about their mom.

"In the waiting room. She's all shaken up." Jada's fingers closed over Whitney's on her cheek. "I–I don't know how to take care of her like you do."

The previous night flashed in Whitney's mind—Mama's incapacitated state, the dizzying lights, and the blaring music. Fear welled up, her already fragile heart racing. "I thought I had more time," she murmured. Was it too late in her situation to help Mama get on track? She needed more time to work and raise money for the surgery, more time to prepare Mama to take over caring for Jada. But what could Whitney do now that she was in bed, weak and helpless?

Jada's lips flattened. "Doc said you need to be transferred to another hospital. He advised we apply for medical assistance."

Given Whitney's inability to work now, she couldn't decline any aid offered. But she still had to pay a lump sum. She could look into unemployment benefits or financial assistance, but she was still employed, though for how long she had no idea since Theo intended to sell Oasis.

Her palms felt sweaty. The looming medical bills from Mama's ambulance, then her current hospital admission, the uncertainty of whether they qualified for financial medical aid—it was all too much.

But Jada needed assurance. Whitney laced her fingers through Jada's. "God will provide."

How? She didn't know, but He'd always taken care of them.

Jada's expression grew graver. "They want to operate today or tomorrow."

In other words, as soon as possible. The matter was out of her hands now. She'd used up all her savings to catch up on bills.

Jada's grip tightened, her eyes resolute. "We'll find a way." She then rose, her demeanor reflecting newfound determination when she unclasped her hand from Whitney's. "Is there a specific way to pray?"

A smile lifted Whitney's cheeks. Her sister asking about prayer was a blessing in itself. "Pray what's in your heart."

"I'll pray, now that you're okay."

"Thank you, sweetie."

As Jada left the room, Whitney's gaze drifted to the window. The smog mirrored the uncertainty clouding her thoughts. Memories of Theo at the resort—the laughter, the comfort of his presence—seemed like a distant dream now. Her heart throbbed with a longing for him, not caring about what he did as long as he loved her. No doubt he'd been honest about his love for her.

What if she died before she made peace with him? He was the only man who'd let her experience what romance and love was all about. While she could call him, she had no idea where she'd left her phone or how she'd made it to the hospital.

She closed her eyes, hoping for a silver lining, not only for herself but also for Jada and Mama. And for Theo, with all the decisions he had to make for his businesses.

CHAPTER 24

The rhythmic pounding of the drums should have been cathartic, a release for Theo as he let the sticks dance across the drum set's taut skins—each piece a glossy testament to his success. But today, the opulent music room, with its polished wooden floors and walls lined with shiny awards his company had gleaned and glossy commemoratives from the businesses they'd helped, felt more like a gilded cage. As he played, his motions lacked their usual fluidity, each beat a jarring reminder of his recent missteps.

He should have been transparent with Whitney. Owning the resort or a company was not a crime, so why had he treated it like one? Concealing his identity had been a strategic move for business, but withholding the truth from Whitney was a personal failure. Trust had been within his grasp, but he'd let his emotions dictate his actions.

His drumming grew erratic, and the cacophony of frustration echoed off the high ceilings and vast space, adorned with artwork that screamed luxury. No expense had been spared in the design of the house, much like the rest of his life—except, perhaps, the expense of honesty.

Startled by the unexpected thump on his head, he glanced up. Wade?

"How long are you going to hide out here?" Wade chided.

"I'm over here by the way." At the voice, Theo turned to Logan lingering by the doorway, his stance tentative, as if ready to give Theo the space he might demand. "Not good to brood alone."

Theo's hands stilled on the drums. At the moment, the weight of his wealth felt heavier than the drumsticks in his hands. Family and love—that was the real treasure he feared losing. With Whitney's abrupt exit, it felt like he'd lost a crucial person in his life. Was there a way to fix it?

Yet his brothers stood with him. No matter the size of the room or the price of the drums, the bonds of family filled the space with true value.

"What's with the intrusion? I thought a closed door means "do not disturb.""

"That was yesterday's memo." Wade dropped into a chair and swiveled it around to sit face-to-face with Theo. "Mom thinks you've wallowed enough."

"Not exactly her words. She's concerned about you." Logan walked in and leaned against the wall.

Theo was a grown man, and he shouldn't have his mom concerned about small matters, although, granted, this matter of the heart turned out bigger than he'd expected.

"The undercover idea was partly ours anyway, remember? It's our mess too."

"And Nate's," Wade added, though he winced. "But let's not drag him into a virtual meeting, especially not today with his race."

"There's not going to be a meeting." Theo tossed a drumstick onto the sleek drum surface with a clatter. He didn't need his brothers to babysit his emotions, even if their intentions were good. Nate and Vanessa had left the same night of Whitney's departure. He'd needed to get back to his race this weekend. While Theo had tangled himself in a web, he wasn't ready for a family intervention, not yet at least.

Logan checked his watch, his brow furrowing. "The family's waiting on you for the band to start. Mom and Dad paused the whole thing."

"Why?" Theo ground his teeth. "Just because I'm not in the mood for music doesn't mean everyone else should miss out."

"Cut it out." Wade huffed. "You're sulking over Whitney and the whole fiasco."

"Yep," Logan chimed in. "Time to learn and not dwell on what should've been with Whitney and whatnot."

Theo bristled at her name. He'd lost someone he truly cared for. And now she saw him as a liar. That hurt even more.

"Maybe today's the day to reach out to her." Logan, being married, seemed to have practical advice. "Clear the air."

Wade nodded his agreement. "She might be anxiously waiting for your call, but you've been busy"—he made air quotes—"since she left."

Today would mark the third day since her departure.

Theo let out a heavy sigh. "I'll give her the space she asked for." He stood, resolved to not let his doubts hold him back. Whitney had wanted time to think about things, and the least he could do was give it to her.

Logan gripped Theo's shoulder. "Don't wait too long. And hey, on the bright side, since you're in a dampened mood, I figured you should be the first to know. I'm going to be a dad."

"Really?" Theo's heart lifted, and the room's atmosphere lifted with it.

Wade leaped up, embracing Logan. "I never get tired of being the cool uncle."

"Are you excited?" Theo asked, and Logan drew out a breath.

"I like the idea." He nodded, seeming doubtful. "Just not sure I have what it takes to be a good dad."

"Eric is your man." Wade punched Logan on the chest.

"If anything, that little peanut will have enough uncles and aunts to figure this parenting stuff out with you."

Logan's eyes shone in the recessed lighting, his chest expanding. "Thanks, guys."

The news brought a genuine smile to Theo's face, pushing aside his concerns. He clapped Logan on the back. "Let's go celebrate then."

At least he had a family to bounce back to. But what did Whitney have?

Her family loved her, no doubt, but she supported them. Who was there for her right now?

While she was on her own, he could pray God supported her through this. *And, God, maybe, just maybe, there can still be a chance for Whitney and me?*

***

The ballroom seemed to dwarf Theo's family gathered in the palatial space. A grand piano anchored one end. Its ivory keys tinkling under practiced fingers added refined charm to the familial warmth. The ornate high ceilings and the gauzy drapes framing the vast windows scarcely contained the genuine laughter and shared affection that truly adorned the space.

Theo, smiling over his brother's joyous announcement, hid a pang of sorrow amid the toasts and congratulations. He lifted his glass of sparkling juice with a practiced ease, mirroring his siblings at his table—Julia, Eric and his wife, and Iris and her husband—who basked in the happy news.

"I'm really sorry," Julia murmured, her gaze meeting Theo's with a sincerity that caught him off guard. "I didn't know you hadn't told Whitney about yourself."

He offered her a half smile. "We're good." His voice held steady despite the tumult within. "I should've been honest from the start."

"Right?" Julia sounded more like herself again. "Glad I'm not the only messed-up one in the family."

"Misery loves company, heh?" he whispered through a laugh, lifting a glass to his sister.

The room burst into another round of applause as Dad ascended to the platform and drew a name from the basket to decide who would orchestrate the next year's reunion. "Wade!"

Approving cheers responded, and amid the celebratory chaos, Theo's phone vibrated in his pocket. His heart raced. *Please, let it be Whit!*

He fumbled the phone free and frowned at the unknown caller flashing on his screen. Usually, he'd dismiss it, but intuition nudged him to pick up. He slid from his chair and stepped onto the porch where delicate fairy lights wove magic through the evening air. He answered, his voice threading through the quiet hum of the outside world.

"Theo? It's Jada." The girl's voice, laden with fear, set his heart racing.

"Is everything okay?" The tightness in his chest foretold the answer.

"It's Whit... her heart. She's in the hospital. She needs surgery right away!"

Adrenaline coursed through him. The situation sounded dire.

"We really need the money." Jada's voice dipped to a guilty whisper. "I didn't know who else to call."

"I'm glad you called me. What hospital is she in?"

He strode back inside, his mind already racing through the steps he needed to take, the festive sounds now a distant clamor against the pounding in his ears. "Can you text me the hospital's name?"

He couldn't trust himself to remember any details. He approached his siblings, needing to locate the pilot. "Have you seen Jovan?"

Eric's frown mirrored Theo's concern. "Everything okay?"

"Whit's in the hospital." The words heavy, their gravity hushed the surrounding chatter.

The news cascaded through the room, the festive atmosphere ebbing away as family members rallied around him. "I need to find a surgeon or whoever..."

He swallowed hard, panic setting in, his usual composure fraying. This wasn't a business proposal he could solve.

"I'll go locate Jovan." Iris left. At least, that task could be taken off his hands.

Eric's hand was already on his phone. "I'm calling Ryan." He spoke of a family friend and doctor. "He'll know the best cardiologists in Houston."

"I have a contact for a cardiac surgeon." Logan was quick to share his connections at the most reputable hospital in San Francisco. "Let me see if she's available to fly to Houston."

Wade chimed in, his voice a testament to his powerful network, a friend of a friend, was a cardiac surgeon who also could possibly fly to Houston at a moment's notice.

His legs numb, Theo lowered himself on the chair. Surrounded by his family, their faces awash with concerned determination, he savored the solidarity of their unity.

His mother, with her soothing presence, gripped his shoulder. "We're going to make arrangements to leave. We're all coming with you."

Uncertainty sucked Theo into a darkening void, a fear of losing Whitney. "If anything happens to her..."

"Nothing is going to happen. We have to hope," Mom and Joy spoke simultaneously, their words staunching the fraying of his nerves. His family was a formidable force, and with them by his side, hope was not just a whisper, but a shout into the void.

Amid the whirl, his anxiety began to spiral, an all-too-familiar tightness constricting his chest. Loved ones in hospitals could mean lives lost or restored. Which was Whitney's fate?

"You all don't have to come with me," he managed to say, his voice steadier than he felt. It might be easier if he went alone.

"You hate hospitals." His mother spoke through the din. Her eyes met his, her acknowledgment of his fear, a soft touch in the chaos. "Whenever we're at hospitals, you tell jokes to avoid what's happening."

All along, he'd thought that was his secret, thought he'd acted brave in the hospital, but Mom knew him inside and out. Tears stung his eyes, not only from the fear and worry but also from the warmth enveloping him—his family's unwavering support.

Eric brought a thread of hope, speaking of a cardiologist ready to step in. Wade's news of a cardiac surgeon on standby offered a second lifeline. And then Logan spoke of another surgeon from San Francisco, ready to fly out at a moment's notice. Theo's breath caught in his throat, their collective efforts a testament to their love.

"Thank you." His whisper, thick with emotion, stuck in his closed-off throat. "I can't lose her."

"You won't." Mom squeezed his shoulder. A swell of hands enveloped him, a tangible manifestation of their support.

As his father's voice rose in prayer, calling on God for guidance, peace, and safety, a sacred stillness fell over the room. The collective amen was a chorus of strength wrapping Theo in a blanket of faith.

In that moment, the Stone family exemplified a bond beyond blood relation. It was about showing up, standing together, and facing whatever came their way as one. The reunion festivities had ceased, but in their place stood something more profound—the affirmation that, when it truly mattered, they were there for each other, without hesitation.

While that would see him through, would it be enough to help Whitney? Undoubtedly, God had heard their prayers, but sometimes He answered no. What would His answer be this time?

CHAPTER 25

In the hospital waiting room, the pervasive scent of antiseptics mingled with distant wafts of coffee to create a comforting yet uneasy ambience, and a collective concern and hope lingered. Theo's family, typically rambunctious, were subdued, their murmurs blending with intermittent phone chirps, intercom doctor announcements, and shuffling shoes on the tiled hallway floor.

Theo's attention riveted on the door, anxious for an update, his palms sweat, and his heart thudded. The clinical environment, with its stark-white walls and pervasive disinfectant, resurrected painful memories long buried deep within him.

"Deep breaths," Logan murmured beside him.

Mom's revelation of his deep-seated fear of hospitals somehow stripped Theo of his usual defenses, leaving him raw and exposed. He shifted in the padded vinyl chair, his posture so stiff and an ache spread across his back. Burying his face in his hands, he created a physical barrier against the emotions threatening to overwhelm him. Eyes closed, he sought forgiveness from God and pushed aside the fear that his lies somehow hastened her crisis. After all, how did a physical heart react to heartbreak?

He had yet to see her since their arrival, right after she was transferred to this facility. The cardiac surgeon, a call made possible by Ryan Harper, was on standby.

Daylight began to filter through the windows, casting long shadows across the room, deepening his foreboding. By the window, his mother, sisters, and sisters-in-law formed a tight cluster around Madonna and Jada, offering them a comfort Theo felt incapable of providing.

Other family members moved around the room, each coping in their own way, but Theo remained anchored to his spot, paralyzed by uncertainty, fearful moving might mean missing a crucial update.

When Iris and Joy walked out with Jada, the rest of the women headed off, and Madonna was left alone. Her disheveled appearance and slumped posture spoke of her turmoil.

Compelled by a sense of responsibility and compassion, he approached her. As he took a seat, her tear-streaked face turned toward him.

"Hello, Madonna."

"This is all my fault." Her voice, husky and strained, broke the silence before a sob strangled her words. Her hands trembled as she wiped away tears, each a testament to her internal struggle.

Theo reached out, his hand hesitating in the air before touching her arm. "No, it's not." He struggled to maintain his voice, needing to be a calming presence in the sterile atmosphere. "If anything, I'm to blame."

Whitney had been fine with her mom lying to her—until Theo compounded those lies.

"No." Madonna shook her head. "You are a good man. I'm her mother. If I hadn't been such a mess, she wouldn't be here now. She's, um, taken care of me and Jada, sacrificing so much for us."

"Hush now." Theo rubbed her arm. "Whitney doesn't see it as your fault. She loves you. That's why she takes good care of you and Jada."

Madonna's sorrowful eyes met his, one side of her mouth lifting. "You think so?"

"I *know* so." The ache wrenched his heart. "God gives us second chances. Whitney will pull through this. She'd want you to be strong too."

His words ministered to himself as much as to the distraught woman beside him. *After all, wouldn't she want you to be strong too, Theo?*

Madonna's eyes closed as another sob shuddered through her. "God, if you bring back my baby girl, I–I won't touch any more alcohol or drugs again. I'll be the mother she deserves."

Feeling her pain and understanding the responsibility Whitney shouldered, he wanted to offer words of comfort to alleviate Madonna's guilt. But some wounds needed more than words to heal. So he sat there, offering his presence as support while she poured out her heart in silent prayers and vows. And, sitting there, he made a solemn promise—a pledge to live truthfully and cherish the second chances he hoped they'd both receive.

A woman in a white coat walked through the door, and Theo stood, Madonna and the others mirroring his action. "I'm Dr. Robertson." She removed her surgical mask. Fatigue lined her eyes, yet her presence radiated a positive energy. A smile softened her expression as she acknowledged Logan and he thanked her again for the last-minute arrangement. They'd intended to go with the cardiac surgeon Ryan recommended, but he'd been reeled into an emergency surgery shortly after the call. Blessedly, they'd had backups.

"Any time." She exhaled, refocusing. "The procedure was successful."

A collective sigh resonated through the room, exhaling in unison. Gratitude weakened Theo's knees, and he dropped into the nearest chair. Madonna's hand found his, squeezing it, and he returned the gesture, their shared relief palpable.

"She's stable and resting."

"Can we see her?" His voice cracked.

Dr. Robertson nodded. "She's still in the ICU. Visits should be brief at this stage. One person at a time, please."

All turned toward Theo.

Madonna, somewhat disheveled, squeezed his hand again, then released him to go. "You go first. I need to... some time to get ready."

The walk toward Whitney's room felt like the longest journey he'd ever taken. His heart pounded in his chest as he made it to the double doors and pushed them open to reveal a sanctuary of recovery. Beeping monitors punctuated the silence, and calming lights facilitated rest. Whitney lay there, so fragile yet peaceful, a stark contrast to the vibrant force he knew her to be.

He approached her bed with reverence, kneeling. Tears blurred his vision, and his hand trembled as he took hers, brought it to his lips, and kissed it. "You are one of the strongest people I know." Emotion lodged in his throat. "I'm so sorry for not being truthful, for not being the best boyfriend I promised to be."

How his heart ached with things left unsaid, with relief that she was still here, her chest rising and falling! "I love you so much."

Whitney's eyelids fluttered open, their gazes locked, and their spirits connected. "You're here," she whispered, the faintest smile curving her lips. "You hate hospitals."

"Yes," he said gruffly. "But there's good in them too."

Without treatment, she wouldn't be alive. While others like his mom died, many recovered.

"I love you," she said, her voice still weak, but that meant he was forgiven. What must've been a goofy grin wobbled across his face when she closed her eyes and said, "I'm glad you're here."

"Yes." His thumb stroked the back of her hand. "And I want to be with you every step of the way." Gently squeezing her hand, he stood with renewed devotion. This connection was still fragile yet unbreakable, an unspoken promise of a new beginning.

He wanted to give her the whole world, but that started with the simple things she might enjoy. When she was moved to the recovery room two days later, he went on a quest to find wisteria. Yes, she'd wanted them for her funeral. But she was alive, she was going to live, and they were her favorite flowers.

He envisioned an abundance of wisteria, enough to transform her hospital room into a fragrant sanctuary. But reality proved more challenging.

His first stop was the wedding venue, where he'd bought wisteria last month. Unfortunately, he learned that the blossoms were usually unavailable by now, and his heart sank. Refusing to give up, he headed to the hotel and sought out the concierge who might know where to find the elusive blossoms. After some searching, the concierge informed him no local nursery had wisteria available, and they weren't sold in any local stores.

Theo's research on the internet earned him several positive results. Botanical gardens in Massachusetts, Michigan, and Wisconsin, and a vast field for sale in Vermont. The idea of purchasing an entire farm for the wisteria overrunning the property crossed his mind, but for now, he focused on acquiring a single bouquet for her bedside.

Just after seven, he walked through the lobby, and the concierge told him of a local residence that might have wisteria still blooming late in the season. So Theo set off to find the house. Located in the suburbs, the quaint two-story nestled among well-tended gardens. The evening sky was darkening as he approached the property.

The house seemed deserted, no lights in the windows, no car in the driveway. He knocked on the door and waited, glazing around. The next house was set well back from this one, an old truck parked in the driveway.

The wisteria, visible just over the wooden fence to the backyard, swayed gently in the breeze. Their purple blossoms seemed to beckon to him, where the vines entwined around an old wishing well. With no one home to grant permission, he walked to the fence and reached over it.

While it wasn't too tall, he'd overestimated the reach. The flowers weren't as close as he'd expected. When he stretched as far as he could, his fingertips barely brushed the blooms. Then a growl froze him in his tracks. Heart pounding, he turned his head toward a large dog, its eyes fixed on him.

Turning back now would mean returning to Whitney empty-handed, an outcome he couldn't bear. And if the dog kept barking, it would capture the neighbor's attention. Perhaps he could get back there, pet the dog, and retrieve the flowers peacefully. He grasped the rung over the fence's latticework, heaved himself up, and swung down, landing on the other side.

The dog, now fully alert, started barking furiously.

"Easy there, buddy," Theo whispered, trying to sound calm, moving to pat it. It calmed—until he inched closer.

Theo decided to focus on the wishing well and the beckoning blooms. Staying calm despite his racing heart, he edged closer, keeping one eye on the dog.

The animal growled louder, its body tensed and ready to leap.

Theo snagged a handful of wisteria, breaking the branch they clung to, sending a shower of the fragile blossoms shaking loose from the rest of the vine, the sweet fragrance a stark contrast to his adrenaline rush.

The dog charged.

Theo's heart raced as he bolted toward the fence. He tossed the fragile flowers over the fence, grabbed the top, and jammed a foot on the lateral board along the bottom. Just as he started to heave himself up, the dog latched onto his pant leg. Theo shook his head, grinding his teeth as he hoisted himself over, the dog snapping at his heels.

Breathless and scratched, he landed on the other side and scooped up the precious wisteria. He glanced back, unable to see the still barking dog, now thwarted by the fence. Then he turned toward the neighbor's house. No one appeared to be watching.

It hadn't occurred to him that he'd stolen the flowers until he sat behind the wheel of the rented Civic he now intended to buy since it held so many memories of him and Whitney. For now, he needed to strategize his return and explain the dilemma to the house owner, with some form of payment. The last thing he needed was to be deceptive again.

CHAPTER 26

Whitney's eyes fluttered open to a blur of pale-white walls, soft hospital sheets, and soothing wisteria scents mingling with a sterile aroma. As her gaze sharpened, she fixed it on a familiar figure sitting across from her bed — Theo, with his head bowed and hands clasped, as if bearing the weight of the world

The wisteria on a nearby table caught her eye. The delicate fragrance wafted through the room in a comforting reminder of life's persistent beauty. Theo had been there for her ever since her surgery and even when she'd moved to the recovery room.

"Hey," she murmured, her voice weak.

His face, previously etched with worry, relaxed into a tender smile when his gaze rose to her.

"I love the wisteria," she whispered, her chest expanding.

"As long as they don't remind you of a funeral." He moved his chair closer, teasing her over wanting wisteria at her funeral.

Despite the IV drip and the steady beep of the heart monitor—a grim reminder of her situation—she chose to focus on the brighter side. "Wisteria reminds me of springtime, new beginnings... life." Her voice a mere breath flowed from the depth of her newly recovering heart.

"I'm glad they remind you of life." He took her hand, painting it with butterfly kisses. "I want you to have a very long, beautiful life."

This late in June, wisteria blossoms would be scarce. "Where did you find them?"

He chuckled. "Let's just say it involved an adventurous encounter with a dog," he admitted, hinting at a comedic escapade. Then, at her urging, he recounted his floral escapade.

Whitney's attempt to laugh resulted in a breathy exhalation, coughing due to lack of energy. "You went through all that trouble just for me?"

Leaning closer, he brushed a stray lock of hair from her forehead. "For you, Whit, I'd search for the impossible." His gaze held hers, a world of unspoken feelings and promises lingering in that look, leaving her no doubt he'd do anything for her.

Her gaze lingered on him, gratitude sluicing through her veins. "Thank you for everything... the medical help." Her neck flushed at the memory of her outburst in Brazil.

"It wasn't all me." His expression tender, he recounted how his family rallied to find her a cardiologist and cardiac surgeon. "I wouldn't have known where to start. Logan flew one in from San Francisco. It seems like it was all part of a greater plan for you to be back here in time."

Whitney nodded, the tightness in her chest easing, but she had to address the pressing issue lingering between them. "What about the resort? What are you planning to do with it?"

"I've decided to keep it." His thumb brushed the back of her hand. "It'll need some work, but it's doable."

"But you're based in Brazil." She furrowed her brow. "How will you manage it from there?"

"You live here with Jada and your mom. That means Houston is going to be my secondary home as well." His thumb still caressing her, he smoothed over her worries with a reassurance that their lives were drawing closer together.

Her lips curved into a hopeful smile. She wanted to understand him more, the man behind the billionaire façade. "Can I ask what led you to the media industry? I read about your work online."

A touch of melancholy glossed his eyes. "Well, TSF is deeply personal. It stands for Theo, Stone, and Felicia—my mother's name. The media industry... It was an unexpected path."

Whitney shifted closer to the edge of the bed, wanting to conquer any distance between them, afraid she might miss or skip an important detail.

"After losing my mom, I found an escape in stories—films, books, anything that took me to a different world." His thumb stopped its movement, his gaze distant, as if reliving the memory. "They helped me deal with the loss."

Whitney's heart ached.

"As I got older, I wanted to give that same escape to others. To create stories to comfort, inspire, and maybe even heal." He squeezed her hand, a passion lilting his voice. "As for going to Brazil, I was too attached to my family and needed to prove to myself I was a grown man who could survive being far from home."

Her admiration for him grew as he confessed his fears of being away from his family, afraid something would happen to them while he wasn't around. That attachment helped him form a habit of returning to the US once a week, on top of his weekly phone calls from his parents and siblings.

Seeing the man behind the mogul, a man driven by a deeply personal mission, she saw the layers of his character unfold. His vulnerability about his fears and unwavering commitment to his family sketched a portrait of a man deeply rooted in emotional bonds and personal development.

Her ignorance of his wealth had perhaps been a blessing. It allowed her to connect with his true essence, not merely his accomplishments. She'd come to appreciate him as a genuine, heartfelt individual, not just his successes.

"Hello?" They both turned to see Daniela waving, a cheery yellow balloon bouncing with her motion.

"Good morning, Daniela." Theo released Whitney's hand, rising to make room for her friend.

"I didn't mean to interrupt." Daniela, still hovering in the doorway, smiled her apology. "I was on my way to work and wanted to check on you."

Theo leaned in and kissed Whitney's forehead. "I'll leave you two to catch up."

His departure was a tender reminder of his respect for Whitney's life outside their relationship, and as he left the room, her healing heart felt full.

"Look at you." Daniela tied the balloon to the wisteria vase. "Where did he find wisteria this time of the year?"

"He broke into someone's yard." Whitney relayed his adventure.

Daniela's laugh was a familiar comfort as she settled into the chair Theo had vacated, the sound refreshing, so relieved she could talk about her romantic life with someone else. "That's... romantic in a wanted-by-the-neighborhood-watch kind of way."

Whitney couldn't help but smile, despite the absurdity. "Yeah, he's... he's really something." The perfect first-and-last boyfriend she could ever ask for.

Daniela leaned forward, her eyes sparkling. "I mean, the way he looks at you, Whitney—it's like you're his entire world. It's the kind of stuff you see in those cheesy rom-coms you can't help but love."

Warmth spread through her. Whitney knew what Daniela meant. "He's so wonderful," she echoed, replaying every gaze he filled with unspoken words and every touch that lingered a moment too long.

"Your mom and Jada were singing his praises at the café." Daniela dipped her voice to a conspiratorial whisper. "They seem to think he's Superman without the cape."

"Jada adores him." Jada seemed so comfortable around Theo and even trusted him enough to call him when the need arose. But knowing that Mama was also taken with Theo brought a sense of relief.

"Your mom said you're heading to rehab in two days?"

"That's what I heard." Whitney shifted to her back, tired of being on one side. "I would rather be at home." Even if home wasn't practical for her six-to-eight-week recovery time.

"Whatever rehab center you're in, you'll be surrounded by love."

"Theo's handling it." He'd be around, and so would Mama and Jada. He'd already assured her everything would be taken care of and he'd stay with her every step through her recovery whatever that meant.

Daniela clasped Whitney's hand. "You've got a good one there, Whitney. Just make sure you let him spoil you a little, okay?"

Whitney nodded, feeling lighter than she had in years. "He spoils me without me asking anyway." She hadn't yet disclosed Theo's ownership of the resort, but what she had told Daniela didn't seem to deter her positive feelings about Theo. "Thanks for coming. It means a lot."

"You deserve it after... well, everything."

They chatted for a while longer. Surrounded by the scent of wisteria and knowing her friend and family and Theo were there for her, Whitney felt a sense of normalcy return. She wasn't as fearful as she'd been. She no longer had to carry her burdens alone.

***

As Whitney stepped through the ornate gates, Theo was at her side to steady her in case she faltered. Mama and Jada had already come ahead to await her arrival at the rehab center, a sprawling ranch-style house, nestled within manicured lawns.

"This is more like a resort than rehab." Whitney hugged his arm close.

Inside the foyer, an expansive wisteria bouquet sweetened the space. The scent trailed into the living area, a breathtaking expanse of modern elegance and comfort. Plush cream-toned sofas formed a welcoming semicircle facing a massive stone fireplace. Beyond them, floor-to-ceiling windows framed the vibrant garden and a shimmering pool, its waters reflecting the clear blue sky.

"Don't worry. I didn't scale any fences for these." Theo chuckled, gesturing to the wisteria bouquets gracing every surface. "They're all legally obtained, I promise. I, um, actually purchased a heritage farm overrun with wisteria vines in Vermont."

Her eyes widened. "What are you going to do with a place like that?"

"We can take a trip whenever we want to savor the wisteria." He helped her settle into the plush sofa. "Or have some delivered whenever we need them urgently."

Warmth spread across her chest. He'd had wisteria flown here from Vermont.

A woman in crisp sky-blue scrubs emerged, her smile warm and reassuring. "Welcome, Whitney."

"This is your nurse." Theo settled on the sofa next to Whitney.

"I'm Lori. I'll be taking care of you here."

Jada waltzed in behind a server who carried a tray of fresh fruit, sparkling water, and gourmet snacks. She shook a finger at Whitney. "Looks like you'll be dining like royalty."

Mama followed and settled in one of the chairs, like Jada seeming comfortable amid the luxurious surroundings.

"I guess I'm not the only one getting pampered," Whitney joked, a smile breaking through.

Theo's eyes gleamed. "Welcome home away from home and hospital."

She chuckled at his lighthearted humor.

The living room, with its high ceilings and open space, felt like an extension of the lush gardens outside. Natural light spilled in, creating a serene atmosphere that seemed to whisper promises of peaceful days and healing.

With Theo close to her, she savored his comforting scent now blending with the wisteria, and contentment coursed through her. She could heal here in this tranquil retreat, not only from the surgery but also from years of pent-up fears and overwork.

She settled back, still amazed by the ambience, nothing like a clinical rehabilitation center—no antiseptic odor, no sterile corridors, just the sweet fragrance of flowers infusing every corner with serenity.

"Whit." Theo captured her attention as he interlaced their fingers. "I've leased this place for you, Jada, and your mom."

"Yes!" Jada burst out, unable to contain her excitement. "I've got my own room, and so do you. And—"

"Jada, dear," Mama cut in, tugging Jada to sit in the empty chair next to her, "let Theo finish."

Something pinched deep in Whitney's chest, and she rubbed at it, unsure if it was the lingering effects of the surgery or the idea of Theo shouldering all their expenses. "What's happening here?"

"I decided to leave the trailer park." Mama clasped her hands as if in prayer, her eyes carrying a weight beyond what Whitney had seen her carry before.

"We still owe this quarter's rent."

"We're squared up with the old place," Mama added. "All taken care of, baby."

Whitney had noticed a change in Mama these last days, a clarity and sobriety.

"While you were in surgery, I spoke to God and Theo." Mama faltered as she recounted her fears during Whitney's operation. "I've failed you girls too many times. This time, my promise to God is different. I want another chance to be the mother you and Jada deserve."

Whitney's breath caught in her throat, and she swallowed. Mama had made promises in the past, but today, her tone held the sincerity Whitney had longed to hear.

"Theo did some research about classes I can take. I'm moving into a facility with some accountability."

Was Whitney dreaming?

Theo's comforting arm snaked around her waist. She rested her head on his shoulder. Overwhelmed by his kindness, she couldn't even speak through the lump in her throat. He'd spoken to her mom while she was in surgery. What more signs of assurance did she need to know his love for her was real?

As Mama thanked Theo for his generosity and encouragement while Whitney was in the hospital, tears welled up in Whitney's eyes. She tilted her head to look at him, still at a loss for words.

"It's okay, baby." His voice was a soft comfort as he drew her close. "We're a family now, and we'll face this together."

Jada's voice broke through the emotional atmosphere. "Does this mean we're moving to Brazil?"

Her innocence brought a momentary lightness, eliciting chuckles from Theo and Mama.

"We could, but you have your life here," Theo replied. "And there's the matter of your sister agreeing to marry me first." Waggling his thick brows, he cast a playful glance at Whitney. "Then maybe, after you graduate and if it's okay with your mom, we can all pray and decide to move if it's in God's plan for us."

"I'd be okay with changing schools now," Jada remarked, always up for adventure.

Time to temper her sister's enthusiasm. "There's a lot for us to consider, Jada. Theo's business in Brazil, then here, and—" She paused, realizing that, while marriage might not be imminent, she was content in the present with love and support surrounding her.

"I should start thinking about coming clean at the resort," Theo mused.

"I'd love to witness that." Whitney grinned to imagine the staff's reactions. "The HR manager is the only one in on your secret, right?"

"And now you." He confirmed with a nod.

Gratitude washed over Whitney. Despite their challenges, they were on the brink of a new beginning, and she was surrounded by love. Her mother's resolve to change, Jada's unwavering enthusiasm, and Theo's support were more than Whitney could have asked for. Life was unpredictable, but she was where she needed to be. Only God could have foreseen all this, sending Theo and his family when she needed them the most. Without His intervention, she may not have gotten her surgery on time, and Mama might never have chosen to conquer her addiction.

Theo hadn't been the only one wearing a disguise. For her own reasons, Whitney had hidden her fears and needs, not only from her family and friends but also from God. Trying to do it on her own, she'd donned a mask and concealed her lack of faith behind continual self-sacrifice. But only by revealing her true self, her fears, and her vulnerability, could she build genuine relationships with God and those He put in her life.

EPILOGUE

Theo paused at the display window in one of San Francisco's shopping centers, captivated by the array of rings sparkling under the bright lights.

"Oh no." Wade's voice buzzed in his ear as their group crowded around the window. "Don't tell me you're seriously considering this."

"Come on." Nate, with his characteristic enthusiasm and spontaneity, nudged Theo toward the jewelry store entrance. "Let's take a look. No harm in that, right?"

Theo's name had been drawn as Nate's best man for the upcoming wedding. This responsibility had brought Theo and his brothers to the tailor shop for their suits, and now, they found themselves at the store across the way, discussing Theo's possible next steps to a future with Whitney.

Inside, a petite Asian woman with a smooth bun welcomed them. Theo's heart quickened at the thought of a proposal, but alongside this flutter of nerves came a calm certainty.

"You've only been together for, what, a month?" Wade leaned over the glittering collection. With Wade's fear of commitment and change, his reservations didn't surprise Theo.

"Three months, actually." The time had flown, but each moment with Whitney contained a lifetime of meaning. Theo's smile grew as he cuffed his brother's arm. "Don't worry, even if I get married, we can still talk about sports."

"Moving things fast is the way to roll." Nate, always spontaneous, pointed to a particularly striking ring. "And that's the one to rev things up, bro."

"If you want her to decline your proposal." Wade snickered. "Then yeah, take the sunflower ring."

Amid their banter, Theo settled on a delicate ring—an elegant solitaire diamond set in a simple yet sophisticated platinum band.

The diamond was impressive but not ostentatious. It would suit Whitney's taste. Its timeless design spoke of enduring love, just like what he felt for her.

While Wade continued to grumble about the pressure of relationships, Theo requested the ring be taken out for a closer look. Holding it, he could already picture it on Whitney's finger.

After some consideration, with Nate's and even Wade's reluctant approval, Theo purchased the ring. The size might need adjusting, but that was a minor detail. The important part was the commitment it symbolized, a commitment he was ready to make.

As they left the store, he plotted the proposal. He'd do it in Pleasant View, Colorado, during the week leading up to Nate's wedding day. It would be the perfect setting, especially with Whitney's mom present. Excitement gave him a fresh buzz, a future with Whitney becoming more real with every step he took.

With Whitney's mom in rehab and showing positive progress, the atmosphere around Whitney had lightened considerably, making this an opportune moment. His revelation about his true identity at the resort had been met with shocked disbelief, but ultimately, understanding. Handing over the resort's management to Whitney, he encouraged her to take her time, to heal, and to learn—she was taking online hotel management classes, giving her the freedom to imprint her style on the establishment.

Meanwhile, Jada was flourishing, immersed in her summer volleyball camp, and looking forward to trying out for the middle school team as soon as cross-country began in the fall.

As they settled into Pleasant View, Theo planned a special evening for their second day in town—a family dinner at a restaurant that would serve as the perfect setting for his proposal.

Now, ambient lighting spilled across the rich wooden interiors while windows offered panoramic views of the surrounding mountains. The tables, meticulously set with sparkling crystal glassware, were interspersed with delicate floral arrangements. Wisteria, its purple hues and sweet fragrance, infused the air with a sense of springtime even if it was August. The chatter of his nieces and nephews blended seamlessly into the soft laughter, conversation, and background music.

Over seventy family members, including some family friends, occupied the tables nearby where Theo sat next to Whitney, who was listening to Rohan, her grace and beauty captivating. Her midnight-blue dress flowed around her like a gentle wave, its subtle shimmer catching the candlelight. Her hair cascaded in glossy waves, framing her face and enhancing the natural radiance that always seemed to surround her.

As the evening progressed, glasses clinked in toasts for Nate and Vanessa. After a sumptuous meal while dessert was served, the perfect moment arrived. His palms perspired as he rose to his feet. He avoided Whitney's gaze, fearing she might not be ready for such a significant step.

The music ceased, thankfully Nate and Wade were in on his plan. Theo took a deep breath to steady himself, then pushed back his chair, making space as he prepared to address the room and cleared his throat.

"Excuse me, everyone." His words cut through the low hum of conversation, drawing immediate silence. As all attention riveted on him, he focused on Whitney. Her eyes—wide with curiosity and lit by the candlelight—added to the gravity of the moment he was about to create.

"I don't usually stand and interrupt the gathering." Nerves tangled his words. "But tonight feels special."

Maybe he should have paid more attention to those chick flicks his sisters adored. Perhaps they would have prepared him for this. He took a deep, steadying breath. "You see, when you find someone who resonates with your soul, who stands by you, and who illuminates your life just by being a part of it, you recognize the blessing you've received."

Emotions closed over his throat as he tried to articulate his feelings. He reached for her hand, and the chair scraped against the floor when she stood in front of him, her eyes shining.

"Whitney." His voice dipped, now a tender whisper. "You've brought so much joy and purpose into my life. I can't imagine my future without... you in it."

He let go of her hand to reach for the velvet box in his coat pocket, then knelt on one knee, the room gasping collectively. Whitney's hand flew to her mouth as he produced the ring, the solitaire diamond glinting.

His heart pounded in his chest, sensing everyone's gaze fixed on them. He then asked the question that would change their lives forever. "Whitney Reed, will you marry me?"

The room was so silent, it was clear that they were all waiting for her response. The next seconds felt like an eternity.

"Theo!" She gasped, then moved her hand to her chest, nodding as tears fell on her cheeks. "Yes. I will."

Everyone erupted in cheers and applause.

He slid the ring onto her finger, then kissed her. The moment was electric, filled with love and hope, a perfect beginning to their new journey together.

The ride home in the limousine was a stark contrast to the joyous occasion they'd left. The interior, usually a space for celebration, now felt subdued. With a gentle glow on her radiant face, Whitney held his hand. Outside, the mountain landscape blurred past tinted windows.

Whitney's mother and sister, along with the girls, had driven in the family Escalade while Theo and Whitney rode in the family limousine with a few of his brothers and Nate's bride-to-be, who was cozily seated next to him, occasionally sharing her water with him.

Owen was perusing his phone, the silence almost pensive, broken only by the hum of the engine, the clink of glassware, and the muted music.

Wade, usually the life of any gathering, sat quiet, his gaze fixed on the passing scenery. Sensing something amiss, Theo squeezed Whitney's hand before turning to his suddenly moody brother. "Everything okay, Wade?"

"Albert's dead."

Wade's words dropped like stones in still water, resonating in the limousine's close confines, and shock jolted through Theo. "What? When did this happen?"

"At the restaurant." Wade rubbed his forehead, his palm hiding his gaze. "I got a call."

Nate clamped a hand on Wade's shoulder. "He's coming to the wedding! You just talked to him last week, right?"

Wade nodded, his movements slow and heavy.

Albert was one of Wade's best friends—well, technically, they'd all been his friends since he'd spent several sleepovers at the house during middle school and high school years. Theo's chest constricted, and Whitney ran a hand of comfort on his back as if aware of the inner turmoil. Death. So unpredictable.

***

The day after the proposal, instead of reveling in the pre-wedding festivities, they found themselves mourning Albert. His death cast a solemn shadow, the burial ceremony offering the finality of goodbye. Theo was overcome with compassion for Claire, who had lost her brother in a sobering reminder of life's fragile nature, contrasting with the joy and promise of his recent engagement. Across the room, he caught Whitney's eye.

Mourners gathered in small clusters, their conversations a murmur against the piano music. The room, awash with flowers, somber hues, and low lights, offered a comforting embrace to those grappling with loss.

Theo stood at the end of a loose line with his family as they waited to greet Claire. At the receiving end, Claire cradled her brother's baby, her demeanor embodying a quiet resilience.

"Hi, guys." Despite the tears that reddened her eyes, she managed a smile born of inner fortitude. The baby cooed, blissfully unaware of the sorrowful occasion.

"Hello, my darling." Mom kissed Claire's cheek before squeezing the baby. "We're here for you—anything you need."

"Thank you, Regina." Claire dabbed her eyes with a tissue.

Dad followed, shaking Claire's hand and conveying his sympathies.

Stepping forward, Theo added his own words of comfort.

Then, one by one, his family members shared similar condolences.

"It means a lot that you're all here," Claire assured them.

Wade stopped before her, Albert's passing having affected him the deepest of their brothers.

"Claire, if there's anything you need, I want to be there for you and Bella." Wade ruffled the baby's curls, and she giggled, tugging at his tie. He reached for her, but the baby clung to the neckline of Claire's dress.

A subtle shift marked Claire's demeanor as she looked up at Wade, a momentary flicker in her eyes, a hint of something beyond gratitude. It was fleeting, but clearly, there was a connection amid shared sorrow.

She shifted the baby to her other arm, her smile faint as Wade gently squeezed her shoulder. "Thank you, Wade. For coming."

Albert had been a single father, and it only made sense that Claire would be the child's legal guardian.

When they excused themselves, leaving Claire to greet others, Wade lingered, his gaze locked with Claire's. She waved at him before he fell in step with Theo.

"I can't start to imagine what she's going through," Wade mumbled as they moved toward the seating area. His jaw set, displaying his protective instinct. "And... oh, Bella."

"We can all pitch in and help anyway," Theo said at their table. Whitney smiled at him, a warm smile that made him eager to start his life with her as soon as Nate's wedding was over. Surely, she'd agree to set the date before the year ended. He certainly was ready. He'd never been as sure about anything as he was about the way he felt about Whitney. With a bittersweet sense of peace, he sat next to her and slid his arm around her waist.

She kissed his cheek. "Are you okay?"

He nodded, kissing her back. He was more than okay with her in his life. Life was unpredictable, often marked by tragedies, but also by connections. In the cycle of loss and healing, new paths were opening, and in them, he saw the possibility of new beginnings, even in the wake of goodbye.

-THE END-

Checkout the Rest of Rose's Books
THE BUCHANAN SERIES

1. *First Site*
2. *Something right*
3. *Bright Side*
4. *Short Sighted*
5. *New Light (A Christmas Novella)*

ROMANCE IN THE ROCKIES SERIES

1. *Complex*
2. *Choices*
3. *Beyond Repair*
4. *Stand Out*
5. *Crystal Clear*

THE CAREGIVER SERIES

1. *The Doctor's Nanny*
2. *The Entrepreneur's Nurse*
3. *The Physician's Helper*
4. *The CEO's Companion*
5. *The Investor's Wife*
6. *The Soldier's Trainer*
7. *The Realtor's Attendant*

THE BILLIONAIRE REUNION SERIES

1. *A legitimate Date*
2. *A Sudden Romance*
3. *A Necessary Compromise*
4. *A Genuine Disguise*
5. *A Convenient Marriage*

www.ingramcontent.com/pod-product-compliance
Lightning Source LLC
Chambersburg PA
CBHW030108260626
47156CB00008B/2571